I0578906

DREAMer

Emily Gallo

All rights reserved. No part of this book may be reproduced in any form or by any electronic or mechanical means, including information storage and retrieval systems, without written permission from the author, except in the case of a reviewer, who may quote brief passages embodied in critical articles or in a review.

Trademarked names appear throughout this book. Rather than use a trademark symbol with every occurrence of a trademarked name, names are used in an editorial fashion, with no intention of infringement of the respective owner's trademark.

This is a work of fiction. Names, characters, places, and incidents either are the product of the author's imagination or are used fictitiously, and any resemblance to actual persons, living or dead, events, or locales is entirely coincidental.

The author may be reached at ecegallo@gmail.com

www.emilygallo.com
http://emilygallo.blogspot.com/

ISBN: 9798566576268

Copyright April 2021

Acknowledgments

Enormous gratitude to my stellar editors, Daniel Nauman and Chris Saur, for always knowing the better way to say it.

Thanks also to my audio producer and cover creator, Glenn Tucker, who has tech savvy as only one of his many talents. Thanks to his granddaughter, Zolie Judge, for allowing me to use her image on my cover.

Thanks to my husband, David Gallo and my friend, Rafiki Webster, both of whom not only give me great advice, but also have to listen to me spew out my crazy ideas.

Thanks also to my assistant, Christopher Barboza, who has brought me to a whole other level of marketing and publicity.

Much appreciation to Cindy Triffo and Lorie Leonard for their expertise with the Spanish language.

And as always, I want to thank Tin Roof Café for providing me a place to write with my endless cups of Earl Grey tea.

Other novels by Emily Gallo:

Venice Beach
The Columbarium
Kate & Ruby
Roads Not Taken
Murder at the Columbarium
The Last Resort

Emily Gallo was born and raised in New York City and now lives on two and a half acres in northern California and in 750 square feet on the beach in southern California with her husband David, their Schiller hound Gracie and their rescued cat Savali.

The future belongs to those who believe in the beauty of their dreams.

Eleanor Roosevelt

PROLOGUE

It was pitch black and still hot, even though it was the middle of the night. His snoring had been loud and incessant. She knew he had drunk himself into a stupor and wouldn't hear her. She was scared, but she was more scared to stay. She didn't know what she would find, but it couldn't be worse than this. She was so thirsty and tired, but she had to keep running. She had to keep hoping. It was all she had. Dawn would come soon and it would only get even hotter. She didn't know how much time had passed, but she had to keep going. She was so tired . . . so tired . . . Maybe she could stop running and walk now. There were no big trees to hide behind, but she saw a rock formation she could climb into and rest. As she settled into the crevice she heard the coyotes. She felt somewhat protected in this niche, but then she heard the rattle. She jumped up. It was still dark so she couldn't see the snake, but she heard it loud and clear. She was afraid she would step on it, but a bigger animal might attack her if she climbed out. There was no choice but to keep running. The coyote's howl seemed further away than the snake's rattle. She kept her eyes on the ground, checking for the snake. It sounded closer and closer and finally she saw it, coiled, its fangs bared. She screamed and ran the other way, but then thought it would be better not to run. She started backing away slowly, her eyes never leaving the rattlesnake. She found some soft sand under a bean mesquite. She wanted to sleep, but she was too afraid. Her eyelids got heavy, though, and she did doze off. She awoke when it got lighter and lighter and hotter and hotter. She wanted to find some shade, but knew that there was little chance of that. She stopped hearing the nighttime sounds of the wild animals and she turned around and walked briskly. She happened upon a road so she stopped and sat down next to a large rock. She was too tired and too hot to run anymore. She didn't know where she was, but she had to rest and she hoped that the animals and snakes would stay away from the road. She had no idea what lay before her, but she knew this was her only chance . . .

1

KATE BRUSHED BY LAWRENCE AFTER HE UNLOCKED THE HOTEL ROOM DOOR AND SHE FLOPPED ON THE BED. "What a gorgeous place!"

"The hotel?" Lawrence asked dubiously. "I mean it's fine but I wouldn't call it gorgeous."

"No, Anza-Borrego."

"Oh, yeah. I knew you'd like it. But you don't want to be here in the middle of summer."

"I was afraid the desert would be hot even now. The guidebook said the best time to visit is October to April."

"It is October."

"Yes, but it's the beginning of the month. Anyway, I want to come back in the spring when the wildflowers are blooming." Kate took out her phone and started scrolling through the pictures of the state park. "I liked Slot Canyon the best. What about you?"

"I kind of liked the metal sculptures."

"Well, this has been a fabulous day. I really needed to get away from LA and this was perfect. And I found us a nice restaurant in town."

"Okay, but I want to shower first."

"Go ahead. I'll shower after you. I almost wish we were staying another day," Kate mused as she continued scrolling. "There's a lot we didn't see."

"We'll come back in the spring," Lawrence called over his shoulder as he entered the bathroom. He stopped and turned around. "Hey there's a nice big shower in here. You could join me."

"Yes, I could." She jumped up and swatted his rear.

"Hey, you! Act your age."

"Why?" she asked as she pulled him close. "Just because we're on Medicare doesn't mean we can't have a little fun."

Lawrence grinned at her. "I wonder if we would still be getting wet together if we were married for forty years instead of four."

"And we haven't even been together through all those four years," she murmured, kissing him. "With me in the Peace Corps and all."

"I know," Lawrence sighed. "It feels like we lost a couple of years. And we don't exactly have years to lose."

"We'll make it up," she said, pushing his tee shirt up over his satiny ebony skin. "Right now."

The lovemaking that started in the shower continued into the bed and they finally set out for the restaurant an hour later. "What's the name of this restaurant?" Lawrence asked.

"Coyote Steakhouse."

"Steakhouse?"

"I know," laughed Kate. "But they have seafood and vegetarian dishes."

"Can we walk to it?"

"Yup. That's one of the reasons I chose the Palm Canyon Hotel. It's close to everything in town." The sky glowed gold and coral behind the silhouette of the San Ysidero Mountains as they walked to the restaurant.

They were seated promptly and ordered a bottle of wine while they waited for their food. "What time do you want to get going tomorrow?" Lawrence asked. "Check out is probably not til 11, but I thought we could check out early and see a bit more of the park before heading home."

"That sounds like a good plan," Kate replied. "We could check out by eight and leave the park right after lunch."

"That should give us time to meander our way home and check out some of the places on the way."

Naturally Kate consulted her phone. "There's the Hale telescope at the Palomar Observatory. Have you ever been there?"

"No. Where is it?"

"It's on Mount Palomar. It's run by Cal Tech but open to the public." Kate checked the map on her phone. "It looks like it's about an hour and a half or so from here, off Route 76."

"I thought we would take Route 78 home."

"Well, that's the point, isn't it? Take our time and meander on some back roads?"

"I wasn't complaining," Lawrence shrugged. "It would be more fun to go home a different way anyhow."

"Would you want to stop at some wineries in the Temecula area?"

Lawrence shrugged again. "If you want."

"Let's play it by ear," Kate said definitively as she shut down her phone. "Let's just enjoy our dinner and take a walk around town and check out some of the art galleries."

After dinner, they ambled down the streets of Borrego Springs, but found the galleries already closed for the day. They dallied at the brightly lit display windows and discussed the merits or lack thereof of the art they could see and then made their way back to the hotel.

They checked out early the next morning and were again at Anza-Borrego State Park visitor's center when it opened for the day. After a hike through Palm Canyon and Font's Point, they wound up back at the visitor's center at noon and bought a couple of protein bars. "I'm sure you noticed how desolate it is around here," Lawrence said. "We might not find a place for lunch for quite a while. Would you rather eat here in Borrego Springs before we leave?"

"Let's get on the road," Kate replied. "These protein bars will hold us for a while."

"It's hot now down here, but I bet it's going to be cool on the top of Mount Palomar."

"I'll leave our jackets in the back seat just in case."

"Good idea. So what does your phone say? We go out Montezuma Valley Road again, right?"

Kate opened the map app. "Yep."

"Okay." Lawrence drove out on Palm Canyon Drive and veered left onto the curvy, steep highway. "At least the drop offs are less nerve-wracking when climbing," Lawrence murmured, "but it's harder to enjoy the far views."

"Yeah," Kate said as she craned her neck to see out his side window. Beyond the peach colored rock lay the Borrego Valley far below — and further east broken land fading into blue gray desert haze. Somewhere out there was the Salton Sea. Lawrence then swerved to avoid a rock in the road, so Kate decided it was prudent to keep her eye on the road, too. They drove silently for a while, listening to music and lost in their own thoughts. "Was that a young girl?" Kate suddenly blurted out.

"What?" Lawrence slowed down. "Where?"

"Back there, sitting by the side of the road." "Lawrence, turn around. We need to see if something's wrong."

Lawrence climbed through more blind curves before he found a spot he could make a U-turn. He coasted down until the girl appeared again, sitting forlornly against a boulder, her back to a thousand-foot precipice. "How old do you think she is?" he asked as he pulled over.

"I don't know. Maybe twelve?" Kate opened her door and half-stood within the opening. "Are you alright?" she called to her. The girl stared at her, but didn't answer. Kate walked over to her and realized she was frightened. "Do you need help?" The girl said nothing.

Lawrence got out and forced a friendly smile across his face for the girl's benefit. "Is she okay?"

"She won't talk to me." Kate looked up and down the endless empty curves that made up the road. "Should we call 911?"

"Is there even cell service up here?" Lawrence wondered as he pulled out his phone.

"There's the valley below," Kate said with a sweep of her hand.

"Yeah, but we can't see Borrego Springs." He tried to make the call. "Nope. No coverage."

"We can't leave her here," Kate said as she turned toward the girl who was still staring at her and breathing hard. "Who are you with? Are your parents somewhere? Are you lost?" The girl finally averted her gaze and looked over the side of the cliff. Lawrence and Kate glanced at each other. "Do you think she was in an accident and she's trying to tell us that the car went over the side?" Kate murmured.

Lawrence reluctantly went to the edge peered over the cliff while Kate stayed with the girl. "Do you see anything?" she called out to him.

"Not really." he answered.

"It's not like there are tall trees, are there? I mean you'd see a car wouldn't you?"

"I guess so." He walked back to Kate. "I suppose we should take her with us and see if there's a sheriff in the next town. What is the next town and how far is it?"

"I think it was called Ranchita, but I'm not going to be able to get the map up on my phone if there's no service."

"Do you think it's a regular town with businesses?"

"Maybe. I recall a store of sorts there when I was looking for restaurants."

"Okay. Then let's take her to Ranchita and hope they're big enough to have a sheriff or at least cell service."

"Well, if nothing else, we'll be able to use a landline and call someone."

"The question is whether she'll come with us," Lawrence commented dubiously.

Kate took the girl's hand. "Will you come with us and we'll take you to the nearest town?" The girl didn't budge. "Are you hungry? We can get you something to eat there." The girl still didn't move. "You can't stay here alone. Please come with us."

"We're not going to hurt you. We want to help you," Lawrence added. Kate put her arm around the girl's shoulders and after a shudder and a sigh, the girl reluctantly got up and walked with Kate back to the car. Lawrence held the back door open and the girl got in.

They arrived at the town of Ranchita about fifteen minutes later. There wasn't much there, but there was a tiny market and gas pump so they parked the car in front. Kate got out and opened the back door. "Let's find something to eat here." The girl got out and took Kate's hand. Kate smiled at Lawrence and walked into the store with the girl.

Lawrence went to the cashier to talk to him while Kate walked around the store with the girl, picking up different items and showing them to the girl, hoping the girl would react to something. But the girl did and said nothing. Kate picked out some crackers and peanut butter and a six-pack of water, and then joined Lawrence at the cash register. "He said there really isn't a sheriff or anything here and we should probably go to Julian, about a half hour away."

Kate looked at her phone and pulled up the map app. "Okay I see how to get there. Can you pay for these, Lawrence? I want to take her to the rest room."

"Sure," he answered.

After all three had used the rest room, they piled back into the car and Kate gave Lawrence directions to the town of Julian as she dipped the crackers into the peanut butter, opened a bottle of water, and handed them to the girl who gobbled them down. "She probably hasn't eaten in a long time," Kate said. "Are there restaurants in Julian?"

"Yeah, Julian's kind of a tourist town."

"It is? Why?"

"The cashier at the market said Julian is known for its apple pie."

"I guess we'll just have to force ourselves to have some then," Kate teased. "Anyway, I think we should take her to a restaurant before bringing her to the sheriff's station. Who knows when she might eat again."

"I agree. We need to eat, too. It may take us a while to get this straightened out."

They got to Julian and found a town filled with restaurants and other businesses, a far cry from Ranchita. ""Who knew?" Lawrence laughed. "There are some really high end places here."

"Well, I think we can try those another time. Let's find a more kid-friendly restaurant for now." They walked by a mall-like place and the aroma of Mexican food filled the air. Kate watched a semblance of a smile cross the girl's face. "Let's go here."

"Where?" Lawrence asked. "Oh, this taco bar here?"

"Yeah, she almost smiled when she smelled them."

"I wonder if that's why she hasn't talked? Maybe she doesn't speak English."

"Well, let's see what happens when we go in to eat," Kate replied.

Sure enough, the girl ate two tacos heartily and even let a real smile cross her face. Lawrence and Kate enjoyed their food as well, surprised at how good it was in the middle of nowhere. "I don't know if I have room for the famous apple pie," Lawrence said sitting back in his chair. "Hey, since this is a taco restaurant, why not ask someone here to try to talk to her? They must be Spanish-speaking."

"Let's just find the sheriff's office. They'll probably have a translator. And we can get some pie later on our way out." They got up and Kate, once again, took the girl's hand. Lawrence, meanwhile, asked the cashier where to find the sheriff. "Can we walk there from here?"

The cashier laughed. "Sure. Nothing's too far from anywhere else here."

"Look at all these bakeries and even a cider mill," Kate said as they walked down the street. "I guess this place really is known for its apples."

When they got to the building that housed the sheriff's department, the girl stiffened and wouldn't walk another step. "Well this is a fine how-do-you-do," Lawrence muttered. "What's this about?"

"I don't know. But she's not moving." At that moment, a uniformed deputy came out of the building and the girl let go of Kate's hand and started running. "Oh no!" Kate said and went after her. Kate was a jogger and in good shape for her age, so she caught up with the girl quickly and grabbed her. "It's okay, sweetie. We don't have to go in there."

Lawrence approached them. "Luckily the deputy didn't notice you both running away. What are we going to do? Shall I go talk to them?"

Kate sighed. "I'm not sure. Maybe we need to think about this some more. Maybe we should take her home and make some calls and figure it out."

"You want us to kidnap her?" Lawrence asked in disbelief. "And what about if there was an accident or something. We can't just take her and not report it?" The girl started to pull away from Kate. "Lawrence, she's not going to stay with us if we approach the sheriff. Let's take her home for now."

Lawrence shook his head. "I think this is a mistake." He grew sullen as they walked back to the car, but he took the time to stop at a bakery and buy an apple pie to take home.

2

THEY ARRIVED IN LOS ANGELES THREE HOURS LATER. Lawrence had recently retired from teaching English at UCLA and Kate had recently returned from her two- year Peace Corps stint in Africa. She had also been an English teacher, but in high school, following in her father's footsteps. Her father had become a best-selling author after his retirement from teaching, and Kate and Lawrence had talked about collaborating on writing a novel. There hadn't been much movement, however, in that pursuit. They had only met a few months before Kate left for Africa, so their marriage had been quick and they were still learning a lot about each other. They had moved in to Lawrence's condo in Westwood, but they had started talking about a move.

"I'll let you two out here while I go park the car," Lawrence said as he pulled up to the front of their building.

"This is where we live," Kate said to the girl whose eyes had been popping out of her head as they drove through the streets of Los Angeles. "I don't think she's been to a big city before. She's mesmerized." Kate got out of the passenger side and opened the back door so the girl could join her on the sidewalk. "I'll take these jackets and the food. Can you get both suitcases?"

"Sure," he answered. "I'll get the mail on my way up."

Kate gave the girl the apple pie to hold and beckoned her to follow as she picked up the coats and the bag of food from the back. The girl looked up at the top of the high rise building, obviously in awe, as she followed Kate inside. When the elevator door opened, Kate entered and held the button for the girl, but she wouldn't budge. "Are you afraid? It's an elevator that will bring us to our apartment. Come on inside."

The girl was scared but took a tentative step. Kate put the bag of food down and took the girl's arm. "It's okay. Really. It's not going to go through the roof or anything."

The girl still wouldn't move, frozen in fear. A man and his dog arrived and got in the elevator. Kate realized she couldn't hold them up, so she got out of the elevator and joined the girl in the lobby. "Why are you still in the lobby?" Lawrence asked as he approached the elevator.

"She was afraid to get in the elevator."

"Well, what are you going to do?"

"I don't know. Any ideas?"

"Take the stairs," he replied.

"Good idea!"

"I'm not joining you, however, with two suitcases."

"I just hope she'll join me." Kate started walking towards the door to the staircase and turned to the girl. "Let's do this instead." The girl followed and happily climbed the stairs on Kate's heels. They arrived at the 5th floor and walked to the door of the condo. Kate put her package and the coats down so she could rummage through her purse for the key.

"I've got my key out in my hand," Lawrence said as he came down the hall towards them.

"Oh good," Kate sighed. Lawrence opened the door and held it open for Kate and the girl. "I'll bring her to the guest room after I drop the food off in the kitchen." The girl stood still as Kate took the pie from her hands and as Lawrence took the suitcases into their bedroom.

The girl glanced around the house and noticed the photographs on the wall. She walked up to a collage of pictures of a young child. The pictures were at different ages from babyhood to about five. There was a wedding picture on the wall next to it. "That's Lawrence's son, Michael on his wedding day," Kate said as she arrived to stand next to the girl. "His wife's name is Carla and that's his granddaughter, Danielle. Let me show you where you can sleep and use the bathroom. But we can have something to eat first, if you want." Of course, the girl didn't answer or move, so Kate took her hand and pulled her gently to the hall where the guest room and bathroom were located.

Lawrence was in the kitchen when Kate entered a few minutes later. "Did you show her the bedroom and bathroom?" he asked as he took some eggs and cheese out of the refrigerator.

"Yes, she and I both used the bathroom. Are you making us all an omelet?"

"Yeah, and a salad. Then we'll have room for some of that apple pie."

"Sounds like a plan," she said as she took the vegetables out of the refrigerator and started tearing up lettuce. "When shall we call the sheriff's department in Julian?"

"Go ahead," he replied. "I'll make dinner."

Kate went into the living room and took her phone out of her pocket. She Googled the Julian sheriff's office and found the phone number. "Hello? I um . . ." she paused. She wasn't sure what to say. She didn't want to report the girl, especially realizing that Lawrence had been right. They had kind of kidnapped her. But what was she reporting then? A possible accident by the side of the road in a place she couldn't describe and how did they know anything? They hadn't seen a car or even tire marks that might have shown one going off the road.

"Hello? Are you there?" the dispatcher on the other end asked.

"Uh, I just wanted — oh never mind. I'm sorry to have bothered you." She hung up quickly.

"What did they say?" Lawrence asked when Kate returned to the kitchen.

"I didn't know what to tell them. I'm not ready to report the missing girl yet. Please let me try to get her to talk first. I'm going to call a friend who speaks Spanish in the morning. Maybe that will help her to talk to us."

"I don't think this is a good idea. I mean not reporting this to the sheriff right away. And what if there was an accident?"

"I know. But . . ."

"I'll call."

"Okay, but just say something about there maybe is an accident. Please don't say anything about the girl yet," Kate pleaded.

Lawrence sighed. "Okay. Take over making dinner." He walked out of the room.

Kate finished making the omelet and the salad and went to get the girl. She had everything on the table when Lawrence re-entered. "What did they say?" Kate asked as they all sat down to eat.

"I had to tell them that we saw a girl by the side of the road, so that there was some explanation for thinking there might have been an accident. I just didn't mention that we took the girl with us."

"Were you able to describe where it was?"

"Just by how long we had traveled from Borrego Springs and how far it was from Ranchita."

"Did they ask about the girl?"

"I kind of hinted that she ran off."

"Thanks, Lawrence. I'll try to get some information out of her tomorrow, and if I can't, then —"

"Then what?" he interrupted. "Then we call back and mention that we kidnapped her?"

"I'll think of something." And once again, the girl gobbled her food . . . like she hadn't eaten in days.

"Do you want pie now or later?" Lawrence asked as he cleared the table.

"What time is it?"

"I don't know, nine or so."

"Let's have it now and then I can help her get ready for bed." Lawrence set down plates of pie wedges in front of Kate and the girl. "No ice cream?" Kate teased.

"Sorry. You'll have to eat it dry." They smiled and the tension in the air dissipated. The pie was delicious and even the girl seemed to relax a bit.

Kate took the girl back to the bedroom with a stop in her own room first to pick up some clothes for the girl to sleep in. She pantomimed taking off her clothes and held up the pajama bottoms and T-shirt to show what she should put on next. "You can sleep in these." Kate left her alone to get undressed and went back to the kitchen. Lawrence was at the sink, his back to her. She went up and tapped him on the shoulder. She hugged him tightly, kissed him on the lips when he turned around, and then went back to the guest room where the girl had just finished putting on her sleeping clothes.

"I'm going to take your clothes and wash them so they'll be clean tomorrow." But just as Kate picked them up off the bed, the girl grabbed them. "I'll give them back to you in the morning," she pleaded. She rubbed her hands together to demonstrate that she wanted to wash them. Then she pointed to some of the dirtiest places on the clothes. The girl seemed to understand at that point and loosened her grip. Before she handed them to Kate, however, she quickly took some items out of the pockets and then dropped the clothes and leapt into bed, holding the objects and hiding them under the covers. Those items were probably important in figuring out where the girl was from, and perhaps where she was going. Somehow, Kate needed to figure out how to get them from her. And she also knew it was not going to be an easy task.

"What are you doing?" Kate asked when she went into the living room after putting the girls' clothes in the washer. Lawrence was engrossed in reading something on his laptop.

"Looking up some places in Los Angeles that work with undocumented immigrants to get them asylum."

"Don't you think you're jumping the gun?" she cautioned. "We don't know that she's an undocumented immigrant."

"It can't hurt to get some advice. There's a group working at UCLA called the Civil Rights Project."

"Well, before you call them, I think we might be able to find some answers to who she is. She grabbed some stuff that she had in her pockets when I took her clothes to wash them. If we can take a look at what she has, it might give us some insight."

"Did you ask her for them?"

"No. She hid them under the covers. I need to get at them surreptitiously, I'm afraid."

"How are you going to do that?"

"Maybe when she's in the shower?"

He shrugged. "And then what? Hide them from her? You're not going to have enough time to get much information from them."

"Well, it's a start."

Lawrence sighed and shut down his computer. "Let's go to bed."

3

KATE WAS ALREADY IN THE KITCHEN ON HER SECOND CUP OF COFFEE WHEN LAWRENCE STUMBLED IN. "I thought I was the one up early," he mumbled.

"I couldn't sleep too well."

"The thought of getting arrested for kidnapping can keep one awake."

"Jeez Lawrence, why do you keep worrying about that? I'm worried about this poor child and what we can do to find her family."

"I *am* worried for her, but the fact is that we haven't been straight with law enforcement of any kind and that is not going to help the situation. We haven't a clue about what we've gotten ourselves into." Lawrence rubbed his forehead. "Kate, You're not a Black man living in this country. You cannot understand how much I have to worry about in everyday situations."

Kate took in a sharp breath and looked away. "You're right about that." She searched for words of support. "I guess my mind just doesn't go there. The privilege of being a White woman is only slightly less than a White man's. I can get myself out of any situation and I've always made up the difference with spunk." She looked back at him, trying to express with her eyes a sorrow much deeper than she cared to dive into. She approached him and offered him a little kiss of consolation, which neither found satisfying. They retreated to opposite ends of the kitchen, brooding over the different perspectives. "I did get one idea," Kate finally said. "When she wakes up, I'll bring her in the kitchen for breakfast and maybe you can go in her room and look for those items."

"In the bed?"

"I guess. That's where she put them last night."

"Are her clothes washed and dried?"

"I need to put them in the dryer. I thought I'd wait until she's up so she can't change into them yet."

Lawrence shook his head. "I don't like it, but I'll do it. Besides what we've talked about, it isn't very nice to look at things that she obviously doesn't want us to see."

Kate shrugged. "Do you have any other brilliant ideas?"

"I've already told you mine. You didn't care for them."

She sighed. "I tell you what. Give me a day or two to see if I can figure out anything or at least get her to communicate with us. I'm going to call my friend Lucy and have her talk to her. She speaks Spanish so maybe she'll open up to her."

"Fair enough. Have you seen if she's awake yet?"

"No, I'll go check." Kate left and returned with the girl. She nodded to Lawrence.

"*Buenos días*," he said and watched for some acknowledgement. The girl did look him in the eye and the corners of her mouth turned up slightly. He smiled at Kate and left the kitchen.

Lawrence had no trouble finding the items the girl had hidden. They were still under the covers. There were some postcards, a couple of photographs, a bit of jewelry, but most importantly a birth certificate that said her name was Lourdes Moreno and that she had been born in a hospital in Fresno. He then looked at the postcards and noticed the pictures were of typical California tourist places: Golden Gate Bridge, Disneyland, Monterey Aquarium, San Diego Zoo. But the postmarks were from places he had never heard of: Tranquillity, Firebaugh, Stevinson. They were written in Spanish and were addressed to Marisol Sandoval in Tijuana. One of the photographs was of the girl standing with a couple and a teenage girl. The girl looked to be a few years younger in the picture. The other photo was of the older girl standing with a group of young people. He took out his phone and snapped pictures of the birth certificate and the written side of one of the postcards. He hoped that Kate's friend Lucy could read the postcard and there would be some information that could prove helpful. He put the items back under the covers and left the room.

Kate and the girl were eating breakfast when Lawrence arrived back in the kitchen. "I made French toast. Do you want some?" Kate asked.

"Sure."

Kate went to the stove and turned on the burner under the frying pan. "Do we have anything to discuss?" she asked pointedly.

"Yeah. Are you going to show her the shower?"

"Just as soon as the dryer is finished so she'll have clean clothes to put on. Then I'll call Lucy."

"Well, I have something to show Lucy as well."

Kate looked curiously at Lawrence and then the girl to see if there was any reaction but the girl was focused on her food. "Okay. The dryer should be done in about twenty minutes."

"Maybe I should shower while the French toast is cooking," he replied.

"That's fine. I'll put the burner on low."

"I'll be quick." Lawrence left, Kate stood at the stove, and the girl cleaned her plate.

"Do you want more?" Kate asked but then sighed when she got no response. "*Más?*" she asked again, trying to remember any Spanish phrase she ever knew. But of course, the girl said nothing. Nor did she shake or nod her head. It was frustrating to Kate, but she tried not to show it. She merely placed a couple more pieces of French toast on the girl's plate and she started eating them right away.

"Is my French toast ready?' Lawrence asked as he entered the kitchen.

"Oh, man. Sorry. I gave away your pieces. I'll make you some more." Kate hurried to the refrigerator and took out the eggs.

"Don't bother. Regular toast is fine. Why not show her where the shower is. The dryer seems to have stopped."

Kate nodded and got the girl's clothes out of the dryer. She pantomimed washing herself, rubbing her hands up and down her arms and face. "How about a, uh, *baños*?" she said to the girl, and then turned to Lawrence. "I think the word for bath is something like that."

Lawrence laughed. "Is it too early to call Lucy? Well, we can always consult Google."

The girl got up and took her clothes from Kate. "Hey, I think she understood," Kate chirped as they left the kitchen. Kate showed her how to turn on the bath and the shower. "And here's a towel and washcloth." She returned to the kitchen.

Lawrence had his phone images ready. "Look at this! It's her birth certificate!"

Kate took the phone and looked at the picture. "Lourdes is her name? And she's from Fresno? You'd think she could speak some English if she was born here."

"Maybe she speaks perfectly good English, but is choosing not to," Lawrence replied. "Or maybe some sort of trauma has made her mute."

"You know, there are different kinds of mutism, not just related to being deaf or a physical deformity," Kate's face became pensive. "There was a girl in my school when I was teaching up north.

She wasn't in my class, but her teacher said she wouldn't speak in class or to any adult, but she would talk to the other kids."

"Maybe I should call Michael and Carla to bring Danielle over."

"We could try that."

"But what's weird is that there were also some postcards of various California tourist spots. Those were addressed to Marisol Sandoval in Tijuana."

"Well, maybe she wanted to mail them to someone named Marisol."

"They were all postmarked from small towns in the Central Valley, so someone had mailed them to her." Lawrence looked closely at one of the photos. "This one's from a place called Tranquillity."

"Hmm. So is she Lourdes or Marisol?" Kate mused. "We could try calling her both and see how she reacts."

"Does Lucy just happen to speak Spanish or is she Hispanic?" Lawrence asked.

"Just happens to speak it. But she has spent a considerable amount of time in Mexico so probably knows more than we do about the culture." Kate glanced up at the clock. "I'll call her at nine. That's a reasonable hour. I'm going to take my shower now."

Lawrence spent the interim on his laptop in the living room trying to decipher what was written on the postcard. It was a painstakingly long process trying to translate one word at a time and it became clear that there wasn't much of value in the actual words. The sentiment was the usual type of postcard sentiment: miss you, can't wait to be together. But there was one interesting reference to not be afraid and stay out of the streets. "What'cha doing'?" Kate asked as she plopped onto the couch next to him.

"Trying to translate this postcard. I'm not sure the postcards will be much help."

"What do they say?"

"Nothing really."

"Are they signed?"

He shook his head no. "Where's Lourdes or Marisol?"

"I haven't checked if she's done in the bathroom. Anyway, I want to talk to Lucy without her in the room first to explain everything. And I'd like to wait for Lucy to use the two names."

"Why not us?" Lawrence asked. "We could try to see if she answers one or the other. Maybe she will and she speaks English and everything will be simplified."

"I just feel like she would respond better to someone speaking Spanish. Also, I think she might react better if it's over the phone."

"Really? Why?"

"I don't know. Do you care that much?"

"Well . . . no."

"I didn't mean to sound harsh. I'm just following my gut."

"Whatever. This is your thing anyway." He closed his laptop and stood.

"Are you angry?"

"I wouldn't call it angry. Just irritated. It doesn't matter. Why don't you try Lucy." Kate watched him go to their bedroom, probably to brood.

She picked up her phone. "Hey Luce, it's Kate. How ya' doing'?"

"I'm good. Just getting ready to meet Julia for a latte."

"Oh gee, I miss you two. Do you have a few minutes?"

"Yeah, what's up?"

Kate took a deep breath. She hadn't thought about how to tell the story and what exactly she was asking Lucy to do. "Uh, Lawrence and I went to Borrego Springs over the weekend and —"

"Oh, I love that place! Where'd you stay?" Lucy interrupted.

"Um, the Palm Canyon."

"Most people don't know about Anza-Borrego. Had you been there before?"

"No. Anyway, on our way home yesterday we came upon a young girl on the road by herself."

"Hitchhiking? Man, you can't do that anymore like we used to."

Kate sighed. Lucy was not making it easy. "No, I don't think so. She's so young. She must have been with her parents, but she was all alone on the road. We picked her up and planned on taking her to the sheriff in Julian."

"How old is she?" Lucy asked.

"We don't know because she won't talk to us. She looks around twelve or so. We think she's Hispanic, so I thought maybe you could talk to her."

"I thought you said you took her to the sheriff?" Lucy asked.

"We brought her to the office, but when a uniformed deputy came out of the building she freaked out and ran. We caught her and took her home with us."

"What?!! Are you out of your mind?"

"We didn't know what to do."

"Why do you think she's Hispanic?"

"Well, she *looks* Hispanic and smiled when we brought her to a tacos place. Plus she had a birth certificate in her pocket that says her name is Lourdes and that she was born in Fresno. But she also had postcards in her pocket addressed to Marisol in Tijuana so we aren't sure what her name is. That's why we thought you could talk to her."

"If she was born in Fresno and she's twelve, she must speak English. All kids learn English in school, even if their parents don't speak a word."

"I don't know. I just thought if you spoke to her in Spanish, she might respond to you," Kate replied.

"The birth certificate could be counterfeit. They're common and not hard to come by. Anyway, I'd be happy to try to talk with her."

"Oh good. I need to go to the guest room where she is." Kate started walking with phone in hand. "I'm remembering that Hmong girl in Alicia's class, the one who was mute. I thought maybe that was the issue. Maybe this girl was traumatized in some way and she became mute —what do they call that again? Selective mutism?"

"Selective or situational. Didn't you help that Hmong girl start talking?"

"I did. It was one of my favorite teaching accomplishments, even though she wasn't my student."

"It was pretty special."

"Here we are." Kate knocked on the door and then, remembering the girl was not going to answer the knock, proceeded to open the door and walk in the room. "There's someone on the phone who wants to talk to you."

The girl was looking at her postcards and looked up at Kate inquisitively, but Kate thrust the phone at her anyway. The girl put it to her ear and Kate watched her face intently and was pleased to see the corners of her mouth turn up. It wasn't a wide grin, but it was definitely a form of smiling. Now, if she would answer . . . but that didn't happen. After a few minutes, the girl handed the phone back to Kate. "Sorry Kate," Lucy sighed.

"But she smiled when you were talking to her. That's huge."

"Then I would guess she is Marisol from Tijuana. I addressed her that way, to see how she would respond. I figure she is an illegal with a phony birth certificate. That's why she reacted to the deputy sheriff so strongly."

"Well, that's a huge help! Thanks Lucy."

"I'm happy to talk to her again, but I have to leave. I'm already late meeting Julia and you know how she gets."

Kate laughed. "Yes I do. Love her dearly, but Julia can be very difficult."

"I'll call you later. My suggestion to you, though, is to call some place that deals with undocumented immigrants. Technically you've kidnapped her."

"You sound like Lawrence."

"Well, he's right. There are plenty of places in Los Angeles that won't have her deported, but could help you."

"Okay, thanks. I'll talk to you later. Love to Julia." They hung up and Kate turned to the girl. "Do you have family here, Marisol?" She watched closely to see how she reacted to the name, even though she wouldn't understand what Kate had said. Marisol looked into Kate's eyes and Kate saw the fear and anxiety behind them. She took Marisol into her arms and hugged her.

4

KATE BROUGHT MARISOL INTO THE LIVING ROOM AND TURNED ON THE TELEVISION. She found a Disney movie on Netflix and patted the sofa for Marisol to sit and watch. "I'm going to make a couple of phone calls. I'll be right back." Marisol didn't respond, of course, but she did seem mesmerized by what was on the screen.

Kate took her phone into the bedroom and lay next to Lawrence as he sat up on the bed, typing on his computer. "What did Lucy say?" he asked.

"We are pretty sure the birth certificate is a fake and her name is Marisol. Lucy addressed her as Marisol and although she didn't talk, she did smile when Lucy talked to her in Spanish. She must be an undocumented immigrant and used the birth certificate to get across the border."

Lawrence stopped typing and looked at Kate. "Okay. Now what?"

"She suggested I look up some Los Angeles agencies that could help."

"Like the one I found at UCLA . . ."

"I guess."

"Did she know where to find these agencies?"

"She was on her way out so we'll talk more later."

"Where is she now?" Lawrence asked.

"Who Lucy?"

"No. Marisol."

"In the living room watching a Disney movie."

Lawrence laughed. "What would parents do without Disney!"

"I thought I might take her shopping for some clothes today. I mean she'll need them no matter where she goes."

"Are you going to talk to one of these agencies first?"

Kate frowned. "Why are you in such a hurry to get rid of her?"

"I'm just not comfortable feeling like a kidnapper. She can stay here as long as she needs to, but I just want some authority to know about her and be doing what's necessary to find her parents."

Kate sighed. "I just wish she'd talk to us. Okay. I'll see what I can find online about immigration assistance."

"You don't even know if she's legal or illegal. Or if her name is Lourdes or Marisol. Or if she's from Tijuana or some tiny central valley town. We should have stayed around Borrego Springs, close to where we found her." Lawrence shook his head and frowned. "Maybe we should go back there."

"You saw how she reacted to seeing the guy in a uniform. She must be illegal," Kate replied. "She was probably taught to stay away from the border patrol or ICE agents who might take her away from her family."

"That's if she's actually from Mexico or Central America."

"Don't you think it's a good bet that she was wandering around on the desert because she crossed the border?" Kate asked.

"Or she and her family are American and somehow they got separated from each other."

Kate was silent. She knew Lawrence was right in many ways. But she also knew from her teaching experience that many children have witnessed unspeakable things, especially those from certain areas of Mexico and Central America. It wouldn't surprise her at all that a child would refuse to talk as a safety valve. She had a pretty strong inkling that Marisol had probably crossed the border somehow and was on the run. Whether taking her with them was right or wrong from a legal standpoint, she was sure it was the compassionate and humanitarian thing to do. "She needs clothes regardless so I'm going to take her shopping and give myself time to think about how to approach this. How about you do the same and we can compare notes in a couple of hours when I get back? Let's both try to approach this without using our own personal opinions. Just look at it from as open-minded a position as we can."

"Alright. That's fair." He reached for her hand. "Where are you going to take her shopping?"

Kate shrugged. "Target I guess."

"See you later, then. I'm going to the gym, the best place to think."

Kate mimed to Marisol that they were going out to buy clothes as she spoke the words in English. She had no idea if Marisol understood any of it, but apparently Marisol trusted Kate enough at this point to just follow her lead. Her obvious wonder at the high rises and at the crowds of people in Westwood as well as the enormity of the Target store was enough for Kate. She felt pretty convinced that Marisol was new to American cities. Fresno may not be the same size as Los Angeles, but it is a city of half a million. After Kate helped her pick out some clothes, she took Marisol to the books department and found a couple of children's books in Spanish. "I don't know if you can read, if you've been to school, or what. But you can enjoy the pictures and maybe read a few words," Kate said as she paid for the items. She took one of the books out of the bag and handed it to Marisol to look at as they headed for the exit. She gave Marisol a sideways glance and noticed that she seemed mesmerized and there was a definite upturn of the corners of her upper lip. Kate smiled knowingly, feeling more and more confident that Marisol was indeed an undocumented immigrant. But where were her parents?

They got home and Kate found Lawrence in the kitchen, setting the table with plates and napkins. In the center of the table was a bag from Chipotle. "She really liked the tacos from that restaurant in Julian, so I thought this might be a good lunch."

Kate grinned at Lawrence. "You're a good man."

"Why wouldn't I give her something she likes?"

"Not everyone would be as thoughtful as you. That's all I'm saying."

"Did you find some clothes?" he asked as he sat down.

"Yes, and I bought her a couple of books in Spanish. They're young children's books with lots of pictures. She enjoyed looking at the one I gave her, but I don't know if she can read the words or just looked at the pictures."

"Why do you think she can't read? She's at least ten years old?"

"In case she's always been working in the fields or just hasn't been to school much. I don't know," Kate replied. "Let's just enjoy lunch and we'll talk about it later." She noticed that Marisol hadn't sat down at the table yet. She seemed to look a bit scared and just stared at them. "What's wrong Marisol?" Kate asked.

"Maybe she wants to use the bathroom or something," Lawrence said as he started taking the tacos out of the bag.

"I guess I'll take her and see." Kate stood and took Marisol's hand. "If you need to use the bathroom, you can go anytime." They walked out.

"Was that it?" Lawrence asked when they returned a few minutes later.

"Yeah, I guess so. She used it, anyway."

They ate their tacos and once again Marisol ate with even more gusto than when they ate dinner last night or breakfast this morning. Tacos were definitely a favorite . . . or more familiar. "I'll wash the plates and see you in the bedroom."

"Okay. I'll set her up with the television again."

Lawrence was already there when Kate flopped onto the bed next to him. "Well, what did you come up with?" he asked.

"The way she looked at the book in Spanish and the fact that she seemed so awed by the tall buildings and crowds of the city, kind of cemented to me that she is not an American," Kate answered. "How about you?"

"That reinforces the gut feeling I'm starting to get. I think she probably is Marisol from Tijuana, not Lourdes from Fresno."

"Then I guess we need to look into Lucy's suggestion of finding an agency to help us?"

"Is that a question?"

Kate nodded and shrugged. "Yes. It's a question to you. I would rather try to find her parents ourselves and not involve the government."

"Dammit Kate! I'm sure there are places to get help that will not notify ICE or the Feds. That's all I meant."

"Okay. I hope you're right, though."

"We'll find out from them how they help before telling them the story." Kate didn't answer. "I tell you what," Lawrence continued. "I'll call a former colleague who might know something about the program at UCLA and see if he can advise us on who to contact."

"That would be great. Let's start there."

Lawrence took Kate's hands into his. "I know you want to protect her, but we wouldn't be much help to her from a jail cell."

"No," she sighed. "I guess not." She got up and went into the living room and sat down next to Marisol on the sofa. She took the girl's hand and held onto it as they watched TV together.

5

LAWRENCE JOINED THEM IN THE LIVING ROOM ABOUT A HALF HOUR LATER. "I spoke with my former colleague. He gave me the name of a place you can call." He handed Kate a post-it note.

Kate looked at the note. "What does ICWC stand for?"

"Immigration Center for Women and Children. They have offices in Los Angeles, San Francisco, San Diego and Las Vegas. That's the number for the LA office."

"Great. I'll go call now." She got up and took her phone into the bedroom. Lawrence started to leave, but changed his mind and took Kate's place on the couch. He didn't take Marisol's hand, however.

Kate sat down on the bed and looked at her phone. She was about to dial the number, but then decided to Google the organization first and read about it, lest she put Marisol in the legal system. The images of children in cages in the detention centers along the border had made a huge impact on Kate. She opened her laptop and then closed it again. She didn't want to take any chances and she worried that by sharing Marisol's story, it might be endangering her. She knew Lawrence would be mad, but she wanted to try to find Marisol's parents without the help of an organization that might, by law, have to report it. Her phone rang startling her. She looked at the caller ID and answered.

"Hi Julia. How are you?"

"I'm great, but Lucy told me what you're up to. Have you lost your mind?"

"Why does everyone think I'm crazy to want to help this poor girl?"

"Now, don't get all pissed off, Kate."

"Well, I guess I am. Haven't you been watching the news for the last few years about these poor children in detention centers at the border?" Kate exhaled loudly. "I'm sorry, Julia, but it feels like you're all judging me based on my political activism. Just because you all don't have the same principled convictions about things like this —"

"Chill, Kate. We're not judging you. It's just a big thing to take on. We're on your side."

"Well if you're on my side then you agree with me about finding her family myself."

"What I meant is that we understand what you're doing and why," Julia replied, "but we don't think it's wise for you or for her. You could get her into more trouble than she may already be in, and you will definitely get yourself and Lawrence into trouble."

"I'm not worried about me. I know Lawrence is concerned —"

"Lawrence has more reason than you to be concerned!" Julia interrupted. "He's a Black man who has kidnapped a young girl!" Kate was silent and Julia was too, wanting that fact to sink in. "You know what I mean!" Julia finally added.

"I guess."

"No guessing. You know, you're putting him in a very vulnerable position."

"We had a discussion about that this morning."

"And you needed a White woman to remind you of that?"

"Okay, okay. I'll talk to him and see if we can come up with a compromise that addresses everyone's issues."

"Look Kate, this isn't about diplomacy. This is about your husband. He's a gentleman and deserves your protection first and foremost. It will do this girl no good to put him in jeopardy . . . let alone your marriage."

"I . . ." Kate choked. "I'll call one of those asylum groups."

"Oh, I wanna hug you!" Julia cried.

"You and Lucy will keep this to yourselves, won't you?"

"Of course! We're your best friends."

Kate hung up and looked up to find Lawrence in the doorway. "How long have you been standing there?"

"I could practically hear Julia in the living room." Kate chuckled. He came over and kissed the top of her head. "I love you."

"I just don't trust all people in government," Kate murmured.

"Believe me, I know, but why not just call the people my friend recommended? See if they have any ideas?"

"I'm afraid to." Kate started to cry. "I thought we could just go to all those small farm towns and talk to other immigrants."

"Kate," Lawrence soothed. "For the very reason you're afraid to talk to anyone, you think other immigrants are necessarily going to talk to you and me?"

"No," she sniffed.

Lawrence sighed. "You are extremely principled and you can be stubborn and rigid when you feel that people's rights are violated. That's a good thing. I'm not knocking it. But sometimes you have to look at the bigger picture."

"Maybe the immigrants we try to talk to would feel more comfortable because a White woman and a Black man are asking the questions. Maybe they would feel more at ease with a person of color . . . not less."

Lawrence shook his head and smiled at Kate. "Okay. I'll give you that one. But it doesn't negate how law enforcement will view this."

Kate shrugged and wiped her eyes with the back of her hand. "We won't know until we try it." She turned to look up at him. "How's this? I will call that Immigration Center for Women and Children without giving my name and ask what they think I should do. Fair enough?"

"Will you follow their advice?"

Kate managed a mischievous glance. "That I can't promise."

Lawrence shook his head again and sighed. "I guess that's a start."

"One step at a time."

"In stilettos?"

"You wish."

She got up and kissed him. "I'm just going to check on Marisol before I make the call."

"I'm going to follow your lead," Lawrence said. "I'm going to call the sheriff in Julian, also without giving my name, just to make sure no one has reported a missing girl."

"Okay." Kate left to find Marisol and Lawrence took out his phone.

Kate found Marisol exactly where she'd left her, mesmerized by the television. She sat down next to her. "Hi sweetie. Do you like the show?" Marisol looked into Kate's eyes and for the first time, actually smiled. Kate hugged her and became even more resolved to find her family herself. But she made a promise to Lawrence that she would keep. She took out her phone and the paper Lawrence had given her with the phone number. She walked into the kitchen and dialed. "Hello? I would like to know what you do exactly."

After talking to them for several minutes, Kate knew that as wonderful a group as these people were, they could not help Marisol. They were lawyers trying to help victims of domestic violence and children who are applying for DACA status or their custodians who have been appointed by the courts. Kate thanked them and hung up. She went back to the bedroom to report to Lawrence. "They could be a great help to Marisol if we found out that she has family here in the United States, or was in the courts and/or immigration system. But they are not going to be any better at finding her family than we would. That is not what they do."

Lawrence nodded. "Okay. I see that. Well, no one has come forward to the sheriff either, but he did ask an awful lot of questions."

Kate wanted to say that she had been right, but she knew better and said instead, "Shall we plan a road trip?"

"I guess so."

"Leave tomorrow?"

"Let's talk about a plan before we decide on when we should leave," Lawrence replied. "Just because no one has reported anything to the sheriff, doesn't mean there aren't people looking for her. I think we need to go back to where we found her and start there. What do you think?"

"I think you're a smart man. I'm going to call Lucy and ask her to explain to Marisol what we are planning. Oh, and guess what?"

"What?"

"Marisol smiled at me. A real smile."

"Really? Maybe she'll even open her mouth and speak soon."

"Maybe. But I'm not holding my breath. That girl I helped in our school . . . it took months of getting to know me."

"Yeah, but she wasn't living with you."

"True. Well . . . we shall see." Kate went back to the living room, dialing Lucy as she walked. "Hey Luce. Here's an update." She gave Lucy the lowdown and sat down next to Marisol. "Lucy wants to talk to you again," Kate said as she handed her the phone.

Marisol took the phone and listened. She looked a little perplexed, stiffening her body with her brow furrowing and her mouth clamped shut. But as Kate watched her, she noticed her shoulders and face relax and she thought she perceived a slight nod of her head. After a couple of minutes she handed the phone back to Kate. "Does she look like she understood what I said?" Lucy asked.

"I think so. She kind of nodded. Well, even if she doesn't, that's what we are going to do."

"You're a brave soul, Kate."

"Why do you say that?"

"Because you could get into a lot of trouble."

Kate laughed. "I'll take my chances. I think they forgive people over the age of sixty for a lot of things. I'll pretend I have dementia or something."

"I'm serious but I know you. When you have your mind made up there's no stopping you. After all, you meet a man and fall in love and choose to go into the Peace Corps rather than stay with him."

"Well, it all worked out, didn't it? He waited for me and I got to fulfill a dream I had for a long time. I got to do both."

"Yeah. But most women wouldn't have taken the chance."

"I'm not most women, I guess."

Lucy laughed. "That's for damn sure!"

6

THE REST OF THE DAY WAS SPENT GETTING READY FOR THE TRIP. Kate gave Marisol a bag to pack with her new clothes, her new books, and her precious possessions: the postcards, pictures, jewelry and birth certificate. Lawrence went to the grocery store to buy snacks and water for the trip while Kate packed and made arrangements for what might be a couple of weeks on the road. She mapped out a route to Tranquillity, the first town they would get to. Firebaugh and Stevinson were further north. She found it odd that the towns of Tranquillity and Stevinson were spelled differently than the norm. She wondered if the towns' populations were entirely Hispanic and that the names were an English derivative of the Spanish in some way. She had always known that being a teacher in California, she should have learned more Spanish since so many of her students had been from Mexico and Central America. But there had also been many Southeast Asians and how many languages could she have learned?

Marisol ate ravenously again at dinnertime, as if she hadn't eaten in many days. Kate and Lawrence glanced at each other, both wondering if it was more that she was afraid she wouldn't get anything to eat in the future. They turned on another movie for Marisol while they finished cleaning up the kitchen and the last minute packing. "I have the route to Tranquillity figured out," Kate said as she zipped up her suitcase. "We should take all back roads to see if she recognizes anyplace."

"Wait a minute," Lawrence replied skeptically. "I thought we were going back to where we found her, first."

"We are. But I wanted to see the roads so we'll know in case there isn't any cell phone service. We're going to be out in the boondocks."

"Okay. Just checking that you hadn't changed your mind about that. You know, she's probably never been to those small towns if she's, in fact, Marisol and not Lourdes, born in Mexico, not Fresno."

"I know," Kate nodded. "That's most likely the case. Lucy said it's common for family members to mail birth certificates to Mexicans who are trying to get into the United States. I'm guessing that's what happened. Lourdes is probably a cousin of hers, around the same age."

"What do you think we should do when we get to Julian?" Lawrence asked.

"I'm not sure why we are going to Julian. You asked the sheriff and no one has reported anyone missing. We need to just go back toward Borrego Springs and look around there."

"I guess you're right. I can call him every couple of days and ask. But we will need to stay someplace and get at least one good meal. I only bought snacks for the car ride, to keep us going after breakfast. Have you found hotels and made reservations?"

"We have to play it all by ear. We have no idea how long we'll be in any one place. We might be in rural areas, but there are always crappy motels around."

"Maybe I should throw in my old tent and sleeping bags, just in case."

Kate looked at him and laughed. "I don't know, Lawrence. I kind of vowed several years ago that I was done with camping."

"Me too. But just in case?"

Kate shrugged. "Is there room?"

"I think so."

"I guess it can't hurt." She looked at the clock. "Shall we go to bed? We do want to get started early."

"Yeah, sure."

"I'll get Marisol." Kate went to the living room. "Hey sweetie, time to go to bed." She turned off the television. Marisol got right up, seemingly understanding what Kate said. She went toward the guest room without Kate having to take her hand and bring her. "Do you speak English?" Marisol paid no attention, just went into the bathroom and closed the door. Kate stood silently, trying to decide if she needed to wait for her to show her it was bedtime, but then decided to let her be and went back to her bedroom.

"That was quick," Lawrence said as she opened the door.

"It was weird. She seemed to understand what I said about being time to go to bed."

"What makes you say that?"

"She just got up and went into the bathroom when I turned off the television."

"It's a common routine. Turning off the television after dinner means it's time for bed."

"I guess. It's hard enough that she doesn't understand English, but this muteness is worse," Kate sighed. "At least if she'd speak to us I could use Lucy or a Spanish dictionary and we could communicate."

"Do you have a Spanish dictionary? At least we could try talking to her in Spanish instead of English."

"No. Just our phones and laptops and translate apps."

"I wouldn't rely too much on the net and cell service where we're going. A book might be a good idea. Let's buy one in the morning."

"You're so smart," she teased. "Must be that PhD."

"Yeah, that's it." He embraced her and they both fell on the bed, a tangle of arms and legs.

After they made love, Kate put on a bathrobe and went out to check that Marisol had, in fact, gone to bed. She opened the guest room door quietly and peeked in. Marisol was sitting up in bed, looking at her pictures, crying softly. Kate went in and sat down next to her. "We are going to find your parents or your relatives." She pointed to the woman in the picture a younger Marisol was in. "Is that your, um, *madre?*" Marisol looked up into Kate's eyes. "And your *padre* and . . ." Kate tried to remember the Spanish word for sister. "Oh yeah, uh, and your *hermana?*"

No response from Marisol, but she didn't try to hide her tears. Kate took her in her arms to hug her and felt Marisol's body heaving in sobs. They sat for several minutes and finally Kate felt her take a deep breath. She pulled away and kissed the top of her head. Marisol got back under the covers. Kate took the pictures and put them into the backpack. She turned out the light and left the room, closing the door behind her.

7

THE SUN HAD JUST STARTED TO COME UP WHEN KATE OPENED HER EYES AND LOOKED AT THE CLOCK. Six thirty and Lawrence was still fast asleep. That was unusual, since they had gone to bed fairly early. But then, like most men, he didn't have the problem Kate had with insomnia. Her mind went a mile a minute when her head hit the pillow while Lawrence fell asleep and stayed asleep, able to compartmentalize and not dwell on worries and concerns. She got up and opened the door to Marisol's room, but she too was still fast asleep.

Kate made coffee and sat down in the living room with her mug and an old-fashioned map of California. It was still easier for her to use paper maps instead of her phone. She liked to be able to see the whole picture. She wanted to take a different route than they had taken going down a few days ago. Might as well make a vacation of sorts out of it, seeing different things. Anyway, they would end up leaving at rush hour so the 405 and the Santa Monica Freeway going toward downtown Los Angeles would be crazy. She decided instead to go north on the 405 to the Valley where they could catch the Ventura Freeway East and then the 210 through Pasadena. It's not like there wouldn't be traffic, but it should be better than going through downtown. Then they could get on 60 toward Riverside and catch the 215 to Temecula where it crosses 79. She wanted to drive some smaller roads before going on Montezuma Valley Road, where they had found Marisol, but she wasn't sure there were any. The map didn't show them, but she hoped they could find some without getting totally lost.

"What'cha doing'?" Lawrence asked from the doorway.

"Checking on our route."

"I thought you had it all planned out."

"I did, but I forgot to take rush hour traffic into consideration. We can't go through downtown."

"That's true. So have you figured it out?"

"Yeah."

Lawrence got a cup of coffee and sat down next to her. "Maybe we could stay tonight in Palm Springs."

"I think they have a major music festival there some time in October," Kate said.

"We don't have to go to the festival. I just thought it might be fun."

Kate shrugged. "We can stay in Palm Springs if you like, but I don't think this is the time to be going out of our way in vacation mode."

Lawrence sighed. "I need to tell Michael and Carla what's going on." He went back to the bedroom to call his son and daughter-in-law, while Kate went to wake Marisol.

"Do you want to eat now or shower first?" she asked Marisol. "Remember, we are going back to Borrego Springs today." Kate rubbed her arms simulating washing herself and bringing a utensil to her mouth to pantomime eating. But Marisol just looked at her blankly, so Kate decided for her. She pointed to the bathroom and said, "*Baños* first while I make breakfast." Then she left for the kitchen, hoping Marisol understood. She must have because when she arrived in the kitchen she was dressed in one of her new outfits from Target.

"Let's eat hearty so we don't have to think about our next meal for a while," Lawrence said as he appeared, also showered and dressed.

"I made oatmeal so add some bananas and blueberries and you can have a piece of toast as well. That ought to hold you," Kate said, patting his stomach after she put the bowls on the table.

"I found an old Spanish dictionary, by the way," Lawrence added. "I'd forgotten I had it."

"Oh good. I wish I had time to study it."

"I'll drive and you can skim it and come up with some phrases that would be helpful for us to know." Kate got up and started to clear the table. "I'll clean up," Lawrence said. "You go take your shower. I assume Marisol had hers?"

"Yes. She's all ready to go. I can turn on the television for her." Kate turned toward Marisol, but the girl was at the sink, washing the dishes. Kate and Lawrence glanced at each other with raised eyebrows, but said nothing. Lawrence finished clearing the table while Kate went to the bathroom to get ready.

Marisol knew how to wash dishes in a modern kitchen just fine, although Lawrence still felt that he needed to stay in the kitchen and make sure. He busied himself packing the snacks he had bought the day before and the only thing he had to show her how to do was the garbage disposal. "You need to run the water at the same time," he said as he turned on the faucet and the switch. She jumped back away from the sink when it went on, surprised by the noise as well as its purpose.

They were on the road by nine and as Kate had expected, traffic was the usual nightmare. She studied the dictionary and gave Lawrence directions while Marisol alternated looking out the window with looking at her photos. Kate decided to try her Spanish skills and turned around. *"¿De dónde eres?"*

"What did you say to her?" Lawrence asked.

"Hopefully, where are you from?" Kate waited a few seconds and then added, "Tijuana?" Not surprisingly, Marisol did not answer. *"¿Viniste de México? ¿Cruzaste la frontera? Queremos ayudarte a encontrar a tu familia."* Still no response. "I told her we were trying to help her find her family."

"Give it up, Kate. She'll talk when she's ready."

"I guess. Hey, maybe some Spanish music would help." Kate fiddled with the radio until she found a station. She turned around again to see if the expression on Marisol's face changed at all. She didn't smile, but Kate did notice that Marisol swayed her body in time to the music. Kate smiled at her and then smiled at Lawrence who nodded. Maybe music, that international language, would break the ice.

They finally reached Temecula and Lawrence said, "Okay, there's the sign for Route 79."

"Wait," Kate replied as she opened the map. "Let's go further south on 15 until we hit Route 76. That road goes by Mount Palomar."

"Why do you want to go that way? You want to do that Palomar Observatory tour today?"

"No. Just that I think we should go on a different road than we were on the last time to see if she recognizes anything along the way. 76 meets up with 79 before getting to Borrego Springs."

"Okay. That's fine." He passed the exit for 79. "But we found her on 79 didn't we?"

"No. On Montezuma Valley Road. Or maybe it was on San Felipe. Oh jeez, I can't remember, but we'll know it when we see it."

"There's an exit for Pala Road. Is that 76?" Lawrence asked.

"Let me see. Yes, I think so. Sorry. I'm not being a very good navigator. Maybe I should drive and you read the map."

"You're doing fine. You can drive on the way out." Kate was fiddling with the radio again, trying to find another Spanish station as the other started cutting out. "I could use a break from that," Lawrence said with a sidelong glance.

Kate grinned. "Me too." She turned off the radio and they drove in silence as the exurbs gave way to the golden hills and green black oaks until they reached the intersection of 76 and 79.

"This is where I turn?" he asked.

"Yeah. You'll drive on 79 for a short distance until we get to San Felipe Road and it's a short distance to Montezuma Valley. Then turn on that."

After a few minutes Lawrence asked, "Should I stop the car?"

"Why? We haven't even reached Ranchita yet. She was already with us when we stopped there, remember?"

"Oh yeah. That's right." They drove through Ranchita and continued down Montezuma Valley Road. "Does she look like she's recognized anything?"

"I'm not sure. She's looking out the window pretty intently. Lawrence! Stop here! That's the rock she was sitting on! I'm sure of it."

Lawrence pulled over to the side of the road. Kate looked through the dictionary for a few minutes. "What are you looking for?" he asked.

"How you say 'do you know where we are?' Not easy to find. I wish there was Internet here. It would be a lot easier." She opened her door and got out. She opened Marisol's door and said, "*¿Sabes dónde estamos?*" Marisol looked like she had seen a ghost. She drew her legs in with her arms and hugged herself into a tight ball. "Come sweetie. Show us why we found you here." Kate reached her hand to take Marisol's hand, but she scooted further away to the other side of the car.

"Don't force her," Lawrence said. "It will only erode the trust she has in us now." He got out of the car and looked over the sides of the road, trying to see perhaps what he missed last time around. He saw nothing, however.

"I don't think this is the way to find out anything," Kate sighed. "She's too scared. Maybe we just need to head on up to those small towns near Fresno and see if we can get some leads there."

"Alright," Lawrence exhaled, not hiding his irritation. He went to the trunk, opened it, and took out some power bars and water bottles. He got back in the car and handed Marisol one of each.

Kate got back in. "Smart move, Lawrence," she said, kissing his cheek, "but I'll just have a bottle of water."

"That wasn't sarcastic was it?"

"Not at all. You're right to make her feel comfortable and continue to trust us. You're more thoughtful than I am."

Lawrence grinned shyly. "Thanks." He turned the car around and climbed back up Montezuma Valley Road. Kate took his hand. "This time let's just stay on 79."

"Sounds good. But let's stop in Ranchita for a rest room break."

"Another good idea. I guess those PhD types are handy to have around."

"And I'm thoughtful, too," he said, winking at her.

They stopped at the market in Ranchita to use the restroom and got back on the road, hitting Route 79 about half an hour later. As they approached the town of Aguanga, Kate noticed a sign for Route 371 to Anza and the Cahuilla Casino and Hotel. "Oh wow. I had a friend in the Peace Corps who lives here. She got a job teaching on the reservation."

"Have you been in touch with her since you both got back?"

"Not really. Just a few emails every now and then. It was one of those things where we said we should stay in touch since we were both from Southern California, but then real life got in the way."

"Do you want to stop?"

"Maybe it would be a good idea to talk to her. She may know something since she lives around here."

"You mean about Marisol?"

"Well not about her precisely, but she may have some info about undocumented immigrants that cross the border and wind up here."

"We don't know that Marisol is one of those."

"Well, it can't hurt. Let's see if she's available and can talk to us."

Lawrence sighed and turned onto Route 371. Kate decided to ignore the sigh knowing full well that there will probably be many of them on this trek.

8

THEY FINALLY CONNECTED WITH KATE'S FRIEND, RACHEL, AND MET FOR LUNCH IN THE CASINO'S RESTAURANT. Marisol's eyes were bugging out of her head at all the lights and sounds coming from the slot machines. They ate as Rachel talked about living on the reservation and her job at the local elementary school in Anza. She used her political activist background to serve as a liaison for the Cahuilla tribe with the city and county and in exchange, lived in a suite at the casino hotel. Kate admired Rachel's devotion to community organizing while balancing a teaching job to provide income, retirement, and health benefits.

"It's great to see you Kate and to meet Lawrence and Marisol, but why are you here?" Rachel finally asked. "I mean this isn't exactly a tourist's mecca."

"Well," Kate hesitated. "I thought perhaps you could help us find Marisol's family."

"Hmm. Not exactly my line of work," Rachel mused. "But tell me more."

Kate related the entire story of finding Marisol and that she won't speak and finding the photos and postcards and having Lucy talk to her in

Spanish. "I don't want to call any of the authorities. I fear she could be deported or be placed in a detention center."

"She may have escaped from one."

"Really?"

"Or run off before being put in one."

Kate frowned. "I was hoping since you live in the general area where we found her, you might have some ideas."

"But do you really think she's from around here?"

"I don't know," Kate shrugged.

"We do have many Hispanics living here among the Native Americans and Whites and the majority are illegals. I could ask around to see if anyone knows anything. They know my line of work and trust me."

"That's what I was hoping for."

"It will take me some time, though. I mean, like a couple of days. Do you want to stay here or go home? I'll call you with any information."

Kate looked at Lawrence who shrugged. "Up to you," he said.

"I think we should continue on our way up to the Fresno area," Kate replied.

"It would sure be easier if she'd talk," Rachel sighed. "Wait, you know what? Let me see if Yolanda is around. She comes from Mexico and got her green card recently. Maybe Marisol would talk to her."

"Oh, thank you!" Kate gushed. "Maybe she will talk to someone she can relate to better than Lucy."

Rachel took out her phone and scrolled through her contacts. "Ah, here it is." She pressed on the number and turned to Kate. "She works here at the casino. Maybe she'll have a break soon."

"Can she answer her phone if she's working?" Lawrence asked.

"She's a maid in the hotel. No one is watching her while she cleans. So yes, she can. I helped her get her green card. Hi Yolanda, it's Rachel. I'm fine. How are you? No need to thank me. You did all the work. I just showed you how. I was wondering if you had a break soon. I need you to talk to a friend of mine who is here. Okay." Rachel looked at the time on her phone. "In about ten minutes we'll meet you in the lobby. Thanks." She hung up. Lawrence took out his wallet and picked up the bill. "Oh no. My treat," Rachel said, snatching the bill from his hand. "I get a huge discount."

"Fine, but you need to take this." Lawrence handed her two twenties.

"No, I'll just charge it to the room. Most of the time they don't even ask me to pay those charges."

"Then give it to Yolanda," he answered. "For her assistance."

"It's really not necessary."

Lawrence sighed. "Then give it to some cause that helps others get green cards. Please take it."

Rachel rolled her eyes at Kate and took the two twenties. Kate smiled back, knowing full well what she meant – men! They got up from the table and walked to the lobby. As they passed a restroom Marisol tugged on Kate's sleeve and pointed to it. "Oh. I think Marisol needs to use the bathroom." Kate smiled at Lawrence. "She actually initiated that."

Lawrence smiled back. "Maybe we should all use it now since we'll be getting back on the road after this, right?"

"Unless Yolanda has some great insight," Kate replied. "But either way we'll probably be on the road. Always a good idea to use a restroom whenever you can."

"Speaking like a true mother," Lawrence winked and went into the men's room.

"Are you coming too, Rachel?" Kate asked.

"I'll wait out here," Rachel laughed.

When Kate and Marisol emerged from the ladies room, Rachel was talking to a young woman who looked to be in her twenties. "Kate, this is Yolanda."

"Hi Yolanda. And this is Marisol. Did Rachel explain the situation?"

"*Sí*. She no talk?"

"No," Kate shook her head. "I don't know if it's because she doesn't understand us or if she is so traumatized by whatever might have happened to her."

Yolanda looked at Rachel questioningly. "*No entiendo.*"

"Doesn't matter. Just see if she'll talk to you in Spanish," Rachel replied.

Yolanda started speaking to Marisol rapidly in Spanish and the light came on in Marisol's eyes. She nodded and smiled at Yolanda, but still didn't speak. Yolanda continued talking a mile a minute with Marisol occasionally reacting with a nod or shrug, but Yolanda fell silent as Lawrence approached. Kate could tell she was uncomfortable in his presence.

"Oh," Kate said brightly, "this is my *esposo*. Lawrence, this is Yolanda."

Yolanda flashed a little knowing smile at Kate's attempt at Spanish as Lawrence extended his hand. "Hello Yolanda."

She shyly took his hand, studying him curiously out of the corner of her eye and let it go quickly as she turned back to Kate and Rachel. "She say yes when I ask if she crossed the border. I ask if she is alone and she say yes."

"Where are her parents? Or family?" Kate asked.

Yolanda turned to Marisol and spoke in Spanish. Marisol looked at the floor and shook her head. "I don't think she know."

"Did she come with them?" Yolanda spoke to Marisol again and Marisol shook her head no.

"Where was she going? Could you ask her that?" Kate added.

More shrugs from Marisol when Yolanda asked her. "She not know."

"One last question. Could you ask her if she has family here and where they live?"

Yolanda took Marisol's hand and spoke affectionately, but again Marisol just shrugged. "She not know," Yolanda said. "Sorry."

Kate sighed and said, "Thank you Yolanda. It is a help knowing that she crossed the border. It's more information than we had before. And thanks, Rachel."

"Let me see what else I can find out," Rachel answered. "Maybe we can learn more when I have a chance to talk to some people who are, shall we say, under the radar."

"That would be great." Kate turned to Lawrence. "Shall we get on the road?"

"Yeah." He looked over to Rachel. "How long is the drive to Fresno from here?"

Rachel grinned. "Can't say I've had the pleasure of making that drive."

Kate whipped out her phone and scrolled a bit. She tapped and said, "Fresno" into the map app. She made a face. "More than five hours," she announced.

They said their goodbyes and drove out of the parking lot. "It's kind of late to start on such a long drive," Lawrence ventured.

Kate looked at her phone again and then took out the map. "We don't go through Los

Angeles or take the 5," Kate said, laying the map over his hand on the steering wheel. Go back on 371 to 74 towards Riverside. Then we can go north a ways on 215, hit the 15 and then 138 and 14 to Palmdale and Lancaster—."

"Just tell me when and where to turn," Lawrence interrupted.

Kate neatly folded the map. "Just don't let your annoyance affect your driving."

"I'll try," he replied coldly.

They drove in silence for quite awhile, Lawrence stewing while Kate kept on the lookout for the next exit to take, all the while mentally twisting new ideas for finding Marisol's family. Finally Kate spoke. "I feel like maybe I should be doing this alone. Would you rather go back to LA and I'll take Marisol up to the Fresno area by myself?"

"No, Kate. That's not the issue at all. It's not about me. Just forget it. I agreed to do this so let's do it."

"I would just feel better if you had a better attitude about it."

"Let's just drop it. Why don't you look on your phone and find us a destination for dinner and a motel."

Kate scrolled. "Reception is erratic. Tehachapi looks like a good place to call it quits for the day, mileage-wise, but Bakersfield would give us more options, motels and food-wise."

"Whatever," Lawrence replied with a yawn.

Kate turned around to face Marisol. "Are you hungry?" She mimed putting food in her mouth and chewing. As expected, Marisol didn't answer, but Kate had hoped she would at least start nodding or shaking her head for yes/no responses as she did for Yolanda. She reached for a bag of nuts and a bottle of water, and extended them to Marisol. Marisol looked at her and took them hesitantly and placed them on the seat next to her. "I wish she would at least nod or something. She obviously didn't want the snack."

Lawrence sighed. "Try to put yourself in her shoes. She's probably petrified."

"After all that—" Kate stopped herself.

Lawrence shot her a look. "We have no idea what she's been through and no idea what she's thinking."

"I know, I know," Kate lamented. "I'm just frustrated. Oh, I see a sign for San Bernardino." She looked at the map on her phone. "Bakersfield is only about two and a half hours from here. Do you want me to drive?"

"I'm fine. You continue to be the navigator."

"It's pretty simple from here. We want 215 and then 15 and then 138 and then—"

"One at a time!" Lawrence interrupted.

Kate sighed. "Why are we arguing?"

"Because WE are frustrated." Lawrence was quiet for a minute. "It's all right. Don't worry about it." He patted her arm. "We're fine."

"I love you, Lawrence."

"Love you back."

9

THEY FOUND A MOTEL IN BAKERSFIELD WITH A MEXICAN RESTAURANT NEXT DOOR, KEEPING WITH THE IDEA OF MAKING MARISOL FEEL MORE COMFORTABLE. After dinner the three went back to the motel. It was pretty late by then so they settled in the room and turned on the television. They found a Spanish language movie and put it on. They had decided to forego paying for a separate room for Marisol, two queen beds in one room was sufficient. Kate was concerned about leaving Marisol alone in a room, anyway. She was still afraid she would bolt. Lawrence wasn't pleased about it, but then he wasn't pleased about any of this. Lawrence curled up on the bed with a novel and Kate sat at the desk with her guidebook, map and phone. "Hey, this looks interesting," she said as she googled on her phone. "Have you ever heard of Colonel Allensworth State Park?"

"Hmm?" Lawrence answered sleepily. "No, I don't think so."

"Allensworth was the only town founded and governed by African-Americans."

Lawrence looked up from his book. "Where is it?"

"On our way to Tranquility, more or less. It could be an interesting diversion. Apparently many of the buildings are still there."

"When was it a town?" Lawrence asked, sitting up and showing more interest than he had in quite a while.

"Let me see," Kate said as she scrolled through her phone. "Uh, it was founded in 1908. This is what Wikipedia says: 'The small farming community was founded in 1908 by Lt. Colonel Allen Allensworth, Professor William Payne, a minister named William Peck, a miner named John W. Palmer, and a real estate agent named Harry A. Mitchell. It's dedicated to improving the economic and social status of African Americans. Colonel Allensworth (1842–1914) had a friendship with Booker T. Washington and was inspired by the Tuskegee Institute.' Pretty cool, huh?"

"Can I read about it?" Lawrence asked, reaching for her phone. Kate happily handed it over, relieved to see him excited about something.

Kate looked at the map. "We could head up 99 to 46, towards Wasco. It's only a short distance on 46 to 43 and then we go north."

"Sounds good." He handed Kate back her phone. "How long to the park from here?"

She went to the map on her phone. "Less than an hour."

"Then how far would it be to one of those towns we're going to?"

"Less than two hours."

"Okay. Let's do it."

Kate got up, went to the bed and gave Lawrence a big hug. "This will be fun!" she exclaimed. She looked at the time. "I wonder how much longer this movie is?"

"Can't you show her how to turn it off with the remote?"

"I can try." Kate got up and handed the remote to Marisol. "Press this when the movie is done," she said pointing to the power on/off button." Marisol looked at her with a confused look on her face. Kate turned back to Lawrence. "I don't think she understood me. I'll just wait up with her until it's over." She climbed into bed next to Lawrence and opened the guidebook, but her eyes closed and she fell fast asleep.

When Kate and Lawrence woke up the next morning, the television was off so apparently Marisol had known what to do. "Did you sleep as well as I did?" Lawrence whispered.

"I must have. I didn't hear a thing," Kate answered.

"Did you wait up with her until the movie was done?"

"I fell asleep so she must have turned it off."

"I'm going for a walk, so you ladies can get up and shower and do whatever you need. I'll take my shower when I get back."

"Okay. Can you bring back some breakfast? I don't think they have any breakfast buffet at this motel."

"Sure." Lawrence went into the bathroom and ten minutes later he tiptoed out the door, dressed in shorts and a hooded sweatshirt. Marisol was still asleep, so Kate went in for her shower.

Lawrence walked out into the parking lot and glanced up and down the street, trying to decide which way to go. He remembered seeing what looked like a nice old residential neighborhood a few blocks away when they left 99 to get to the motel. Lawrence put in his ear buds so he could listen to a podcast as he headed in what seemed the right direction. Soon he found himself on streets named after trees, where dappled shade cut the growing heat of the day. He smiled to himself. Tree streets seemed to always be some of the oldest, nicest neighborhoods of any city.

The houses were large and nicely landscaped with expansive lawns in front. He noticed an especially attractive Craftsman and thought Kate would enjoy seeing it, too. He took out his ear buds and stepped back and off the sidewalk onto the driveway to get a better angle with his phone. As he started to take pictures, he heard a woman shouting at him but couldn't make out what she was saying. He turned around and saw a woman with a German Shepherd in front of the house across the street. "Excuse me?" he said. "I didn't hear you." Before the woman could answer, her dog ran across the street, barking ferociously at Lawrence. The dog didn't attack him, just kept barking at him. He saw the woman on her phone, doing nothing to control her dog. "Hey lady," he called to her. "Could you please get your dog?"

The woman ignored him and continued talking on the phone. Lawrence turned back to taking pictures of the house, hoping the dog would just stop. He tried talking to the dog hoping to calm it down a bit. Sweat broke out all over his body. "Please call off your dog," he shouted, trying not to sound too desperate.

"I'm videotaping you!" she finally shouted. "This is my neighborhood. You don't live here!"

"No I don't, but I am allowed to walk on this street."

"I've called the police!" she screamed at him. "They are on their way now!"

"I'm not breaking any laws," he retorted. "But I assume there's a leash law here and therefore you are the one breaking the law."

"This is my home and my neighborhood!" Her voice was shrill and almost as annoying as the barking dog. "You need to go back where you came from!"

At that moment, two police cars pulled up and four cops approached with guns drawn. "You've got to be kidding me," Lawrence mumbled to himself.

"Get down on the ground, arms and legs spread!" the older one of the cops yelled. Lawrence did as he was told. Black men do not argue with the police.

The woman came closer. "He's taking pictures of that house! Casing it to rob I'm sure!"

"Is it against the law to take a photograph of an interesting-looking house?" Lawrence asked.

"Let me see your ID!" the policeman said.

"Oh shit," Lawrence said to himself. "I don't have one on me," he said aloud. "I'm staying at a motel around here and just went out for a walk. I didn't bring my license." One of the cops knelt down and patted him down. "I don't have anything on me except my phone."

"Sit up! And keep your hands in the air!"

"Look, let me call my wife. She can come and bring my identification."

"Shut up and don't move!"

Lawrence shook his head in disgust and that just angered the cop even more. "What have I done wrong? This isn't a gated community. The streets are open for anyone to walk on."

The cop kicked him and sneered, "You bothering this lady?"

"Not at all. Her dog was actually bothering me. Isn't there a leash law?" Lawrence worked at keeping calm, but it wasn't easy.

"Well, she says you were bothering her."

"What did I do?" Lawrence looked at the woman who turned her head away from him and didn't answer. He turned back to the cops. "Look, this is ridiculous. If you want me to leave the neighborhood, I'll gladly walk out of here and go back to my motel."

"You're not going anywhere buddy, other than the police station."

"What the hell did she say I was doing to her? I told you I was just taking pictures of this house because it's an interesting style. She sicced her dog at me!" Lawrence was yelling at this point, unable to keep his temper in check.

"Cuff 'im!" the cop said to his partner.

Lawrence felt his cheeks burn and his breath get shallow. "Are you fucking serious? Let me call my wife, for God's sake. And by the way, I'd like to register a complaint against this woman. Her dog is off leash."

"It doesn't work that way," the vocal cop said as his partner pulled Lawrence's arms to his back and put on the handcuffs.

Lawrence was enraged, but knew enough to keep his mouth shut at this point. There were too many instances of police killing Black men in the news lately. The cop who handcuffed him shoved him into the back seat of the cruiser, bumping Lawrence's head on the roof of the car as he did. "Shit man, watch it!" Lawrence complained.

"Shut up, boy!" Lawrence glanced at the two cops from the second car, who hadn't participated. They looked young and scared and not interested in speaking up.

The cops in the front seat bantered with each other, ignoring Lawrence, which was just as well because Lawrence had already decided that he wasn't going to say another word until he could call Kate to come to the station. He hoped that seeing that his wife was White would be enough to mitigate things and they would release him. Then they could get the hell out of this godforsaken place. But it wasn't Bakersfield, per se. He knew this could be happening anywhere, even liberal bastions like Los Angeles or San Francisco. This wasn't the first time he was stopped for being Black, and wouldn't be the last.

10

KATE RUSHED INTO THE POLICE STATION, BREATHLESS AND ANGRY. "Where's my husband, Lawrence Ellison?" she snapped.

A female officer jumped up from her desk behind the counter. "He's your husband?"

"Are you shocked?"

"Uh—well he just didn't say—"

"That I'm White?" Kate fairly screamed. "Should he have?"

The officer drew in a deep breath and stood herself tall. "I'll let them know you're here." She picked up the phone, punched a few keys and relayed the news of her arrival. "They'll be right out, Mrs. Ellison." She then picked up a tablet from her desk. "Is that with two Ls?"

"Yes," hissed Kate as she circled the room. "But *my* name is Ms. McCoy."

A few minutes passed and the arresting officer came through a door. "Are you Lawrence's wife?"

"Yes I'm Mr. Ellison's wife. Where is my husband?"

"Hold on, we have some paperwork to take care of."

"What kind of paperwork? Have you arrested him?"

"Not exactly. Just holding him and asking him some questions."

"What kind of questions?" Kate asked, her voice rising. "More like what kind of bullshit!" she yelled.

"Now calm down, missy."

Kate inhaled and exhaled loudly, then spoke firmly. "Why exactly are you holding him?" The cop stared at her coldly. "Don't waste your time," Kate growled. "I'm not easily intimidated."

"We had a complaint."

"Yeah, and so do I," she shot back.

"It's our job to follow up on complaints."

"I didn't say it wasn't. I was merely asking you what the complaint was."

"Look, he doesn't live in the neighborhood and he was taking pictures of a house. The complaint, a woman, felt afraid."

"And she felt afraid because he is Black!" Kate shouted.

"I can't answer that," the cop replied.

"And you brought him in because he's Black!" she added vehemently.

"No, because he had no ID."

"But he had his phone, which he used here to call me to bring his wallet!" She shoved Lawrence's driver's license into his hand.

"Why don't you just wait here and I'll finish the paperwork and bring him out."

"And you wonder why people protest and call you racist pigs," she muttered as he left.

Just then a police captain came out of an office. "What the hell is going on in here?"

"Nothing much, sir. Just getting ready to release Ellison."

"The Black man on the tree streets?"

"Yes sir."

"Can you do that without yelling and screaming?"

"Yes sir. Just an ID check and the form to fill out."

The captain started to return to his office when the female officer called out from her desk, "Sir?"

"Not now, Morrison."

"Case related, sir."

The captain went to her desk and Morrison tilted the tablet for him to view. "That's the mayor of Los Angeles, isn't it?"

"Mm," she affirmed. "And that's Ellison with him, handing out scholarships. PhD and UCLA English professor, retired, sir."

The captain blew air between his teeth and turned around to come face to face with Kate hanging over the counter. "Uh, this is regrettable—"

"Terribly," Kate agreed with just a touch of sarcasm. "Imagine how much nicer a day it could have been for all involved if my husband had been allowed to call me on the street to bring him his wallet."

"Your husband looks remarkable for his age."

"No one should be treated this way! His age and occupation shouldn't have anything to do with it!"

The door opened and Kate ran up to Lawrence and hugged him, then grabbed his face and studied him. "I'm okay, Kate," he sighed as he turned away. "Let's just get the hell out of here."

"Did they arrest you?"

"No."

"Then what was the paperwork they had to do?" she asked hotly.

"I had to sign some papers."

"For what? So they aren't liable if you decide to sue them?"

"Kate," Lawrence sighed. "This is the world of being Black. Let's go!" He yanked her towards the entrance.

Kate glared at the cops and turned abruptly to leave. "Well, I didn't sign anything," she said loudly as she walked out.

"Where's Marisol?" Lawrence asked when they got to the car.

"I couldn't bring her here with all the police around. She'd freak out. Besides, they might start asking questions about her."

"Did she understand that we'd be back?"

"I'm sure she did. Our suitcases are still there."

"She wasn't afraid?" he asked.

"I don't know. I hope not." They jostled around each other in a silent decision about who was going to drive. Kate got behind the wheel and drove back to the motel.

Marisol was obviously happy to see them when they opened the door to the room because she actually smiled and ran up to them. "Hi Marisol," Lawrence smiled back, trying to appear like their absence was of little consequence. "I'm taking a shower now," he said over his shoulder.

Lawrence was in the shower for a long time, so Kate packed what she could into the car until he was ready to go. "We'll find somewhere for breakfast on the road," Kate said. "I want to get out of this godforsaken place!"

"I think it's lunch at this point," Lawrence said. He was quiet for a moment, obviously trying to frame his words. "You're not thinking of pursuing something with the police department here, are you?"

"I'd like to," Kate replied grimly, "but the feeling is slipping fast. I know it would be a foolish waste of time and money. It just makes me so mad . . ."

Lawrence took her free hand. "I learned long ago you've got to pick your battles. If I lived here . . . if it was part of my career . . ." He shrugged. "Better to give a donation to the big players like Black Lives Matter or the ACLU."

"I feel in the same boat as Marisol now," she sighed. "It's awful to feel hostile towards the very people who are supposedly entrusted to help you.”

They drove in silence for some time until they entered Shafter. “Hey, there’s an IHOP. Shall we stop?” Lawrence asked.

Kate made a face. “I guess IHOP is the best we’re going to do in these parts. Marisol needs to eat, anyway.”

“It doesn’t matter at this point,” Lawrence shrugged. Kate turned into the parking lot.

Kate pointed out the pictures of pancakes on the menu to Marisol. “Can you point to the one you want?” she asked. Marisol just looked at her, not understanding or choosing not to make any decisions.

Kate gave Lawrence a look and he said, “I guess I’ll just order her plain pancakes,” he said. “What do you want?”

“I don’t know. Maybe just poached eggs and fruit with a side of rye toast.”

“You’re at the International House of Pancakes and you’re not having pancakes?” he teased.

“That is correct,” she smiled.

The waitress came over and Lawrence ordered for all of them. “Oh, and do you know how far is it to Allensworth?” he asked.

“Where?”

“Allensworth. The state park.”

“Never heard of it,” the waitress said and turned away.

“And aren’t you surprised?” smirked Kate.

Lawrence chuckled. "Nope."

Kate took out her phone and scrolled and tapped. "It's only about forty-five minutes away."

"I'm really looking forward to it."

"I'm glad. You need a nice diversion after what you've been through."

"Those settlers had to feel the same way," Lawrence mused.

They ate their food, got back on the road, and were at Colonel Allensworth State Historical Park by two. The stark setting and patches of alkali depressed Lawrence, but Marisol seemed to enjoy it. There was a state park ranger who took them around and explained the history of the various restored buildings: the dairy barn, the blacksmith, the store, the church, the school. Marisol got on the school teeter-totter and Lawrence perked up and pushed down the other end.

"Oh, let me take a picture!" Kate cried.

"Okay, grandma," Lawrence grinned.

Kate turned to the ranger. "Do you speak Spanish?"

"*Sí.*"

"You can see how Marisol is really taking in this place," Kate explained. "Normally she's really shy and doesn't speak much at all, but I think she'd really open up if you could translate for her."

"No problem." The ranger spoke to Marisol directly and offered his hand. She took it shyly and the ranger did the whole tour again in Spanish, and although Marisol didn't speak, she was clearly captivated. Kate and Lawrence enjoyed tagging along, watching her relaxed demeanor and feeling themselves release their own tension. Occasionally they would hang further back to be alone, to touch one another and feel the lost promise of a past ideal. The sun dipped lower, glinting off the alkali, making long shadows off the salt brush. They did not leave until closing.

11

THEY HAD DINNER AT A MEXICAN RESTAURANT . . . AGAIN. It was right next door to their motel in Hanford, so it was the easy choice, but Kate was pleased that the menu offered atypical fare with a lot of vegetarian choices. "What are you planning to do tomorrow when we get to Tranquillity?" Lawrence asked after they had ordered.

"I plan on calling Lucy and Rachel after we get back to the motel to see if they have any ideas on how to look for Marisol's family."

"Rachel might have some ideas, but Lucy?"

"I want Lucy to explain to Marisol exactly what is going to happen the next couple of days as we drive around these little valley towns."

"Do you think she recognizes Hanford? Tranquillity isn't very far from here."

"I doubt it," Kate admitted. "In fact, I'm thinking more and more that she just got over the border. Maybe even by herself."

"Really?" Lawrence asked in amazement. "What kind of parent would let their child come to America alone?"

"It may not have been the original plan," Kate answered. "Maybe they got separated or maybe her parents were even killed. There are also stories of parents letting their kids go alone, feeling like they'd have a better chance of making it. Or she could have been with a coyote or some other border crosser that was only planning on taking her across and leaving her. Maybe someone else was supposed to meet her. There are lots of possibilities."

Lawrence rubbed his forehead. "This is feeling crazier and crazier."

"Well not as crazy as this morning," Kate sighed. "I wish I could let things bounce off me the way you seem to be able to do."

"I'm used to racism," Lawrence replied, dropping his hand on the table. "It's as blatant as the Confederate flag in these small towns, as subliminal as when a colleague at UCLA is surprised or annoyed that you actually know more than they do. It's not like looking for someone who doesn't really want to be found among forty million residents."

Kate frowned. "Who says they don't want to be found?"

"Marisol's relatives aren't waving a flag, are they? They're not White; they're probably not even legal. Not only do they have to deal with racism . . . they have to deal with the law. They have no recourse. They have to live and work undercover. They have no freedom to recover what they've lost. They can only move forward."

"Well, I'm free enough to help them if I can."

The server came with their food and Marisol ate with fervor, having been so active at Allensworth all afternoon. Yet, Kate observed, it was her usual approach to a bounty of food—eat because you never know when you'll eat again. "I guess the kind of discrimination that I've experienced doesn't hold a candle to what you go through," Kate mused.

Lawrence looked at her cautiously. "It's pretty easy for a woman to play the White male patriarchy, isn't it? Unless you're petty and manipulative."

"Some women make a career out of it," Kate admitted. "It's a field that has never interested me—simply because I'd have to shed most of who I am to become a player. To become a piece of décor or an echo and lose one's voice entirely." She glanced over at Marisol sweeping beans and rice with her fork. "Oh, I do wish she'd speak to us."

"Well, I know that silence is sometimes the best self defense."

Kate grabbed his hand and leaned across the table and kissed him. She then turned to Marisol and said, "*¿Te gustó la cena?*"

Marisol nodded. "Did you see that?" Lawrence exclaimed. "She just answered you. What did you ask her?"

Kate smiled broadly. "I asked if she enjoyed her dinner. Google comes in handy for a lot of things. *¿Puedes hablar?*" she said to Marisol and then turned to Lawrence. "I asked her if she could talk." Marisol looked at her solemnly and then nodded ever so slightly. Kate smiled at her and then turned to Lawrence, "There is hope."

"I'll say," Lawrence replied. "The trust is there now, I think."

They finished eating and paid the bill. As they left the restaurant to walk back to the motel, Marisol stood between Lawrence and Kate and took each of their hands. Kate and Lawrence grinned at each other and the threesome acted like a happy family. "It's definitely looking more and more hopeful," Kate said.

Lawrence turned on the television and found Marisol a Spanish station with what appeared to be a family situation comedy. "I have no idea what this is, but it looks harmless enough and it's in Spanish," he said to Kate as he took out his book and settled into one of the queen beds in the room. Marisol hopped onto the other bed and Kate sat at the desk, scrolling through her phone to find Rachel's number.

"I think I'd better walk outside. I don't want my talking to disturb you two." She left the room just as Rachel picked up. "Hi Rachel, it's Kate."

"Kate, hi. Where are you now?"

"We're in Hanford, leaving for Tranquillity in the morning. That's one of the places her postcards are from. I called to ask you if you had some ideas on who I should contact there. I don't really know where to begin."

"The population of Tranquillity can't be very large."

"Yeah, I looked it up. The population is like eight hundred or so."

"How many are Hispanic?"

Kate thought for a minute. "I think it's about sixty percent."

"That's what I figured," Rachel said. "The problem is, first of all, the language difference. But more than that is the trust issue. They are not going to talk to you willingly, of course, because they're scared to death of ICE."

"I know. This trip has been quite eye opening for me. I've done my share of marching and public protesting, but I had no idea what it's like for the ones I was supporting. Lawrence was brought to the police station in Bakersfield this morning because some stupid woman decided that Black men aren't allowed to be in her neighborhood."

"Unbelievable! How awful! This still goes on in this day and age. Was Marisol with him?"

"No, thank goodness. She would have freaked."

"Thank God for that," Rachel said. "Anyway, I think you need to have some Spanish phrases up your sleeve to talk to anyone," Rachel said.

"I'm going to call my friend Lucy next to talk to Marisol and explain what we're doing," Kate replied. "I'll ask her for some phrases. I was thinking that it might be helpful that Lawrence is Black and Marisol's Hispanic. Hopefully that will soften things."

"Lawrence's race could help or hinder. There are Latinos that don't like Blacks."

Kate scoffed. "Jeez, what a mess race relations are in this country."

"Everywhere," Rachel sighed. "Not just here. Anyway, I'd try to find a liaison—a shop where farmers go. You know, tractors. Fertilizers. Good luck and let me know how it goes."

"Thanks. I will." Kate hung up and immediately dialed Lucy. She explained what was going on and what had already happened. "Let me go back in the room so I can write down some of those phrases and you can talk to Marisol. I'll call you back from inside."

Kate found Lawrence snoring with the open book on his chest and Marisol engrossed in the television show. Marisol smiled at her and Kate couldn't resist giving her a hug. She dialed Lucy and gave the phone to Marisol. Kate watched Marisol and noticed that she was nodding as Lucy talked, another positive sign. After a few minutes Marisol handed the phone to Kate. "Do you think she understood what I told her?" Lucy asked.

"Yes," Kate answered. "She was nodding. She's been responding with nods and smiles lately. We hope she'll start talking soon."

"That's great. Now, do you have that pen and paper ready?"

"I do." Kate wrote quickly, using several pieces of the hotel pad. "Okay. I think I have it. I hope my pronunciation won't get in the way of their understanding me."

Lucy laughed. "You'll do fine. Keep me posted on how things worked out."

"Oh yes. I hope you don't mind being at my beck and call like this."

"Not at all. I'm glad to help."

They hung up and Kate saw that Lawrence's eyes were open. "Just got off the phone with Lucy." She turned to Marisol. "*¿Entiendes lo de mañana?*"

Marisol nodded, but didn't smile. In fact, she looked scared and somber. "Why does she look like that?" Lawrence asked.

"She's afraid? Apprehensive? Just like we are." Kate lay on the bed next to Marisol and took her in her arms.

"You would have been a great Mama," Lawrence said.

"I don't know," Kate sighed. She thought back to her own childhood . . . her mother dying when she was young and being raised solely by her father. After Kate's marriage broke up in her twenties, she had decided that motherhood and marriage were not in the stars for her . . . until she met Lawrence.

12

MARISOL WAS THE FIRST ONE AWAKE AND SHE TOOK OUT HER PICTURES AND POSTCARDS. Lucy had explained that the postmarks on the postcards were the reason Kate and Lawrence were bringing her to those specific towns. When Kate and Lawrence woke up, she hurriedly put them away. Kate noticed this and whispered to Lawrence, "Do you think she doesn't want us to find her relatives?"

"Why do you say that?" Lawrence asked.

"The look in her eyes."

"My guess is that life with us is a hell of a lot better than the one she's been used to, even if we aren't her real family. They could be dead for all we know." He gently turned Kate's face toward him. "We can't keep her, you know."

Kate sighed and started to speak, but stopped herself. The option of keeping her was actually becoming appealing, but she knew better than to open up that can of worms. "What time is it?" she asked.

Lawrence looked at the clock next to his side of the bed. "A little after six."

"I think I'll go for a jog this morning. I have some podcasts I need to catch up on."

"I'll stay here and keep Marisol company. Probably best if I don't go out alone in these towns anyway."

Kate shook her head. "You can't live like that."

"This isn't Westwood."

She kissed him and got up, grabbing some jogging clothes out of her suitcase. *"Buenos días,"* she said as she patted Marisol's head on her way to the bathroom.

Kate returned an hour later with two coffees, a pint of milk and three bagels slathered with cream cheese. "You thought it was time to give Marisol a taste of some other cultures?" Lawrence said as he peeked into the bag.

"Well, I was a bit surprised to find decent looking bagels in Hanford," Kate grinned. "Maybe we'll get lucky and have sushi for dinner."

"Right. I'm sure there will be tons of Japanese restaurants in Tranquillity," he chuckled.

Marisol took her bagel and stared at it for a minute, then glanced at Kate who separated the two halves and bit into one of them. Marisol copied her and took a tiny bite first and then gobbled the first half and bit into the second. "I guess she likes Jewish food," Kate winked at Lawrence.

They finished eating and were on the road to Tranquillity by nine. Kate had to keep watching the map on her phone since the route was somewhat complex. There was no direct way to get to Tranquillity. "So what's the next road I'm looking for?" Lawrence asked as he drove onto State Route 198.

"Stay on 198 until you see a sign for 41 toward Fresno."

"I thought Tranquillity was west of here. Isn't Fresno east?"

"Yes, but 41 is a north/south road so we have to go on that for a little while. Basically we are going to Helm but I doubt they would have a sign for it. It's not a large town."

"And what do we do at Helm?" he asked.

"Then we take a smaller road through San Joaquin for several miles to get to Tranquility. I'll talk you through that when we get to Helm."

"How long does the map say it is to Helm?"

"Forty-five minutes." Kate scrolled through her phone for a few minutes. "Wow! Helm has fewer than two hundred people and it's one hundred percent Hispanic according to Wikipedia!"

"All migrant workers probably."

"I'd guess so. Maybe Marisol's family lives in Helm and we should stop and try to talk to someone there."

"It would be hard to find someone willing to talk to us in a place like that," Lawrence said. "They may be illegals themselves and wouldn't want to bring attention to themselves or rat on someone else."

"That may be the case everywhere we go, I'm afraid," Kate sighed.

Lawrence wanted to say what she just said was the reason why they should have left this up to the authorities, but he kept his mouth shut. They drove in silence for a while until Lawrence turned onto Route 41. "What am I looking for now?"

"Uh, Mount Whitney Avenue."

"Then I take a left? Since I need to go west?"

"Yep. Then right on Lassen Avenue. It's also State Route 145. That takes us right into Helm."

"Okay. Mount Whitney to Lassen. In the middle of this hot, flat valley."

"Maybe it helps people cool off in the middle of summer, pretending they live on a mountain." Kate flicked at the map. "We're at the same latitude as Mount Whitney. Maybe if it wasn't so smoggy we'd see it."

"What's Marisol doing?"

Kate turned around and smiled at her. "She's just looking out the window. She seems content, so I guess she understood what Lucy told her."

"Or she might think we're totally nuts," Lawrence responded irritably. "We have no idea what her story is. We're just working off speculation."

"Well, it's all we've got right now," Kate sniffed. "At least she is learning to trust us and maybe she'll start talking soon if she can. And here's another way of looking at it, Lawrence. She could have been picked up by some very unsavory characters rather than us."

"That's true." Lawrence grumbled. The cotton fields suddenly gave way to the town of Helm, if you could call it a town. The buildings were fairly run-down and many were empty. The stores were all mom-and-pop shops, nothing corporate. Even the gas station was a no-name brand. The houses were tiny, probably all rentals for the migrant workers. But there did seem to be more houses than what would be needed for just two hundred people. They passed an elementary school and a high school. Marisol leaned across the back seat, curiously looking out one window and then another. "Can there really only be two hundred people here?" Lawrence asked. "There seem to be more houses and the fact that they have their own schools here."

"Maybe the two hundred number is simply the legal count," Kate replied.

Marisol continued to look around, paying much more attention than she had driving through any other place. "Marisol seems so interested in this town," Kate murmured to Lawrence. "Which is strange considering this is probably one of the worst places we've driven through."

"Actually it looks a lot like the Mexico the tourists don't see," Lawrence mused. "Perhaps that's why. So do you want to stop and ask about her relatives here?"

"I guess it can't hurt," Kate replied. "That trailer over there is the post office. That could be a good way to start. Aren't the postmasters or postmistresses in small towns the ones who know everyone?"

Lawrence pulled up in front of the post office. Kate got out and Marisol opened her door to join her. "First time she's wanted to get out of the car without us opening the door for her!" he exclaimed.

Kate smiled at him. "Maybe she'll talk next." Kate walked up to the door of the post office, turning to see if Marisol had followed her. She hadn't, but she was looking at the elementary school building right behind it. There were Spanish words and colorful images on the windows and screaming, happy children running around the yard.

"It must be recess," Lawrence said. "I'll bring her over to the school while you talk to whoever in the post office."

"Are you going to go to the school office?"

"No. Just thought she'd like to watch some kids play and maybe she'd interact with them."

"You can't just go onto a playground. Well, maybe it's different in a small town. When I taught in Venice Beach and Petaluma, it was a reason to call security. Maybe that would be another place to ask, though, at the school office."

"Should I or do you think you'd better?"

"You can. Why shouldn't you?"

"Um, I'm a Black man towing around a little girl who doesn't look like me."

"Now you're being paranoid."

Lawrence sighed. "Not paranoid, just realistic."

"Okay, okay. I'll go after I see what happens at the post office." Kate went inside and Lawrence took Marisol's hand and they walked over to the fence surrounding the schoolyard. They stood watching the kids play and Lawrence peeked at Marisol's face. There was a wide grin. One little girl came to the fence and smiled shyly at Marisol. She said something in Spanish that Lawrence didn't understand, but lo and behold, Marisol answered in Spanish. He started to react excitedly, but then thought better of it. He didn't want to startle her into being mute again. He just watched as the two girls spoke to each other and grinned. A bell rang and the little girl ran back to her classroom. Marisol watched her go and smiled up at Lawrence.

Kate arrived and said, "No help there. I'll try the school office."

"She spoke!" Lawrence gushed.

"Really? What did she say?"

"I don't know. A girl came to the fence and they spoke to each other in Spanish."

"Oh my God! That's wonderful! Let's bring her into the office. I'm sure the clerk would speak Spanish. Maybe Marisol will talk to her."

"The real question is whether the clerk speaks English," Lawrence said.

"Of course they do. Let's go and see." The three traipsed off to the school office, Marisol gladly following.

They got inside and Kate spoke to the office clerk while Lawrence and Marisol viewed the children's art and written work hanging on the bulletin boards in the hall. The smile never left her face and consequently, it never left his either. Most of the writing was in Spanish and Marisol spent a long time in front of each essay. Lawrence noticed that she was not a fast reader and that she moved her lips as she studied every line. It was apparent that she wasn't up to the reading level she should be at her age. He couldn't read the essays himself, but he did notice that the words were short and the handwriting looked childish, so he assumed that they were at a second or third grade level. Kate snuck up behind them and startled him when she poked his sides. "Oh!" He turned around. "She's reading, but very slowly."

Kate watched her for a minute. "I see that. She's probably had very limited schooling."

"What did the clerk say?"

"Not much. She had no idea, actually. She just said that she hadn't heard about any twelve year old in their school or town that was missing, nor that anyone was expecting any young relative."

"You do realize that our chances of finding Marisol's relatives in any of these towns is . . . uh . . . small."

"Yes I do realize that. But I have no other ideas. Do you?"

"Well, my ideas are very old ideas to you, so let's just go on to Tranquillity."

Kate gave him a look and didn't move. "Let me see if she'll talk to the clerk." She took Marisol's hand and brought her back to the office. "Could you ask her in Spanish if she knows where her relatives are?"

The clerk did that, but Marisol didn't answer. The clerk shrugged and Kate took her hand and they left the office. They all got in the car and Lawrence asked, "So, straight up 145?"

"No," Kate answered. "Take this left on Colorado and that goes right to Tranquillity. It's only about fifteen minutes or so. And it's a bigger town than this." She scrolled through her phone for a minute and then turned around in her seat. "*Marisol, por favor habla con nosotros.*"

"What did you ask her?"

"To please speak to us."

"Maybe she will only talk to other kids," Lawrence muttered.

A look of fear and sadness washed over Marisol's face. Her lip quivered and a few tears escaped down her cheeks. Her mouth opened slightly and Kate thought that perhaps she would talk, so she looked back at her phone and scrolled some more. "*Nosotros queremos ayudarte.*" Marisol started to cry. "*Está bien. Nosotros nos cuidaremoss de ti.* I told her that we want to help her and that we will take care of her."

"Do you think she understands you?"

"I hope my accent is good enough to get my point across at least."

"Let's let her be. She'll talk when she's ready."

"Lawrence . . . always the voice of reason."

"You can't save everyone, Kate."

"I know. But I hope I can save Marisol."

13

TRANQUILLITY WAS A PLEASANT SURPRISE, SINCE IT RATHER LIVED UP TO ITS NAME. Compared to Helm, it was clean and tidy, and if not exactly prosperous looking, it had an air of perseverance. There were nicer homes and most had decent lawns and even an occasional tree. The grocery store, though small, was busy, and the customers coming and going showed some diversity. "Hey, there's even a Chevrolet dealer," Lawrence said as they drove by a small lot lined with white pickups of various configurations suitable for heavy farm work. Next to the tiny showroom there was an obligatory black or red one, loaded with luxuries, to entice a landowner.

Kate watched as a muddy truck marked Ybarra Farms entered the service area. "Stop!" she cried out. "I want to talk to the guy in that pickup."

"Just like that?" Lawrence laughed as he pulled up to the curb.

"Well, I've got to start somewhere," she said, jumping out of the car. She trotted over to the man getting out of the cab. "Excuse me, do you speak English?"

The man turned her way and gave Kate an incredulous look. He appeared to be in his forties, very tan, but otherwise he would be considered White. "You're not from around here, are you?"

"Um, no," Kate admitted.

"Didn't think so," he grinned. "What can I do for you, ma'am?"

"I don't know," Kate replied, not sure if he was the right man to talk to. "Well, a girl has been separated from her relatives and I'm trying to find them." She proceeded to tell a very abbreviated, somewhat legal-sounding version of Marisol's story.

"She doesn't speak at all?"

"At first we thought she was mute. But then she talked to a girl through a fence of the elementary school in Helm this morning. Now I'm guessing she just doesn't speak English."

"Well, I speak Spanish just fine, but from what you've told me I don't think I'd be of any help. I'm not a little girl."

Kate managed a chuckle and then shrugged. "Maybe one of your workers might know a family that knows something?"

"They're not very willing to talk to strangers about things like that. They trust my field manager, though. He knows what it's like, even though he was born here. Maybe if I put in a good word for you, he'd ask around. I just have to pick up something here, and then you could follow me out to the farm."

"Oh, that would be great! Thank you so much. My name is Kate, by the way. And that's my husband Lawrence. Marisol's in the back seat."

The man squinted in Lawrence's direction and waved and then turned back to Kate. "I'm Steve, owner and general manager of Ybarra Farms. I'll be out in a minute." He went inside the dealership while Kate went back to the car and informed Lawrence of the farmer's offer. She then looked though her phone and turned to Marisol. *"Vamos a la granja de ese hombre."*

"You're getting to be quite the Spanish speaker," Lawrence chuckled.

Steve came out of the dealership holding a part and waved at them to follow as he got into his truck. Lawrence followed him down the streets of the town and then out midst the fields of cotton, then almond orchards and finally vineyards. Marisol looked curiously at the men and women picking huge clusters of purple grapes and stacking crates. Steve slowed and turned into a driveway marked with a sign that was the same as the one on the door of his truck. They were now in the midst of almond trees again, and suddenly a large house appeared ahead of them. "Wow! I don't think we're in Tranquillity anymore!" Kate exclaimed.

"Apparently this Steve Ybarra does quite well." Lawrence said as he followed Steve's gestures to park in front of a house that could have belonged to the famous wine families, Gallo or Mondavi. It was an enormous mansion with a lovely patio, swimming pool, and a six-car garage.

Steve got out of his truck and walked back to their car. "Come on in. I'll call Javier and see if he can come to the house."

"Thanks so much for all this," Kate gushed as she and Lawrence stepped out and then opened the back door for Marisol. "You have a beautiful home and a gorgeous farm."

"Thank you. Too bad you're not here in February. The almond blossoms make for a spectacular entrance. So this must be Marisol." She smiled at him as she looked around in wonder. "*¿Cómo estás mija?*" She just smiled back at him.

"What did you say?" Lawrence asked.

"How are you sweet girl? Anyway, come on in." He brought them inside and they followed him into an office with a huge desk and conference table. Off to one side was a wet bar and an overstuffed sofa and chairs for more relaxed meetings, amidst California plein air paintings and rusty farm relics. In all, the room was just slightly smaller than Lawrence and Kate's whole apartment.

"Can I get you anything to drink?" Steve asked.

Kate looked at Lawrence who shook his head and then said, "We're fine, thanks."

Steve got on his phone and pressed a button. "Javier? Can you come to the house? Oh, okay. Sure." He hung up. "He's just finishing up something and will be here in a few minutes. So where are you guys from?"

"L.A.," Lawrence answered as they sat down around the table and started chatting about themselves.

"But what about you?" Kate finally said. "This house . . . there must be an interesting story behind it."

"I think grandpa rolled over in his grave when I built this house," Stave grinned. "He didn't give a hoot about the ag business. All he wanted to do was ride a horse and round up cattle. Before state water came in, this place was worth next to nothing. He got an Okie girl pregnant and they were pretty ostracized all around. I guess they really did love one another because they made it work for the next fifty-six years, and it wasn't easy. There was grazing in wet years, but in dry years sometimes the whole family drove around the valley looking for work in the fields to pay the bills. Then state water came in and Dad built the Brady Bunch house, and then I diversified the farm . . . found the high paying niche markets . . . the grapes you could grow to sell for wine blends." Steve shrugged. "I work hard, but I don't work like they did. It's a real juggling act, being on the field and running the business." Just then the door opened and a Latino man who looked to be in his fifties entered the room. "Ah, this is Javier. These are Kate, Lawrence and Marisol." Javier nodded and smiled, shyly. "Do you want to tell your story?" Steve asked Kate.

As Kate spoke, it was clear to her that Javier grew genuinely concerned and sympathetic. After she finished he turned to Marisol and spoke softly to her in Spanish. She didn't answer, but kept her eyes glued to his. *"Pobrecita,"* Javier said affectionately to the whole group.

"Do you think you can help them, Javier?" Steve asked.

"Let me go talk to the workers, but I haven't heard of anyone expecting a child to come . . . or losing one. Many children were left alone when their parents were deported, however. I asked Marisol if she was in a detention camp or if she just crossed the border, but as you saw . . ." His voice trailed off and he shrugged sadly.

"Do you have children, Javier?" Lawrence asked.

Javier beamed as he put up three fingers. "Three. Two boys and a girl. My daughter, Angelita, is about the same age as Marisol."

"The one time Marisol spoke was when another little girl talked to her," Lawrence explained. "I wonder if your daughter could ask her those same questions. Maybe she would answer them."

"Angelita won't be home from school until four, but we could try. If you can stay, that is."

Lawrence looked at Kate. "It's not like we are on any schedule."

"You're welcome to hang around here if you wish," Steve added.

"How about we go back into town for lunch and Javier speaks to some of the farmworkers and we come back around four?" Kate said. "Does your family live here on the farm?"

"Yes." Javier looked over at Steve and smiled.

"We built this house ten years ago and Javier's family lives in our old house now," Steve said.

"Great," Kate said. "We'll see you back here at four then. Thank you so much." She took Marisol's hand and started to leave with Lawrence, but then turned around. "Javier, would you tell Marisol in Spanish that she will meet your daughter later and that we are going into town for lunch?" Javier put his arm gently around Marisol and spoke to her in Spanish. He smiled at her so tenderly and affectionately that she couldn't help but smile back.

"What a lovely man!" Kate said as they got into the car and turned down the long driveway.

"Who? Javier? Or Steve?" Lawrence asked.

"Both, actually. But I was talking about Javier. He had such a warmth and sweetness about him, especially when talking about his family."

"Hispanic men are very family-oriented."

"Yes. I've heard that. I hope this works."

"You mean his daughter talking to her?"

"Yes. It's the first glimmer of hope I've felt throughout this ordeal."

"I agree. But be prepared. Just because she might talk to Angelita, doesn't mean we'll get any useful information." They drove in silence until they got back into town. "So, what'll it be?" Lawrence grinned. "Mexican food or Mexican food?"

Kate grinned back. "Our choices are Tacos Campa Frank or Mom's Drive-in. You choose."

Lawrence drove into Mom's. "In case we are tired of tacos, this place has burgers too."

"Want to take the food to go? There was a park a couple of blocks down. I think I saw picnic tables."

"That would be good," Lawrence said as he turned off the car.

They all got out and went to the window to order. "Do you want tacos or a burger?" Kate asked Marisol. Luckily there were pictures on the menu that was posted on the window so Kate could point to them. Marisol pointed to the burger, much to Kate and Lawrence's surprise. "Cheese? Ketchup? Mustard?"

"Just order for her, Kate. I'm sure she isn't anywhere near as picky as you are."

Kate scrunched her nose at Lawrence and ordered a burger for Marisol with cheese and pickles and a taco for herself. "I'm not going to eat at an authentic Mexican restaurant and not eat Mexican food."

"I agree. Kind of funny, though, that she has the burger and we have the tacos."

They sat down at a patio table to wait for their food. "On second thought," Kate said. "Let's just eat here and then walk down to the park."

"That's fine," Lawrence answered, and that's just what they did.

Kate watched as Lawrence pushed Marisol on the swing and went down the slide with her. He pushed his side of the seesaw as Marisol giggled in delight. Kate watched lovingly for a while, but then started Googling, trying to find out about the detention centers at the border, wondering if there was any way she could find out if any child had escaped. If this trip yielded no results, she knew that she was going to have to go to some agency or authority. It was a sobering thought.

14

JAVIER WAS WAITING IN FRONT OF STEVE'S HOUSE WITH HIS DAUGHTER WHEN THEY DROVE UP AT FOUR ON THE DOT. Angelita ran up to the car and peered in the window at Marisol who perked up and grinned at her. They got out of the car and Angelita immediately started chatting with Marisol in Spanish while Lawrence and Kate talked to Javier. "I told Angelita your story and to try to get Marisol to talk," Javier said.

"Is that what she is saying now?" Kate asked.

"No. I told her not to jump into asking about where she came from and where she was going."

"She's lovely," Kate smiled.

"*Ella es mi hija querida.* She's my dear daughter."

They watched to see if Marisol answered Angelita. So far she just smiled as Angelita babbled on. And then she started to cry. "I'm sorry, *Papá,*" Angelita said regretfully. "I didn't mean to make her cry." She turned to Marisol and hugged her. "Don't cry."

"What did you ask her that she started to cry?" Javier asked.

"I asked where her mama and papa are."

"This is important, Angelita," Lawrence interjected. "Please see if she will tell you where they are."

"What should I say?"

"Ask her if they are in Mexico or in the United States," he replied.

"*¿Están tus padres en México o Los Estados Unidos?*"

Marisol tried to stop crying and in a quiet, quavering voice she said, "*Mis padres están muertos.*" Angelita hugged Marisol tighter. "*Lo siento,*" she said as tears started streaming down her face as well.

Javier turned to Lawrence and Kate with a dejected face. "They are dead," he said.

Kate covered her mouth. "I guess I shouldn't be surprised," she said, her voice cracking. "See what else Angelita can find out."

"No questions," Lawrence cut in. "Just let Angelita talk to her and maybe she'll open up more."

The adults watched as the girls stood hugging each other. Then Marisol started speaking in such a low voice that none of the adults could hear. She talked a long time and Angelita was wise enough to let her talk without interrupting. Finally Javier walked over to the children and spoke to them and then returned to Kate and Lawrence. "I told Angelita to bring Marisol into our house for some ice cream. You come too."

They all walked down the driveway and turned onto another driveway that led to a more modest, but still lovely house. Javier took them all into the kitchen and introduced them to his wife. "Consuela, this is Kate and Lawrence and Marisol."

"*Hola*, nice to meet you," Consuela said with as warm and inviting a smile as her husband and daughter had. "Come sit down," she pointed to the kitchen table. Lawrence and Kate glanced at each other and then sat down.

"I told the girls they could have some *paletas*," Javier said as he joined them at the table.

"I'll bring it to them outside. The *paletas* can be very messy." She then said something to Angelita in Spanish and Angelita took Marisol's hand and brought her out the back door to a picnic table.

"How about you? Coffee? A beer? *¿Paleta?*" He grinned over his last question.

"Nothing for me," Kate said.

"What's *paleta?*" Lawrence whispered to Kate.

"I think it's an ice cream pop," Kate whispered back.

"I'm good, too," Lawrence said.

Javier sat down. "I think it's best to leave them alone for now. Angelita is a smart girl and will know how to ask her questions."

"I can definitely see she's wise," Kate said. "You should be very proud."

"She is our pride and joy," Consuela said as she took the pops outside.

"Are your sons here?" Lawrence asked.

"No, they are teenagers," Javier replied. "They play sports and hang with their friends until supper. But they are good boys, too. No drugs. Study hard after dinner. So I let them stay in town after school."

Consuela came back in and sat down at the table with them. "Angelita told me that Marisol's mother was killed in Mexico by the gangs. That poor little girl."

Lawrence took Kate's hand. "We shouldn't be surprised."

Kate nodded. "But do you think she could have come across the border alone?"

"She could have come with another family member," Consuela said. "Or with a coyote."

"Have you heard of children coming by themselves?" Kate asked.

"Oh yes, especially now after they started deporting the parents and keeping the children in those detention centers, separating them. It can be safer to come over separately."

"You know, Kate," Lawrence said. "There could be no family members here waiting for her."

Kate sighed. "I suppose that's possible." She looked at Lawrence, forlornly. "And if that's the case . . . I have no idea what to do."

Angelita and Marisol came back in the kitchen. "*Gracias Mamá*, we finished our *paletas*."

"Are you taking her to your room?" Consuela asked.

"*Sí*. I'm gonna show her my video games."

"Has she told you anything else?" Kate interjected.

"Not really about anyone here in America. Just about how her mother was killed."

"That's fine, Angelita," Lawrence added quickly. "Let it come out naturally."

Angelita nodded and took Marisol's hand. "*Ven.*" They left the kitchen.

"Please don't feel like you have to sit with us if you have something you need to do," Kate said to Conseula and Javier.

"I should see what's going on in the field," Javier said. "I'll be back shortly." He went out the back door.

Kate turned to Consuela. "Please feel free to go back to whatever you were doing."

"I was just putting dinner together," Consuela answered. "Will you stay?"

"Oh, I don't want you to go to any trouble."

"No trouble. I'll just make an extra pan of enchiladas. Is that okay?"

"Oh, homemade enchiladas," Lawrence sighed. "That would be great!" Lawrence exclaimed.

Kate stood. "But please let me help. I'd love to learn how to make them."

"I already have the filling made," Consuela explained. "I always have some on hand, just in case. But I'll tell you about making the filling as you help me wrap them. That would be a big help."

"Sounds wonderful."

Kate got her cooking lesson and listened to Consuela talk about her children and how they were going to be the first ones in her family to go to college. Lawrence interjected a few comments here and there, but then decided he would like to take a look at the farm. "Is it okay if I go outside and look around?"

"Sure," Consuela answered.

They sat down to eat dinner when the boys got home. Marisol looked to be in heaven, smiling at everyone, enjoying the enchiladas and listening to the boys teasing Angelita. They spoke in English, but every now and then Angelita would say something to Marisol in Spanish. Kate and Lawrence sat quietly, watching the interaction, hoping Marisol might speak to Angelita, but that didn't happen. Finally Kate turned to Angelita and asked the question that had been burning inside her. "So did Marisol say anything to you when you were in your room?"

"Not much," Angelita answered. "I hoped she would just talk, but she wouldn't say anything unless I asked her a question. I asked her if someone was here waiting for her but she just shrugged."

"I wonder what that means," Lawrence mused. "Why would she shrug?"

"Probably because she doesn't know," Conseula replied.

"I spoke to the workers," Javier reported in a low voice. "No one knows of anybody waiting for a child from Mexico."

"Oh," Kate replied, trying to hide her disappointment. "Well, it was a long shot. I appreciate you taking the time to ask." She turned to Lawrence. "I guess we should head up to the other towns postmarked on the cards."

"It's beginning to look like they really have no relevance to Marisol," Lawrence sighed.

"It's all we have to go on."

"Where would you be going next?" Consuela asked.

"Firebaugh," Kate responded.

"Oh, that's only about a half hour away."

"Are there motels there?"

"Oh yes." Consuela glanced at her husband. "Motel 33."

"Not a beautiful place, but clean," Javier said.

"That's okay," Kate replied. "We're only sleeping there." She stood and started to clear the table.

"Oh please," Consuela fussed. "Don't worry about that. I'll take care of cleaning up."

Kate looked at Lawrence who nodded. "We should get going. Thank you so much for your generous hospitality." She turned to Angelita and smiled. "And thank you, Angelita, for being so wonderful with Marisol. You have helped us so much."

"You're welcome," Angelita replied, a little shyly. "Maybe you can bring Marisol back and I can find out more. I like her. She's nice."

"Would you explain to Marisol that we are going to Firebaugh to see if she has relatives there?"

Angelita spoke to Marisol in Spanish and Marisol hugged her and then got up and went to Kate's side. Kate took her hand and they all walked to the car. "Do you know how to get to Route 33?" Javier said after Lawrence, Kate and Marisol were settled inside the car.

"As long as there's cell service we'll be fine," Kate answered.

"There should be," Javier said. "Will you let us know how things are going?"

"Of course."

"Thanks again," Lawrence said as he started the car. All three waved goodbye as they drove off.

The sun was now low behind the Coastal Range, tinting the landscape with russet hues as they headed north across miles of fields turned under for the season. Soon they saw trees on the horizon, and the first streetlights winking on ahead, and eventually they were in the midst of a jumble of glowing plastic signs for businesses already closed for the day.

"There it is," Kate pointed out.

"Pretty grim," Lawrence mumbled as he slowed in front of the motel.

"Yes, it is," Kate sighed, pulling out her phone. "But it's another half hour to Los Banos, and that's off our route. Oh wait. Here's something off the highway. Riverfront Inn."

"At least it sounds inviting. Direct me."

"Turn right here and then in three blocks on Q Street." In the dusky light the neighborhood resembled Tranquillity, but once on Q there was the sign of water in the form of willows and sycamores to the east.

"There!" Kate shouted as Lawrence kept driving.

"Uh? Looks like condos in Encino."

"I know," laughed Kate, "but look," she said flashing the map on her phone screen in front of his face.

Lawrence spun the car around and pulled into the parking lot shaded by young trees. "A sign would be handy. Oh, there it is." He pointed to a small wooden plaque lit by a floodlight in the grass.

"Who would have guessed? This is so nice. And look, there's a path to the river."

"It will be a good place for a walk in the morning," Lawrence replied as he pulled into a parking space.

"Now to find the office," Kate said as she opened her door. "I hope someone is around."

They checked in and admired their big, comfortable room before unpacking for the night. "I'm so tired," Lawrence announced as he flopped onto the bed after brushing his teeth. "Time for some mindless channel surfing."

Five minutes of a flashing screen put him right to sleep, and Kate gently slid the remote from his hand and turned off the television. In the darkness of the room she could hear Marisol turning under her own covers, and as the sound of sheets ceased, Kate heard a whisper. *"Gracias."*

To Kate it was as if someone switched on the softest illumination, and she wanted to get up and hug Marisol, but thought better of it. *"De nada,"* Kate whispered back lovingly.

15

KATE WAS THE FIRST UP AND JUMPED IN THE SHOWER. The other two were still sleeping when she finished, so she went to the office and picked up some coffees, milk for Marisol, and some donuts. Not a gourmet breakfast, but enough to keep them going until they got to a restaurant. She got back to the room and found Lawrence in the shower and Marisol still asleep. Kate was glad to see her sleeping. It told her that Marisol felt calm and safe, probably something she hadn't felt for most of her life.

After all three were washed, fed and packed, they went out to the river to take a walk. It wasn't the most beautiful hike they'd ever been on, but it was still a nice break from the monotony of the tilled earth they had been driving through the last couple of days. "So have you figured out how we are going to approach finding people to talk to here?" Lawrence asked as they sat down at a picnic table to enjoy the sunlight dancing through the trees. "Are we going to look for a Chevrolet dealership?"

"Very funny. I really don't know. I guess we could go to the local school again, but Firebaugh is way bigger than Helm or even Tranquillity, so I doubt we'd have much success here."

"So what should we do?"

"I guess we need to at least try."

"I think we might have better luck just trying to get Marisol to talk to us," Lawrence mused. "It seems to me she's getting close to opening up. We should just take her home where she feels safe."

Kate sighed. "Maybe you're right."

Lawrence took her hand. "We know people who speak Spanish in Los Angeles. And maybe Danielle could help."

"Your granddaughter? Does she speak Spanish?"

"No, but she's a kid. Marisol seems to talk more to kids, right?" Lawrence asked.

"But Danielle's only six."

"But she's smart. We can coach her with some phrases and stay within earshot."

"Smart . . . like her grandfather," Kate replied, eyeing him wryly. "It's worth a try."

"So shall we skip Stevinson and go home?"

Kate nodded. "I wonder if we can set her up to go to school. They have to educate all children regardless of immigration status. We might have to get her shots, though."

"That sounds like a long term plan."

Kate took a deep breath to keep from overreacting to the doubt in his voice. "Do you want to call the authorities? That's the other option." She gave him a stony look.

"Touché," he smiled.

Kate smiled back. "So we're on the same page?"

"Apparently so."

"Let's find something to eat in town and head home," she said standing up from the picnic table. They walked back to the inn, checked out, and got in the car. "All the restaurants seem to be on N or O Streets," Kate said as she looked at her phone.

"Any choices besides Mexican?" Lawrence asked. "I wouldn't mind a change of pace."

Kate shook her head. "Just pizza and burgers. Oh wait, there's a diner."

"Let's go there."

"Okay. It's on O Street."

They got to the diner parking lot and went inside. It was a bit early for lunch and a bit late for breakfast, but the place was packed. "I guess I'm not the only one looking for something besides tacos, pizza or a burger," Lawrence chuckled. The hostess sat them and gave them menus.

"Whoa! That's a lot of choice," Kate said to Marisol. She pointed to the pictures on the menu and scrolled through her phone. "¿Uh, *qué quieres comer*?" Marisol pointed to a picture of a cheeseburger. "I guess she isn't tired of burgers. I'll have a chef salad."

The waitress approached and Lawrence ordered for Kate and Marisol. "And I'll have the tuna/avocado sandwich." He turned to Kate.

"Healthiest thing I could find on the menu. Other than the chef salad."

"Our meals may be changing now that we have a twelve year old to feed, you know."

Lawrence shrugged. "Or we could try to change her eating habits."

"I think she could do with fewer changes, not more."

"Just a suggestion. She may very well want to leave her past behind. Wouldn't you if you had lived through what she did?"

Kate shrugged and then sighed. "I can't even imagine it." She scrolled through her phone again and turned to Marisol. *"¿Quieres ir a escuela?"*

"What did you just ask her? Something about school?"

"Yep. I asked her if she wanted to go to school."

Marisol smiled and nodded. "Well, that's a clear response to a big question," Lawrence chuckled.

Kate smiled back as she scrolled some more. *"Nosotros vamos a casa y tu puedes ir a la escuela."* She looked at Lawrence. "My accent may be terrible, but she seems to be understanding me. I told her that we are going home and she can go to school."

"And you're learning Spanish."

"Well, I don't know about learning it, but Google is a life saver."

The food came and they all ate in silence. They were hungry and there seemed to be little to say at this point. They were going home with a new plan and both were uneasy about it, but at the same time they were happy with the agreement. Lawrence seemed especially invested in Marisol's progress, like it brought a new dimension to their marriage. After trips to the rest room and paying the bill, they got back in the car. "If I just stay on N Street, it will meet up with I-5, right?" Lawrence asked.

"Yes. Route 33 and N Street are the same. It should be about three and a half hours to L.A."

"I'm glad to be going home. You?"

"Yes. And apparently Marisol is too. When should we have Michael, Carla and Danielle come over?"

"Probably wait until the weekend. Maybe she'll open up to us before that and we don't have to ask Danielle to be the go-between."

"It's a lot to ask of a six year old, but she's intuitive, mature and caring and that's exactly what Marisol needs."

Lawrence smiled. "Yes, she is that."

"I'll go to our neighborhood school and talk to the principal tomorrow. I hope they'll let her in without any papers."

"I thought we needed to get her vaccinated first?"

"I'll find out tomorrow." Kate sighed. "I hope we're doing the right thing putting her in school."

"How would it not be the right thing?" Lawrence asked.

"It's putting her name out there publicly."

Lawrence shrugged. "I think it'll be fine."

"I guess."

They drove in silence for a while, the road ahead a long gray ribbon towards the Coast Range and the Interstate, where semis crawled along like toys in the great distance. A car approached from the opposite direction, and at close range it was clearly a police cruiser. It passed with a whoosh, and all was relatively quiet again until Lawrence looked in the rear view manner. "Uh oh."

"What?" Kate asked. "Is something wrong with the car?"

"We're being pulled over."

"For what? You drive like a grandpa."

"I am a grandpa," Lawrence replied sharply as he pulled unto the shoulder. "Now keep your cool."

"Like hell—"

"Kate," Lawrence warned as he shifted in his seat to get his wallet out. "Get the registration out of the glove box." Lawrence rolled down the window as a paunchy officer approached from behind.

"License and registration, please," the officer announced. Lawrence handed over his license as Kate rummaged through the glove box, trying to find the registration and restrain her annoyance at the same time. "Are you alright, ma'am?"

"I was until you pulled my husband over for driving while Black."

"Kate!" Lawrence hissed.

The officer stared at her, but it was hard to register any emotion on his part due to his dark glasses. Kate returned her attention to the glove box and finally found the registration. The officer took it and compared it to the license. "Actually ma'am," he finally said as he studied the documents. "I pulled you over because a car like yours is missing from Dos Palos. Different plates than this one, but I had to check and make sure these plates weren't stolen. And—at sixty-five miles an hour—I thought I saw a middle aged White woman in the passenger seat, and she's missing along with her car." He handed the documents back over. "But the plates match the registration and the license matches the registration and your anger cannot be confused with a nervous hostage."

There was silence all around for a moment, but with a range of expressions passing over Kate's face, Lawrence didn't take long to fill in the gap. "Thank you, officer."

The officer peered into the back seat. "Is that your granddaughter?"

"Uh," Lawrence hesitated.

"Yes," Kate piped in.

"Yes," Lawrence agreed. He turned and stared at Kate. Both looked desperately at one another, knowing they both sounded totally unbelievable.

"She doesn't seem to like cops much either," the officer said.

Kate twisted in her seat. Her anger was buried by guilt. She had totally forgotten about

Marisol, now pressed up against the seat and door like a trapped animal. Kate reached out to her, but Marisol didn't move. "She—she's had a lot of traumatic experiences," Kate explained, trying to get Marisol to take her hand. Marisol didn't move. "I—I had to take custody of her," Kate continued. Marisol then timidly reached for Kate's hand. "Isn't that right—Danielle?" she gushed, relieved that Marisol finally responded. She dared not look back at the officer.

"She's lucky she has you," the officer said. "Can I give her a sucker?"

Kate slowly turned her head. "What?"

"A lollipop." She watched his mouth as he spoke, which now seemed softer, even a little sad. "I keep them in my cruiser for domestic abuse situations, traffic accidents—anywhere I need to calm a kid down and gain some trust. She's a little old, but—well, who doesn't like candy?" He patted his soft gut. "My favorite is cherry."

"Oh," Kate sighed. "Yes, of course."

"Very kind of you, officer," Lawrence added.

When he walked back to his cruiser, Kate became frantic. "He's going to call ICE!" she cried.

"Stop, Kate!" Lawrence snapped. "Now you're the one being paranoid!"

"How could be possibly think she's our grandchild?"

"He was talking to you, not us. Shhh! Here he comes."

"Could you roll down your window, sir, so I can hand it to her?"

"Certainly."

Kate turned to watch Marisol's eyes grow larger as the glass whirred down opposite her. "It's okay, dear." Kate bit her tongue when she found herself formulating some Spanish in her head.

The officer reached in with a sucker. "I hope you like cherry, too."

Marisol's eyes darted between the offering and Kate, the latter nodding approvingly, but it just wasn't going to happen. "Oh, sometimes she gets so scared she becomes practically mute."

The officer's arm relaxed. "It doesn't always work," he admitted. "And sometimes it takes so long for protective services to appear on the scene. It's heartbreaking." Kate stiffened at the mention of protective services. He had called them! The officer then offered the sucker to Kate. "Would you give this to her after I'm gone? I don't want to delay you any longer."

"Uh . . ." Kate's head felt like it could explode with conflicting thoughts. "Oh, how thoughtful," she finally murmured, taking the sucker.

"Yes, very thoughtful," Lawrence echoed.

The officer straightened up beside the car. "On your way home?" he asked Lawrence.

"Yes."

"It's a long drive. Be safe." He walked back to his cruiser, got in, unwrapped a sucker for himself, stuck it in his mouth and started the engine.

"Let's get out of here!" Kate cried, tapping Lawrence's thigh.

"Not until he's rolling along on his own way." Lawrence started his engine as the cruiser swung an arc on the road and sped off in the opposite direction. He blew out a long breath as he shifted out of park and started off at a leisurely pace.

"You never know, do you?" Kate finally said.

"Nope. I always hold my breath. Keeps you from screaming or saying something you'll regret later." He then chuckled. "And here I thought my car model was a level of protection. It's been a long time since I've been stopped."

"You bought this car for protection? I thought it was just a sign of middle age."

He gave her a look. "Who doesn't want to feel safe?"

"But you should be able to drive what you want to drive, not some social device."

"I'm happy with my car. I got a good deal and it gives me no trouble, mechanical or otherwise."

"Until now."

"Freak coincidence. And I got a lollipop."

"Marisol got a lollipop," she corrected, looking down and twirling the red sucker between her fingers.

"Even better," Lawrence replied.

Kate twisted round in her seat and found Marisol peering out the rear window towards the horizon and the long-gone officer. She turned back to her phone and started tapping out her thoughts to reassure Marisol. *"Todo está bien. Nosotras vamos a casa."*

Marisol smiled faintly at Kate and took the lollipop. *"Gracias,"* she murmured.

16

THEY WERE HOME BY FIVE AND MARISOL PRANCED INTO THE GUEST BEDROOM AS IF IT HAD BEEN HERS ALL HER LIFE. Kate went immediately to the grocery store while Lawrence went through the mostly junk mail and unpacked. It was a true family-like scenario. Kate returned with a roast chicken and made a salad and some vegetables. Their stomachs needed a rest from the fattening meals of the last few days. "Is she going to eat this?" Lawrence asked as they sat down for dinner.

"Weren't you the one who said we could try to change her eating habits?" Kate answered with a playful smirk. She looked over at Marisol who didn't seem to bat an eyelash over the change in her diet. She ate as heartily as she had all along. "Doesn't look like we have anything to worry about," Kate said as she nodded toward Marisol.

"She does eat most anything we give her."

"She must have been starving for so long that anything tastes good to her." Kate patted Marisol's arm and smiled at her. "*¿Buena comida?*" Marisol nodded.

"Hey, you didn't even have to look that up," Lawrence said.

"I guess I am starting to remember certain words. I always knew '*Buena*' was 'good' and I think I somehow knew that '*comida*' was 'food'."

After dinner Lawrence did the dishes, Marisol watched television, and Kate got on her computer to search through the Los Angeles Unified School District website. "I guess our neighborhood school is Westwood and it's a charter school," Kate told Lawrence as he sat down next to her. "That's good, I think. Maybe they can be a little more lenient about letting her in without papers."

"Don't charter schools still have to adhere to district guidelines?"

"Yeah, in some ways. Anyway, I'll talk to the principal tomorrow and see. I'll also call the doctor and make an appointment to get her vaccines." She leaned back into the sofa back and smiled. "I like this."

"Which 'this' are you talking about?" Lawrence asked as he leaned back and put his arm around her.

"Oh, getting back into the school and education culture. But I guess I'm also talking about having a child around."

Lawrence kissed the top of her head. "It is kind of fun."

They all woke up later than usual the next morning. In fact, Marisol was up first and in the kitchen when Kate and Lawrence stumbled in at eight. She had made a piece of toast and poured herself a glass of milk. Kate beamed and said to Lawrence, "Look. She feels at home and knows what to do!" She turned to Marisol. "*¿Quieres huevos?*"

"*Sí,*" Marisol smiled at Kate and Lawrence. "*Huevos.*"

"That's eggs, right?" Lawrence asked. "Like *huevos rancheros.*"

"Very good. Before long we'll be bilingual!"

"*Huevos* coming right up," Lawrence said, taking a skillet out of the cabinet.

Kate scrolled through her phone and then said, "*Vamos a visitar la escuela esta mañana.*"

Marisol smiled and nodded. "*Qué bien!*"

Kate and Lawrence glanced at each other. "She's going to be a regular chatterbox," he said, returning his attention to the skillet. "How should I make these eggs?"

"Oh, scrambled, I think."

"She's going to be disappointed after I said *huevos rancheros,*" he grinned.

"Google it," Kate laughed, poking him in the side.

They finished breakfast, showered, and reassembled in the kitchen. "Are you calling Michael to tell them what's going on?"

"Yes. Maybe invite them for dinner on Friday?"

"Okay," Kate replied. "I've lost track of the days. Today's Thursday, right?"

"Yes. Are you going to walk to the school or drive?"

"Walk. It's just off Overland, south of Santa Monica Boulevard. It'll be nice to show Marisol the neighborhood."

"Maybe she's too old for elementary school," Lawrence mused.

"But her lack of schooling and English will put her there," Kate answered. "And she'd be in one classroom instead of moving from room to room for different subjects. Anyway, I'll see what the principal says. Maybe they've had a similar situation before."

"Good luck. I'm on my way to the gym." He kissed Kate and then turned to Marisol. He hesitated, looked at Kate who shrugged at him, and then hastily kissed Marisol on the cheek. "*Adiós*, Marisol." He smiled at Kate and left.

"*Vámonos*," Kate said as she took Marisol's hand. They walked out after Lawrence.

Marisol didn't let go of Kate's hand for the whole walk to the school. Kate tried pointing out some sights in English to see if Marisol would repeat the words, but she just looked around in awe at the sights. They found the principal's office easily and asked the clerk if the principal was in.

"Yes, but she's observing in a classroom. Can I help you?"

"I'd like to enroll Marisol in your school, but there are some problems with her papers."

"Do you have proof of residence, birth certificate and vaccination record?"

"I have proof of residency, but that's all right now. It's kind of a long story. I'd like to talk to the principal. Will he or she be finished soon, do you think?"

"I don't really know. Maybe you should make an appointment."

Kate thought for a minute. "I guess."

The clerk checked the principal's calendar on her computer. "Well, she actually should be back any minute because she has an appointment in ten minutes. Because of the circumstances maybe she can squeeze you in for a moment so we can get the process started."

"Okay. Thanks." Kate sat down on a bench and patted the seat next to her for Marisol to sit.

The principal arrived shortly and the clerk spoke to her in low tones while the principal glanced at the clock. She then turned to Kate. "I have a couple of minutes. Come in." Kate and Marisol followed her into her office. "I'm Mrs. Flores," she said as she studied Marisol. "Did you want to enroll her? We are only K-5."

"Yes. Well, there may be a problem." Kate spoke quickly of finding Marisol on the side of the road and how she wouldn't speak at all. "I can take her to my doctor for vaccinations, but I can't come up with a valid birth certificate or passport."

Mrs. Flores sighed and turned to Marisol. She spoke to her in Spanish, much too fast for Kate to decipher anything she said. Marisol didn't answer and Mrs. Flores turned to Kate. "I'll put her in a fifth grade, but I will need the immunizations done."

"I'll take care of it right away."

"We have a couple of other undocumented students. Maybe the counselor can help after she seems comfortable."

"She has finally started saying a couple of words so maybe she'll start talking and we can find her relatives."

"Well, I have an appointment, so take the enrollment packet home and get her vaccinated. Then we can enroll her."

"Thank you." Kate took Marisol's hand and left the office after getting the enrollment packet from the clerk.

They took a different route home and Kate immediately called her doctor's office to explain the situation. They told her to come that afternoon at four. Kate opened the packet and realized that there was little for her to fill out or attach to the form. She had few answers to the mystery that was Marisol's past: no birth certificate, no passport, no transcripts. She thought they could try to start Monday if all went well with the doctor and the fact that she doesn't need a proof of age. And Kate had high hopes that Marisol would start talking soon. Maybe Danielle will be the key . . . or maybe a classmate. She gazed at Marisol and thought again of all she had gone through to get here. And how unfamiliar all this must be for her. What strength and resilience this little girl has.

"How did it go?" Lawrence said as he walked into the living room.

"We have a doctor's appointment this afternoon for vaccinations and I filled out the enrollment forms as best I could. The principal, Mrs. Flores, said she'd put her in a fifth grade classroom."

"Sounds good. So she'll start tomorrow?"

"I think Monday. I'll give them the forms tomorrow. Did you call Michael?"

"Yes. I spoke to Carla. They'll be here for dinner tomorrow night."

"I guess I need to think about what to cook for dinner then."

"I can get take-out."

"No. I need to start cooking meals. Marisol needs to see what American food tastes like. I mean other than hamburgers and pizza."

"Well, make it simple," he replied. "None of us needs a gourmet meal."

"Yeah."

They had sandwiches for lunch and the afternoon passed quickly. Soon it was time to go to the doctor's office. Kate hadn't really explained the situation to the nurse on the phone, so when she got there, they were taken aback when she said it was for Marisol. "We'll need to give her a physical," the nurse said.

"That's fine. But I don't have any papers for her."

"I need to talk to the doctor." The nurse went into a door and closed it. When the door opened, it was the doctor that came out.

"Hi Kate. So what's the story here?"

Kate explained the situation, starting to feel a bit annoyed that she had to, even though she certainly understood why. "If you need to give her a physical exam also, that's fine. But I just need the vaccinations so she can attend school."

"She doesn't speak at all? Not even Spanish?"

"Just a couple of words occasionally."

The doctor examined her and Marisol was very compliant. "She seems in pretty good health considering all she's probably been through. I'll have the nurse give her the vaccinations she needs." He left the room and the nurse returned. Marisol was silent and winced a bit when she saw the needles, but again acquiesced.

Baked salmon, a green salad, and rice were on the table when they got home after six. Kate kissed Lawrence. "Oh thank you! Did you shop this afternoon?"

"I figured you would be late and tired, being rush hour and all, so I ran out to Gelson's. I'd like to say I cooked it, but I didn't. They did."

"Doesn't matter to me who cooked it." They sat down and ate.

"And ice cream for dessert," Lawrence said as he cleared the plates.

"Yum."

Dinner was finished and the dishes done. Kate found some English children's books that Lawrence had saved for when Danielle came to visit and gave the pile to Marisol. They went into their respective bedrooms and Kate and Lawrence took advantage of the peace and quiet and the fact that they were finally alone together.

17

A LOUD KNOCKING AT THE DOOR ANNOUNCED THE ARRIVAL OF GRANDDAUGHTER DANIELLE THE FOLLOWING EVENING. "How's the most beautiful girl in the world?" Lawrence said as he scooped her up in his arms.

"Hi Grampa!" she squealed with delight.

"Hi Dad," Michael said, stepping in and giving him a side hug.

"Where's Carla?" Kate asked as she hugged Michael and kissed Danielle on the top of her head.

"She's meeting us here. She had an appointment."

Marisol stood timidly in the doorway of the living room. "Come on in, sweetie," Kate said taking her by the hand.

Lawrence put Danielle down and Kate brought Marisol to her. "This is Marisol. Marisol, this is Danielle." The girls smiled shyly at each other.

"*Hola*," Michael said, shaking Marisol's hand. "*¿Cómo estás?*" Marisol looked down slyly so he turned to Kate. "That about does it for my Spanish.

"I wouldn't be any better without Google," Kate grinned.

"Well, come on in," Lawrence said. "Can I get you a beer?"

"Sure," Michael answered.

"How about you, Kate?"

"I'll have a beer. Would you girls like some juice?"

"I'll take apple!" Danielle said. Marisol just shrugged.

"Two apple juices coming up!" Lawrence announced. He went to the kitchen to fetch the drinks with Danielle skipping after him. Marisol looked at Kate uneasily and then slowly followed Lawrence and Danielle into the kitchen.

"Does Danielle understand what's going on with Marisol and what we're hoping she'll do?" Kate asked Michael.

"Carla talked to her. We'll see how it goes."

"I enrolled her in school," Kate said. "She'll start Monday. The principal put her in a fifth grade classroom. There are other undocumented immigrants at the school, so we're hoping they will help open her up."

"Los Angeles is full of DREAMers."

"I wonder if Marisol even knows that term," Kate mused.

"Guess I really don't much about it either," Michael admitted. "Is a DREAMer simply an undocumented immigrant with aspirations or one that has actually applied for citizenship?"

"I don't really know. I think it's someone who's applied for citizenship. It's fairly clear she came here to escape something awful. I don't know the exact circumstances, just that her mother is dead. I'm hoping Danielle might find out more."

Lawrence arrived with the beers, trailed by the two girls sipping their juice boxes. "What time do you think Carla will be here?" he asked as he joined them on the sofa.

"I don't know," Michael replied. "Her meeting was at four. She didn't think it would take too long, but there's always traffic."

"It's okay." Lawrence turned to Kate. "I took the manicotti out of the oven. It can sit for a while. The salad's made so we're fine waiting."

Just then the doorbell rang and Kate jumped up to open it. "Hi Carla," she said, hugging her.

"Sorry I'm late," Carla answered breathlessly. "I stopped to buy a few things for Marisol." She gave Lawrence a hug and flopped into a chair.

"Beer? Wine?" Lawrence asked.

Carla looked around and saw that everyone else was drinking beer. "Beer's fine." She opened the shopping bag she had placed on the floor next to her. "I bought a few games and puzzles that I thought would appeal to both six year olds and— well, a kid considerably older."

"Let me see!" Danielle exclaimed as she ran to her mother's side.

"You know what, Danielle?" Kate interjected. "Why don't you take the bag into Marisol's room and show her?"

"Okay. Come on," she said to Marisol and took her hand. The girls scurried out of the living room.

"Does Danielle know any Spanish?" Kate asked Carla.

"She knows a little. She has some classmates and friends that are Mexican or from Central America and their teacher uses Spanish in the classroom."

"I hope this works. I don't mean to put pressure on her."

"Oh I don't think she feels pressure. Even if it doesn't work out tonight, we can get them together often to make Marisol feel more comfortable. Danielle's very excited to have an auntie." Carla laughed. "I was going to say cousin, but then I realized if Marisol's your daughter, then she's my sister-in-law."

Lawrence and Kate glanced at each other. "I guess we didn't think about it that way," Lawrence said after a moment of silence.

Carla looked over at Michael. "Oops, I thought you said they were keeping her . . ."

"We are," Kate said quickly. "I mean, for now. We're trying to locate her family and actually haven't discussed much beyond that. We just hadn't used the word 'daughter' before. That's why we were surprised."

"I'm sorry. I didn't mean —"

"Oh, Carla. It's fine. Please, no worries," Lawrence said.

Michael quickly changed the subject. "So how was the park?"

"Park?" Kate asked.

"Didn't you guys go to Anza-Borrego State Park?"

"Oh, jeez. That was like a lifetime ago. It was beautiful. It's a real gem in the middle of nowhere. You should go."

"The canyons and badlands are an interesting contrast," Lawrence interjected. "Anyway, it's nice to get to the desert once in a while. I'd hate to live there, but it's nice to visit. And nice to go somewhere other than Palm Springs."

"And just outside the park are all these enormous metal sculptures of prehistoric and mythical animals," Kate added.

Danielle and Marisol entered the room then. "I'm hungry," Danielle said. "When's dinner?"

Kate stood. "Right now. Let's go eat." She turned to Marisol. "*¿Quieres comer?*"

"*Sí,*" Marisol said, smiling.

Over dinner the adults talked about Danielle's school and how Marisol was going to start school on Monday. When they had finished the main course and Lawrence brought in the dessert, Kate turned to Danielle. "Did Marisol talk to you about anything?"

"Not much. I told her that I didn't have any brothers or sisters and asked her if she did."

"In English or Spanish?" Carla asked.

"I knew that *hermano* is brother and *hermana* is sister so I just said those words."

"And did she answer?" Kate asked.

"She went like this." Danielle nodded her head vigorously.

"Did she say anything else? Like that they're here or in Mexico?"

"We don't even know if she's from Mexico," Lawrence explained impatiently to Michael and Carla.

"She would still have had to go through Mexico to get where you found her," Carla said.

Danielle looked at her mother doubtfully. "I just said *hermano* or *hermana.*"

"And?"

"She said *hermana.*"

Kate turned to Marisol. "*¿Hermana en Los Estados Unidos?*" Marisol shrugged her shoulders. Kate scrolled through her phone. "*¿Sabes dónde está tu hermana?*" She turned to the others. "I asked her if she knows where her sister is." Marisol shook her head no. Kate scrolled some more. "*¿Cruzaste la frontera con tu hermana?*"

"What did you say now?" Lawrence asked.

"I asked her if she crossed the border with her sister." Marisol shook her head again. "I'm thinking her sister lives here and sent for her, perhaps, when her mother died."

"That sounds logical," Michael said. "Maybe her sister sent the money for a coyote to take her across the border and then somehow Marisol got away from him."

"Or maybe her sister was supposed to meet her and didn't show up and the coyote just left her," Carla added.

Kate gave Danielle a big hug. "Thank you. You've been a big help."

Danielle beamed for a moment but then asked, "But why would she go with a coyote across the border? Don't they bite?"

"Oh not the animal, coyote," Carla said. "Coyote is a name for people who smuggle people across the border."

"Smuggle?" Danielle asked.

"Yes. Like, uh . . . pirates or a bandit."

"Why can't people just come across the border?"

The adults looked at each other, not sure how to answer. How does one explain politics to a six year old? Finally Lawrence cleared his throat. "It's like going into a stranger's house without their permission. You have to ask first. But if no one answers the door, and it's raining and you have no other place to go, you sneak in to stay warm and dry."

Danielle seemed to accept that answer. "Well, I hope she can stay. I like having another kid around."

Everyone smiled and then Michael shook his head. "Dad, from now on I'm sending her to you with all the difficult questions."

"I hope she's already asked you about the birds and the bees," Lawrence mused. Everyone laughed.

Kate resisted the urge to question Marisol further. She started to clear away the dessert dishes to distract herself and said to Danielle, "Do you want to take Marisol back to her room and play some more?"

"Sure!" Danielle took Marisol's hand and dragged her out.

Carla joined Kate in the kitchen and started putting dishes in the washer. "So what are you going to do now?"

"I guess keep questioning her. I just didn't want to bombard her since she just started talking. This is a start, anyway."

"Yes. Now you have something to work with. Maybe the school has someone who speaks Spanish who can help you."

"The principal already spoke to her in Spanish."

"Perfect. I think things will fall into place pretty soon. Don't you?"

Kate paused before answering. "I'm not sure. She may truly not know where her sister lives. She may not live in those towns in the San Joaquin Valley. She may have sent those postcards when she was just passing through."

"Are you prepared to keep her if you don't find her sister or any other relative?"

"Lawrence and I haven't really discussed that, but I don't think he wants to."

"Do you?"

Kate sighed and looked away. Carla reached out and put her arm around her shoulder. "I just don't know what I want to do," Kate finally said.

Michael and his family left and Marisol went to bed. Lawrence and Kate got into bed and she turned to him and said, "Carla asked me if I wanted to keep Marisol if we couldn't find her relatives."

"What did you say?"

"That I didn't know."

"Even if we wanted to, what would we do? Adopt her? With no papers?"

"Let's not go there," Kate murmured. "I'm sorry I brought it up. Let's just try to find her sister." She took a deep breath and exhaled, trying to rid herself of the frustration and uncertainty. She then leaned over and kissed him. "You have a wonderful family."

"They're yours too, you know."

18

THE WEEKEND WENT BY QUICKLY. Kate took Marisol to shop for school clothes and supplies and decided to leave long term arrangements well enough alone. When Sunday night rolled around and they had finished dinner, they sat in the living room watching a movie. *"¿Estás emocionada por ir a la escuela mañana?"* Kate asked Marisol after Googling the translation.

"What did you say?" Lawrence asked.

"Are you excited about going to school tomorrow."

Marisol said, *"Estoy nerviosa."*

"¿Una nerviosa buena?"

Marisol smiled. *"Me gusta la escuela."*

"Me too," Kate nodded. She scrolled through her phone. *"Yo era maestra."*

Marisol's eyes widened. *"Quiero ser una maestra también."*

"She wants to be a teacher," Kate told Lawrence.

"Well she's in the right family for that. You, me, Michael and Carla; all of us teachers."

Kate grinned, enjoying the use of the word 'family'. "I wonder if I should stay with her tomorrow."

"I don't think that's a good idea. She might get laughed at by fifth graders."

"I'm just being a mother hen," she said with a twinkle in her eye. "I remember having parents hover in the classroom . . . it was a real pain in the butt." She turned to Marisol. "*Es hora de dormir. Mañana es un dia importante.*"

"You are remarkable, you know that?" Lawrence marveled.

"Well, yes, but what are you referring to?" Kate teased.

"You've learned all this Spanish so quickly."

"I'm working on it. Why not? They say learning a language is a good retirement activity." She got up and said, "*Necesitamos despertarnos a las 6:30.* I'm setting the alarm for six thirty."

Lawrence nodded. "Are you going to walk to school?"

"Yes, I'll take the long route home and get some exercise." She and Marisol both left Lawrence to finish the movie alone.

Everyone was in the kitchen by six the next morning. No alarm had been necessary. Marisol had on her brand new clothes and wore her new backpack. "*Huevos?*" Lawrence asked Marisol who nodded.

"Look at you speaking Spanish," Kate winked.

"I guess now I have to learn 'scrambled' or 'fried'."

Kate watched as Marisol loaded her backpack with all her supplies. She noticed that

Marisol had put her pictures and postcards in with the pencils and notebooks. Kate decided not to comment on it. "I'll just have coffee and toast," she said to Lawrence.

"You got it."

Kate and Marisol finished breakfast and started the journey to school. It was about a mile so they left with plenty of time to get there before school started at eight. Kate saw the principal in front of the school, greeting the students as they got dropped off, and approached her. "Hi. Should I go ask the clerk what her room number is?"

"Why not leave Marisol with me. I'll take her to her classroom. I've already informed her teacher about the situation. She has a particular student in mind to show Marisol the ropes. Her parents are undocumented, but she was born here. She speaks fluent Spanish and English."

"Perfect. What's her name?"

"Yesenia."

"Pretty."

Mrs. Flores took Marisol's hand and spoke to her in rapid Spanish, too fast for Kate to understand, but she figured Mrs. Flores was explaining what she had just told her. Marisol did not shy away. In fact, she answered her back with more words than Kate had heard her speak to anyone else. Things were definitely looking up. She kissed Marisol goodbye and headed to Olympic Boulevard for her walk home, even though it was in the opposite direction. She figured she'd walk towards the beach, but being some five miles away, she probably wouldn't make it that far. It didn't matter. She was relishing the thought of having the day largely to herself for a change, but after walking a few blocks west, she changed her mind and headed back to the apartment. Whether Lawrence wanted to face it or not, there were long-term decisions that had to be made, and research to be done about what was legal and best for Marisol.

Lawrence wasn't home when she got there. She sat at her computer and started searching, but was distracted by the fact that everything seemed to be going so well at the moment. Marisol was in school and talking more and more. It just seemed a natural opening to her future. Maybe school was the right place to start the process of—well, what? She typed and typed for connections and found herself far astray an hour later, studying a site for a bilingual summer camp in the Santa Monica Mountains. Then she heard the front door unlock and soon Lawrence appeared. "Want to go out for lunch?" he asked. "Just the two of us?"

"I don't know. If you want. Where were you?"

Lawrence gave her a look. "The gym, like every Monday morning. What's wrong? You seem distracted."

Kate considered her options and decided to stay safely within the idea of finding Marisol's family. "Just thinking about Marisol's sister. She must be so worried."

Lawrence put his hand on her shoulder. "Marisol is talking more and more every day. We might get a break in the matter soon."

"I know. I guess I'm just not sure what to do in the meantime."

Lawrence shrugged. "It'll work itself out."

Kate laughed. "It seems that we've switched positions. Now you're less concerned than I am."

"I'm just glad to be home and she's in school," he replied, settling back into the doorway. "It's better than running all over the state on a wild goose chase and getting ourselves into predicaments where we may look like kidnappers."

"Don't you want another sucker?"

"Is that a proposition?"

"No," Kate replied, rolling her eyes. "You need to take a shower."

"Will do. And then let's go out to lunch. I'm starving." He wagged his eyebrows. "We'll celebrate later."

"Someone has to pick up Marisol at two-thirty . . ."

"We can do that, too."

"You're going to wear me out."

"That's my plan," he smiled.

Lawrence and Kate arrived breathlessly in front of the school a little after two-thirty. "There she is!" Kate exclaimed as Marisol came out of the building with another girl and looked around. Kate waved and Marisol waved back and then turned to the other girl and said something. Then she ran over to Kate and Lawrence, beaming.

"*¿Cómo extuvo la escuela hoy?*" Lawrence enunciated slowly.

"Whoa," Kate laughed. "When did you pick that up?"

"Oh, when you were in the shower," Lawrence winked.

Marisol had been watching intently as they bantered and then finally replied, "*Escuela era Buena.*"

"*¿Es ella Yesenia?*" Kate asked, pointing to the other girl.

"*Sí. Mi amiga.*"

Kate looked at Lawrence. "Maybe in a couple of days we could interview Yesenia."

"Or maybe in a few days Marisol will just tell us anything she might have told Yesenia."

"Hm. That's true. I've never seen her look so happy and secure. Anyway, let's go home."

They started to walk away but Mrs. Flores rushed over to them. "Just a minute!"

They stopped and watched the principal approach. "I just wanted to let you know that Marisol's teacher said she did really well today. She answered her questions with help from Yesenia, and the bilingual coordinator will be here tomorrow to test her reading and math skills. She seemed to get along well with the other students."

"That's wonderful! She spoke then to her teacher and the other kids?" Kate asked.

"Apparently she wasn't particularly shy and was engaged when Yesenia translated for her."

"We don't want Yesenia to feel like this is a burden," Kate said.

"She's a sweet girl, but also assertive and bright. The teacher said Yesenia was still performing well in her own work, so I think the situation suits them both."

"Is there anything we can do at home to help Marisol along?" Lawrence asked.

"Maybe you can ask the teacher that. But let's wait and see how Marisol does on the tests. We need to know what levels she's on in reading and math before we can answer that."

They walked home, stopping for ice cream on the way. Marisol went to her room while Kate got back on her computer for more research and Lawrence started dinner. "Dinner's ready," he called, "unless you want to have a glass of wine first."

"Let's eat. I'll go get Marisol." Kate knocked on Marisol's door and then opened it slightly. "Marisol?" No answer. Kate opened the door wider and saw Marisol engrossed in one of the books Kate had given her. She was mouthing the words as she read. Kate smiled. "*¿Quieres comer?*"

"*Sí.*" Marisol put the book down after taking one of her postcards and putting it inside as a bookmark.

"*¿Es ella tu hermana?*" Marisol did not answer and Kate was sorry she had said anything to ruin all the good that was happening today. "*Vamos.*" Kate took Marisol's hand, hoping to smooth it over, and they went in for dinner.

The next day went well. Kate went early to pick up Marisol so she could talk to the principal again. Mrs. Flores was still in her office when Kate arrived. School wouldn't let out for another fifteen minutes. "Can I help you?" the clerk asked Kate as she approached the counter.

"I was wondering if I could speak to Mrs. Flores for a minute."

The clerk got up and went into the principal's office. She came out and said, "You can go in for just a minute. Mrs. Flores likes to be outside when the kids are dismissed."

"Thank you." Kate went into the office. "I was wondering how the testing went."

"Well, they haven't been scored yet, but the bilingual coordinator said her reading is most likely on a second or third grade level. She has probably missed a lot of school. Her math is about the same."

"So do we keep her in the fifth grade?"

"Oh yes. She's already bigger and older than her classmates. We can work out a reading and math program for her where she can go to another classroom just for those subjects."

"Are you going to teach her in Spanish or English?"

"Both, I imagine. Don't worry. We have resources to help her."

"What can I do at home?" Kate asked.

"Get her books and read with her."

"In English or Spanish?"

"Are you comfortable reading with her in Spanish?"

"Not really, but I'll do my best. I was a teacher before I retired, but high school English."

"I'm sure anything you do will help. Now I need to get outside. Maybe you should make an appointment with her teacher. You can email her. Her email address is on our website."

"Okay. I will. Thanks." They both left and went outside.

Marisol ran up to Kate, again grinning from ear to ear. Kate decided to take her to the library this afternoon so she could pick out books in both English and Spanish, now that they had a better idea of what she could do. Both of them could sense the contentment emanating from each other.

19

THE NEXT MORNING, AFTER KATE RETURNED FROM DROPPING MARISOL OFF AT SCHOOL, SHE DECIDED TO CALL LUCY AND SEE IF SHE HAD SOME IDEAS ON HELPING MARISOL WITH HER READING. But just as she got her phone out, it rang with an unknown number. Kate let it go to voicemail and dialed Lucy. Lucy didn't answer, but as she was leaving a voicemail, she noticed that the same person was calling again. Maybe she should answer it. "Hello?"

"Ms. McCoy?"

"Yes."

"This is Principal Flores at Westwood School. You need to get down here right away."

"Oh God! Is Marisol okay?"

"She's fine. But there are ICE agents here looking for her."

"What? How did they know?" Kate was furious.

"I'm not sure. We are trying to figure that out, but first we are working on keeping them out of Marisol's classroom."

"Can they do that? Just come and take her?"

"No. The Los Angeles Unified School District has adopted sanctuary policies. But they still try to strong-arm us into thinking they can."

"I'll be right there." Kate dropped her phone into a pocket and ran out the door, then ran back in to grab her purse and hustled to her car. She was at the school in a matter of minutes and parked in front, hoping she wouldn't get a ticket, but also not caring if she did. She rushed into the office and saw the agents talking to the principal and the clerk. "You cannot do this!" Kate yelled.

An agent gave her a withering look. "And who are you?"

"This is the girl's guardian," Mrs. Flores snapped back. "And you do not have my permission to be on the school grounds."

"Like you own the place or something," the agent replied coolly. "We were called in by a district official. Game over."

"This is my school and I am ordering you off the grounds."

"So I've heard," the agent yawned. "We wouldn't be here without a warrant, you know."

"Your warrant is no good here, as I just told you. Schools are safe zones. I, too, am following procedure and have called the school police and our local district administrator of operations. I need your names and badge numbers and your supervisor's phone number."

"It's a federal warrant. Do you want me to search every classroom?"

"You wouldn't dare smear yourself all over the news like that," snarled Mrs. Flores. "Let me see the warrant." The agent casually produced the item and she snatched it from his grasp. "Louise," she called out. "Please make a copy of this and email it to the district administrator." Louise appeared and took the warrant and Mrs. Flores turned back to the agent. "You will wait here until I hear from the Office of General Counsel." She rummaged through some file drawers and took out a piece of paper. "Here, read this. This is the memo from the district pertaining to all this. As you can see, I am following the guidelines." The agent gave a disinterested glance at the paper as the principal turned to Kate. "Can I see you in the hall for a minute?"

Kate followed Mrs. Flores into the hallway. "I don't understand. I thought she'd be safe here."

"Just listen to me," the principal said in a low voice. "Go to her classroom and take her home. I'll be in touch."

"What's the room number?"

Mrs. Flores practically mouthed the words. "Thirty-three."

Kate rushed out, frantically running through the hallways looking for Room 33. She finally found it and yanked open the door. "I need to take Marisol," she panted.

The teacher looked up in shock. "I'm sorry, who are you?"

"I'm her guardian. It's an emergency."

"I'm sorry, but I need to get the okay from the office."

Kate paced impatiently as the teacher went to the intercom. As soon as she pressed the button the clerk responded hastily," Yes, yes. Let her go. Elena cleared it."

Kate hurried across the room full of staring, restless fifth-graders and picked up Marisol's backpack off the back of her chair. "*Necesitamos ir a casa,*" she said to Marisol as she took her hand and pulled her up. Then she turned to the teacher. "Is there a way out of the school without going by the principal's office?"

"Uh, yes," the teacher answered, looking bewildered. "Take a left and down the stairs. What's going on?"

Kate was already rushing out with Marisol in tow. They ran down the stairs and into a playground. Kate looked around frantically, trying to find an open gate. She noticed an ICE vehicle parked out front and tried another direction, but to no avail. It seemed that the only open gate was near the office. She hoped they could slip by without being seen. She looked for shrubs or trees she could stay close to, but the landscaping was high and sparse around the building. The blacktop and lawn beyond were empty. Any activity on their part at this moment would look suspicious, so with nothing more than an air of nonchalance for protection, she guided Marisol towards the gate.

Just as they reached the gate, Kate noticed the agents standing by the door as if they were about to leave. "Oh shit!" she said, but then she met Mrs. Flores eyes looking out the window. The principal took the arm of one of the officers and guided him away from the door. Unfortunately, though, she didn't get to the other agent before he turned around and saw Kate and Marisol. He walked briskly out the door towards them and Kate started to run. But then she decided she would stand her ground and not let them intimidate her. Marisol, however, didn't stay put. As soon as she saw the ICE insignia she bolted. Kate was about to yell after her until she realized that perhaps this was the best thing to do. She let Marisol run away and tried to figure out a way to stonewall the agent.

The first thing that came to her mind was to fake an illness or injury. She put her hand on her chest and sunk to the ground with a moan. Sure enough, the officer ran to her side. "Are you alright?" he asked.

'Could you get Mrs. Flores please," she answered in the feeblest voice she could muster up.

"Do you need an ambulance?"

"No, I think I'll be okay." She saw that Marisol was nowhere to be seen, so she stood up and brushed herself off. "I guess I had a little fainting spell or something. Maybe a little vertigo."

"Can you drive?"

"Sure."

"Looks like you lost someone," he snickered.

Kate walked to her car, praying that Marisol was hiding near it or knew her way home. She glanced up and down the street as she approached the car, but saw no one. She started the car and pulled out of the space after she saw the agent still standing in the playground, watching her car with a sneer on his face. She drove slowly down the street, looking every which way for Marisol. She pulled over after going a block and took out her cell phone to call Lawrence. "Oh God!" she exclaimed when he answered. "Are you home?"

"Yes. What's wrong?"

"ICE went to the school to pick up Marisol and —"

"What?!" Lawrence yelled into the phone.

"Just listen, okay? I'll explain it all later. I was with her on the playground and she bolted when she saw the agent. I'm driving around looking for her, but can you start walking over here and see if you find her along the way? I think she knows her way home so maybe you'll run into her walking. I'll stay around the school and search the neighborhood."

"Okay." They hung up and each went on their assigned patrol. An hour elapsed and Lawrence called Kate. "Where are you now? I've walked up and down every street between here and home. No sign of her."

"I'm driving up and down Santa Monica Boulevard. I thought she might feel less conspicuous on a busy street. Oh Lawrence, what are we going to do? It's not like we can call the police."

"I think you should go home now."

"Not yet."

"We need two sets of eyes looking for her at home. She doesn't even know what button to push on the intercom out front."

"Shit!" Kate exclaimed. "All those little important things I never thought of. Okay. Do you want me to pick you up?"

"No. I'm in front of the school now. I'll go in and talk to the principal and see if there are any new developments."

"Good idea."

Kate drove home and parked the car. Before she went upstairs, however, she searched all around including the bushes and doorways of surrounding buildings. Finally she gave up and went into the apartment. She couldn't do anything, however, except pace from window to window, watching for Marisol. Or for someone watching her. What if Marisol came home and the agents . . .? She tried to push out the fearful, negative thoughts. There wasn't anything else she could do now but wait and see. Lawrence arrived about half an hour later and hugged her tightly. "Mrs. Flores filled me in on what happened. She and Marisol's teacher will both spend their lunch breaks looking for her around the school."

"Did she tell you how ICE got notified?" Kate asked.

"She just said she's looking into it. Apparently the teacher has an idea."

"She does? What's her idea?"

"Mrs. Flores didn't say. I didn't press her."

Kate sighed. "So what do we do? Just sit here and wait?"

"I don't know," Lawrence responded. "Marisol doesn't have a key so she can't get in the lobby and you know she's not going to ask anyone for help."

"Then we need to be outside."

"What? Sit outside the building all day?"

"I guess we could keep driving and walking the neighborhood. The agents have left, right?" she asked.

Lawrence shrugged. "How would I know? No one was at the school, anyway. Look, let's grab a bite to eat here and then go back out."

"Alright," Kate sighed. "That sounds like as good a plan as any."

"You should stick close by. Just keep walking around the block. We don't want Marisol waiting outside the building."

"Yes, of course."

They decided to reverse their tasks so Lawrence drove back and forth to the school while Kate walked the neighborhood around their building. After sunset, Lawrence called. "I think we need to call it a day."

"We can't stop, Lawrence!" Kate retorted.

"Are you planning to keep at this all night?"

"Yes." Kate exhaled loudly. "I am."

Lawrence was silent. He knew that when Kate was determined to do something, there was no stopping her. "Well, I'm going home," he finally said. "It's getting too dark to see anything from the car anyway. I'll bring you some food if you like."

"I'm not hungry right now." She choked back a sob.

"Kate, you're exhausted. Don't be so—"

"I'm staying out here."

"Okay. Okay. I'll call you in a little while." Lawrence drove home and went up to their apartment. He made two sandwiches, ate one over the sink and wrapped the other for Kate. And then he called her again. "Kate, you need to come home. It's too dark. We'll go back out as soon as it gets light in the morning. Marisol's resilient. You know that. She's been through much worse than this."

Kate was silent, but then Lawrence heard the sounds of crying. He waited until she pulled herself together to reply. "I can't leave her out here alone."

Lawrence sighed. "Where are you now?"

"In front of the library on Glendon."

Lawrence gritted his teeth. She was nowhere near their building. "I'll meet you."

"I'm going to start walking east on Wilshire," she replied.

"Okay. I'll walk west and we'll meet up."

"You don't have to come, you know."

"Yes. I do." He hung up and grabbed the wrapped sandwich and a bottle of water. He took a jacket for himself and one for Kate out of the hall closet and started to open the front door, but then stopped and went into Marisol's room. He found a coat that Kate had bought for her but she hadn't worn yet, and put that over his arm as well. Then he left and started to walk towards Wilshire Boulevard.

They met up and hugged. Kate buried her face in his shoulder and let the tears come again. "I can't remember the last time I cried," she finally said.

"We'll find her. Just give her time to come out of hiding."

"I wish we had given her a key."

"We will now."

"I hope this doesn't cause her to go mute again. We were finally getting her to talk. And she loved going to school, but now . . ." Kate buried her face into his shoulder again, shivering.

"I brought your coat," he replied softly. "Here, let me put it on."

Kate pulled away enough to allow him to slip it over her shoulders, and then she looked up at him. "I love you, Lawrence."

"Love you too."

20

MARISOL RAN BLINDLY DOWN THE STREET, NORTH TOWARDS SANTA MONICA BOULEVARD. Here traffic forced her to stop, and she stood panting on the corner, her backpack at her feet. Beyond the river of cars she could see the tall buildings along Wilshire peeking over the leaf canopy on the street ahead, and as her adrenaline gave out, she started thinking more clearly. She remembered Kate driving down that street, the crowded sidewalks of Westwood Village, the really big school where older students bustled about or sprawled on really big lawns. She could blend in, sitting on the grass. The light changed and she picked up her suddenly heavy backpack and trudged across the boulevard and once again into a quiet neighborhood. She tried to look purposeful instead of lost and tired. Once she crossed Wilshire she started trailing a young woman with a backpack, and after a few blocks she started seeing others coming and going in similar fashion. Eventually she found the really big school. She kept walking until she saw one of the big lawns and then flopped down near, but not too close, to a group of students sitting and chatting. Nearby a young man napped with his head on his jacket, and she thought of rest, even napping like him, until her stomach growled. Her old friend, hunger. It took her a minute to remember the lunch Kate had packed for her, and she now dug it out of her backpack, finding it a bit worse for wear after her flight.

When Marisol finished her lunch, she realized she had to pee, so she got up and looked around for a restroom. There was a place across the lawn where people were taking away food, so that seemed a good place to look. Once inside she felt conspicuous and afraid, so she moved off into a corner and watched for women going off alone. No one seemed to notice her, but she soon picked up on a traffic pattern and followed two women down a side hall. Once it was clear they were entering a restroom, she waited a moment and followed them in.

Once outside again, she tried to figure out what she should do next. Should she try to find Kate and Lawrence's house? She knew it had to be in the opposite direction from where she was, so she started walking that way. Soon she was in the midst of some of the biggest houses she'd ever seen. Really rich people, she thought. The streets snaked around in an indirect way and she didn't recognize any as anywhere she had been with Kate. She walked slower and slower, the streets seeming to defeat her. The air grew cooler and she knew that it wouldn't be that much longer before it got dark. And that's when she sat on a stone wall in front of a house and started to cry.

"Are you okay, *mija?*" Marisol looked up into the kindly face of a middle-aged woman. She wore a housedress like her mother used to wear and carried a large purse and a shopping bag. Marisol sniffed and shook her head. "Are you lost?" Marisol stared into her eyes. "*¿Estás perdida?*"

"*Sí,*" Marisol answered softly.

"*¿Dónde está tu casa?*" Marisol shrugged. The woman sat down on the wall next to her. "*¿Cómo te llamas?*"

"Marisol."

"*Mi llamo Juanita.*" Marisol smiled. "*¿Dónde está tu madre?*" Marisol sniffed and shook her head. "*¿Ella está aquí?*"

"*Está muerta.*"

Juanita hugged her and said," *Lo siento.*" Marisol hugged her back and cried into her chest. A car pulled up next to them. "*Mi esposo está aquí.*" Juanita stood up and Marisol stood with her and reached for the woman's hand. Juanita stood frozen, unsure what she should do.

The man in the car got out and said, "Who's that?"

"Marisol. I found her sitting on the wall when I left work. She's lost and speaks no English."

"What should we do?"

"I don't know. I can't just leave her here."

"Call the police?"

"*No policía!*" Marisol cried out.

Juanita squeezed her hand and turned to her. "*¿Quieres venir a mi casa?*"

"*Sí.*"

Juanita looked at the man and shrugged her shoulders. "It's almost dark. Maybe we can find out some more about her tonight. At least she'll be warm."

The man shrugged his shoulders, but then held out his hand to Marisol to shake. "*Me llamo Pedro.*" Marisol smiled and shook his hand. They got in the car and Pedro drove off.

They drove through this neighborhood of large beautiful homes until they got to Santa Monica Boulevard. Marisol didn't notice the familiar street, however, since it was totally dark by this time. Pedro drove east on Santa Monica, past the street her school was on into Beverly Hills and then West Hollywood. The neighborhoods started to get less upscale when they got to Hollywood proper and then even more so as they neared downtown. But that's where Pedro turned onto a side street and pulled up to a small, but neat, bungalow surrounded by other ones. They weren't all as well kept as Pedro and Juanita's, however. "*Aquí estamos,*" Juanita said as she opened the back door for Marisol.

Marisol scurried out and followed the couple through the chain link gate and up the walkway lined, it seemed, with a thousand potted plants. Inside, the bungalow was tiny and sparsely furnished, but clean and neat. "*Siéntate,*" Juanita said, pointing to the sofa. Marisol sat where she was told to and Juanita went down the hall to drop off her things and returned to the living room where she motioned Marisol to follow her into the kitchen. Juanita took some homemade enchiladas out of the freezer and put them in the microwave. "Is dinner ready?" Pedro asked as he entered.

"In a minute." She turned to Marisol. "*Lávate las manos*. Pedro, show her the bathroom."

Pedro brought Marisol down the hall and returned to the kitchen. "Where will she sleep?"

"I'll make up the sofa."

"And what are you going to do with her tomorrow when you have to go back to work?"

Juanita shrugged. "Hopefully she will have told us something tonight and I can find wherever she belongs."

"And if not?"

"I don't know. I can't call the authorities. You know what that would mean."

"You think she's undocumented?"

"Of course she is," Juanita retorted. "If she lived here she would speak at least some English. They learn quickly enough when they move here." Marisol joined them and they started their dinner. When they were about halfway through the meal Juanita said, "Marisol, *nosotros necesitamos encontrar tu casa*."

Marisol just stared at her. "She's not going to answer you," Pedro said. "Maybe she ran away from a bad situation."

"*¿Con quién vives?*" Juanita asked.

"She doesn't want to go back to the people she lives with," Pedro chimed in.

"You don't know that."

"Kate *y* Lawrence," Marisol said all of a sudden.

"Don't sound like Spanish names to me," Pedro said.

"*¿Te gustan?*" Juanita said warily.

"*Sí!*" Marisol exclaimed. "*Mucho!*"

"*¿No sabes dónde viven?*"

"At least she likes them," Pedro butted in.

"*Cerca de la universidad.*"

"So she lives near UCLA," Pedro said. "We already figured that out since that's where you found her."

"Well maybe if we drove her around there tomorrow she would recognize the house," Juanita replied.

"Ay! We'll rent a Cadillac and go in style," Pedro said, throwing up his hands. "We work, Juanita!"

Juanita glared at him. "I'll call Mrs. Wentworth and see if I can come in late. Her house is spotless anyway. It's not like I have to be there all day."

"Don't risk it, Juanita. It's a good job and you don't have to break your back like you did for that *pinche vieja*. Or like I have to do at that damn packing plant."

"*¿Puedo tener más?*" Marisol asked, pointing to the enchiladas.

"*Sí.*" Juanita put another one on her plate. "*¿Cuando viniste a Los Estados Unidos?*"

Marisol shrugged. "*¿Una semana? Dos semanas?*"

Pedro looked at Juanita and turned to Marisol. *"¿Quiénes son Kate y Lawrence?"*

"Mis amigos."

"This is weird, don't you think?" Pedro said. *"¿Eres de México?"* he asked Marisol.

"Sí. Tijuana."

"¿Tienes parientes aquí?" he asked.

"I told you her mother is dead."

"There might be other relatives." He turned back to Marisol. *"¿Tu Padre está aquí? ¿Hermana? ¿Hermano?"*

"Sí. Mi hermana."

"Now we're getting somewhere," Pedro said excitedly. "Her sister lives here. *¿Es Kate tu hermana?"*

"No. Mi amiga."

"¿Dónde está tu hermana?" Juanita said softly and gently. Marisol shrugged her shoulders and looked away. *"¿Sabes?"* Marisol shook her head.

"So I guess we need to find these Kate and Lawrence people," Pedro interjected. "Back to driving around."

"I'll call Mrs. Wentworth." Juanita got up from the table to make the call.

"¿Quiéres un poco de pastel?" Pedro asked as he stood up to clear the table. Marisol nodded and smiled. He brought her a piece of cake just as Juanita entered the room.

"She said that would be fine. I could come in whenever I finished."

"Did you tell her why?"

"No. I just said I had some business I needed to take care of."

They finished eating and Juanita made up the sofa for Marisol. *"Gracias,"* Marisol said as Juanita tucked her in.

Juanita smiled and kissed her on the forehead. *"Buenas noches."*

Marisol slept fitfully, feeling scared and anxious. She wanted to go back to school, but knew she couldn't. Kate and Lawrence were probably worried about her. She had already lost so many people . . . She fought back the tears, not wanting to upset Juanita and Pedro. They were all she had now.

Pedro was up first and tiptoed through the living room. He didn't realize Marisol was awake and she didn't say anything. He was trying to be quiet in the kitchen, but Juanita yelled from the bedroom asking if he was done in the bathroom. "Yes!" he shouted back and then came back into the living room. "Time to get up. *Es hora de levantarse,"* he told Marisol. She got off the sofa and folded the sheets and blanket. Pedro smiled and nodded. She sat down on the sofa, unsure what to do. Should she follow Pedro into the kitchen? Use the bathroom? Or just wait for Juanita? Pedro popped his head into the room. *"¿Quieres comer?"*

"Sí." Marisol went into the kitchen. She would wait to use the bathroom. She had learned how to hold it a long time in her trek across the border. Pedro set a plate of *huevos rancheros* in front of her. *"Gracias,"* she said and started eating.

"You made breakfast?" Juanita said kissing Pedro on the cheek. "*Buenos días?*" she smiled at Marisol.

"*Buenos días,*" Marisol replied.

"*¿Quieres ir al baño?*"

"*Sí.*" Marisol stood and looked at her plate that was still half full. Did she mean now? Or should she finish eating first? She looked at Juanita and said, "*¿Ahora?*"

"Are you going to shower this morning?" Juanita asked Pedro.

"Yes. She should use it now so I won't be late for work."

"*Sí, ahora.*" Juanita said to Marisol.

Marisol left the room and Pedro turned to Juanita. "You drop me off first and then do your driving around. Pick me up on my lunch hour and then I'll drive you back to the Wentworths. Have you thought about what you're going to do if you don't find where she lives before you go to work?"

Juanita shrugged. "Take her with me, I guess."

"That's okay?"

"I think so. But hopefully we'll find these people she lives with." Marisol came back in and sat down to finish her breakfast and Pedro left the room.

They finished eating and getting ready by seven thirty and piled into the car, this time with Juanita driving. They drove a different way than the night before. Marisol guessed this was downtown because there were so many tall buildings, even more than there were in Westwood. She wasn't sure where they were going and didn't ask. She was afraid that Juanita might just drop her off where she found her and then Marisol would have to fend for herself again to look for Kate and Lawrence. They drove past the tall buildings and then there were lots of low buildings with many trucks and a stream of cars going into all the parking lots. Juanita pulled into one of the lots and Pedro got out of the car. "Okay. See you at noon," he said.

Juanita drove away and got onto a freeway, crawling with traffic, eventually getting off on Overland. As she drove north on Overland she asked Marisol if she remembered any of the scenery. Marisol said no, but Juanita kept driving because this was the way to the university and she had said that they lived near there. They drove past Pico Boulevard and then Olympic Boulevard when all of a sudden Marisol called out, *"Mi escuela! Mi escuela!"*

Juanita stopped short and luckily no one was right behind her. She pulled into the school's driveway. *"¿Asistes a esta escuela?"* It didn't seem right that Marisol was going to school and couldn't speak any English. She parked the car and opened her door. *"Vamos a la oficina."* But Marisol didn't budge. She looked around like a frightened animal. There were a few tardy students running into classrooms, but otherwise the playground and street were empty. School had probably just started. *"¿Por qué estás asustada?"*

"ICE!" Marisol mumbled.

"Está bien. Los agentes de ICE no están aquí."

Marisol got out of the car tentatively, still glancing all around. Juanita took her hand and they walked into the office. "Marisol!" It was Kate, running out of the principal's office with her arms outstretched. Juanita grinned as the two embraced with tears running down both their cheeks. After a few joyous minutes, they let go and Mrs. Flores gave them each a Kleenex. "Are you a relative of Marisol's?" Kate finally asked between sniffles.

"No. I found her yesterday afternoon sitting on a wall in front of my boss' house. My name is Juanita."

"I'm Kate. Thank you so much for taking care of her. Where was this? Around here?"

"Not really. Up by Beverly Glen."

"Oh my God! She went all the way there?"

"I thought you might live around there."

"No. She ran away from school, though. ICE agents were here looking for her."

"Oh, that's why she was so afraid to get out of the car."

"Did she talk to you?"

"A little . . . only in Spanish."

"Did she tell you anything about how she got across the border? Or about any family living here?" Kate asked.

"Just that her mother was murdered and that she has a sister. But she doesn't seem to know where her sister is."

"Anything else?"

"You don't know any of this?" Juanita asked.

Kate proceeded to tell Juanita the whole story, not leaving any detail out. She wanted Juanita's help since Marisol seemed to talk to her. When she finished she turned to Mrs. Flores. "Have you found out anything about how and why ICE was here?"

"I have a few people at the district level looking into it," the principal answered.

"I thought schools were safe zones," Juanita piped up.

"They're supposed to be. It's an ongoing battle."

Juanita nodded and stood up. "I need to get to work."

"Can I have your phone number?" Kate asked. "Marisol seemed to open up to you. Maybe you can help us find her relatives."

Juanita recited her phone number and Kate put it in her contacts list on her phone. Then she asked her, "Are you legal?" Juanita gave her a sour look. "I'm sorry. I only ask because maybe you've gone through this and know some way to help."

"Yes. I am legal," Juanita replied proudly. "But I know many who aren't. I'll see what I can find out."

Kate grabbed a piece of paper and pen off the principal's date and jotted down her address and phone number. "Here's my information. And thank you again."

Juanita smiled and hugged Marisol. After she left Mrs. Flores said, "I think you should take her home today. I don't want to take any chances until I have something written from the district."

"Yes. I agree." Kate turned to Marisol. "*Vamos a casa.*"

Marisol took her hand and they left the school.

21

THEY STAYED INSIDE THE CONDO THE REST OF THE DAY, WARY THAT ICE AGENTS MIGHT COME KNOCKING. Kate wanted to ask Marisol all kinds of questions, but her limited Spanish made it difficult. She hoped that Juanita would be willing to help, but she didn't want to call right away. So she got out her computer and looked up the Spanish translations for some of the easier questions. She wrote them out on a piece of paper and then knocked on Marisol's door. "Marisol?" she asked softly and then opened the door.

Marisol was sitting up in bed, looking at a book. She looked up and smiled. "*Sí?*"

Kate came in and sat down on the bed next to her. "*¿Qué pasó en el desierto?*" Then as an afterthought, she added the English translation. "What happened in the desert?" It was important for Marisol to learn English, especially since they weren't sure when she would be able to go back to school. Marisol looked down with a quivering lip. "Were you with your sister? *¿Estabas con tu hermana?*"

Marisol shook her head no. "*Ella no vino.*"

"You were supposed to meet her?" Kate scrolled frantically through her phone. *"¿Ibas a reunir con ella?"*

"Sí. Pero ella no estaba."

"She wasn't at the place you were supposed to meet? In the desert?" Kate was frustrated, scrolling through her phone. She needed a translator. "Who brought you across the border? *¿Quien te trajo al otro lado de la frontera?"*

"Un hombre."

"Coyote?" Marisol shrugged. Kate realized she might not know that term for someone who smuggles immigrants across the border. "He left you alone in the desert in the middle of nowhere?" She looked down at her phone to get the Spanish translation. *"¿Te dejó sola en el desierto?"*

Marisol shook her head. *"Me llevó a una casa."*

"A house? Whose house?"

"Mala gente."

Kate looked up *gente.* "Oh, bad people." Things started to make sense to Kate now, but she wanted to have Juanita do the rest of the translating. It was just too difficult this way and things were probably going to get even touchier. She hugged Marisol. "You are an incredibly brave strong girl!"

After dinner Kate took out her phone and called Juanita. She explained what she had been able to get out of Marisol that afternoon, but reiterated how difficult it was to speak in Spanish just Googling the translations. "I can talk to her, but I think it would be better to do it in person," Juanita replied.

"Can I come to your house or meet somewhere?" Kate asked.

"Maybe I could meet you tomorrow morning before I go to work. You live near where I work, yes?"

"I think so. We are near Wilshire Boulevard and Glendon Avenue. There's a Coffee Bean café on Westwood Boulevard. Do you want to meet there?"

"Okay. At eight?"

"We'll be there. Thanks so much, Juanita."

"I just hope we can help the poor girl find her sister."

"Yes, I hope so," Kate said with not a lot of conviction. She wasn't sure if that was because she didn't think they would find her, or because she didn't want to find her. She was growing very attached to Marisol. She hung up and told Lawrence what was going on, and then looked on her computer to translate for Marisol. "*Nos encontraremos con Juanita mañana.*"

A look of alarm spread across Marisol's face. "*Por que?*"

"Why?" Kate wasn't sure how to answer. She didn't understand why Marisol looked so frightened now. She thought she liked Juanita. She looked at Lawrence for advice, but he just shrugged. "*Habla en Español,*" she replied, looking back to Marisol.

"*¿Puedo quedarme con ustedes?*"

Kate tried to look up what Marisol had asked on her computer. She finally found the translation and hugged her. "Yes . . . *sí* . . . you can stay with us."

Kate and Marisol arrived at the Coffee Bean café early the next morning to wait for Juanita. They didn't have to wait long. Juanita was early too. "*Buenos días,*" Juanita said as she approached the table, smiling.

Marisol smiled back and Kate's apprehension about how Marisol would react subsided. "What would you like to drink and eat?" Kate asked. "I want to buy yours."

Juanita didn't argue. She was quite aware that Kate had much more money than she did. They all went to the counter to order and finally settled into a booth in the back. "What do you want me to ask her?" Juanita said as she took a sip of coffee.

"I guess I want to know how she got here and what happened when she crossed the border. Also, what was supposed to happen that didn't. I mean like was her sister supposed to meet her or was whoever took her across supposed to bring her somewhere? She says the man brought her to a house where there were bad people. But was her sister supposed to meet her there? It's all such a mystery."

Juanita turned to Marisol and spoke in rapid Spanish that Kate couldn't understand at all. Marisol kept chewing on her pastry, her eyes on her plate, and didn't answer right away. Juanita and

Kate glanced at each other, but they both seemed to know not to prod her into answering. Finally Marisol finished her pastry and looked up. *"Mi hermana le pagó al hombre para que me llevara al otro lado de la frontera. Se suponiá que ella me encontrariá. En cambio me trajo a una casa."* She stopped talking and her lip quivered and she narrowed her eyes. *"Ellos eran muy malos."*

"¿Qué querián que hicieras?" Juanita asked.

"Llevar drogas conmigo."

"What did she say?" Kate implored.

"She said that her sister paid a man to take her across and he was supposed to take her to her sister but instead he brought her to a house. Those are stash houses. And they wanted her to be a drug mule."

"Oh God!" Kate exclaimed.

"Y sexo." Marisol muttered.

"For sex too? So you ran away from the house?" Kate asked.

Juanita translated for Kate. *"¿Entonces te escapaste de la casa?"*

"Sí."

"And that's where we found you? The house was near there?" Juanita translated again.

"Sí."

Kate sat back into the bench and exhaled loudly. "No wonder she was so freaked out that she was mute!"

"Do you want me to ask her about where her sister is?" Juanita inquired.

"She doesn't seem to know where she lives, but ask."

"*¿Tienes alguna idea de dónde está tu hermana?*"

"*Ella trabaja en una granja.*"

"*Dónde?*" Marisol shrugged. "She worked on a farm but she doesn't know where," Juanita told Kate.

"Can her sister make enough working on a farm to pay a coyote to bring her across the border? I've heard they cost like four or five thousand dollars."

"It would take a long time for her to make that much," Juanita responded. "Unless she works on a pot farm. They make more than picking fruits or vegetables." She turned to Marisol. "*¿Es una granja de marijuana?*"

"*No lo sé.*"

"She doesn't know," Juanita said.

"Ask her if her postcards are from her sister."

"*¿Son las tarjetas postales de tu hermana?*"

"*Sí. Ella visitó los lugares,*" Marisol replied.

"What did she say besides yes?" Kate asked.

"Her sister visited those places."

"Did she mail them from the towns on the postmark? Would her sister live there?" Juanita translated but Marisol just shrugged and shook her head. "What do you think that means?" Kate asked.

"I think she just doesn't know. I wonder if her sister works in the Santa Barbara area. There are a lot of pot farms there."

"I was guessing the Emerald Triangle in northern California. That's the pot capital," Kate said.

"Where is that?" Juanita asked.

"Mendocino, Humboldt and Trinity counties."

"They are far, though."

"Yes. Maybe you're right. Maybe it's Santa Barbara County." Kate sighed. "This is not going to be easy."

Juanita stood and said, "I need to go to work. Call me if you need more help. And thanks for the coffee and pastry."

"You're welcome and thank you for meeting us."

"*Adiós*, Marisol." Juanita kissed the top of her head and left.

Kate called Lawrence at home. "Hi. Want to go for a drive up the coast?"

"Okay, but why?" he replied. "Just an outing?"

"I thought we might visit some pot farms in the Santa Barbara area."

"Did Marisol say that's where her sister is?"

"She doesn't know, but Juanita suggested that her sister might work on one. They make more than working on a regular farm. I guess that's the newest coveted farmworker job."

"Interesting," Lawrence mused.

"We can pick you up in about ten minutes."

"I'll be in front."

22

KATE SCOOTED OVER TO LET LAWRENCE DRIVE. They drove to Sunset Boulevard, then turned west towards the ocean. There was no hurry so they might as well take Pacific Coast Highway north and go through Malibu. They could get on the 101 in Oxnard. It was definitely a prettier drive and less traffic, even if it took a little longer. Marisol was mesmerized during the drive, watching the ocean as if she'd never seen it before. "Isn't Tijuana near the ocean?" Kate asked.

"I think so," Lawrence answered. "Why do you ask?"

"Marisol seems so enthralled with it like she's never seen it before."

"Well, even if Tijuana is near the ocean, it doesn't mean she lived anywhere near it and maybe never went to it."

"Yeah, I guess. I've taught kids who lived not too far from the ocean, but had never been there."

"Should we pull over and let her really enjoy it?" Lawrence asked.

"Oh. Let's wait until north of Ventura. The beaches are nicer and more accessible up there."

"Do you have a plan?" Lawrence asked. "Or are we going to do what we did in those central valley towns and just wing it?"

Kate frowned, getting a bit annoyed at his skepticism, but not blaming him either. After all, the furthest they got with Marisol was her accidental meeting with Juanita. "I'm hoping that when we get to the Santa Barbara area something will jump out that Marisol will recognize."

"You mean that her sister might have written her about?"

"Yeah, something like that."

"So we will just drive around?"

"Well, there seems to be a large cannabis farm presence in Carpinteria and there's a beautiful beach there."

"That would be an expensive piece of land, wouldn't it?" he asked.

"Well, yeah, so?"

"I mean, wouldn't the farms be more inland?"

Kate sighed. "I don't know. Lawrence, I haven't a clue what to do anymore. I kept thinking that once Marisol started talking, we'd find out what we needed and this would be over. But apparently, she doesn't know where her sister is, and now her sister doesn't know where Marisol is. I'm just trying to bide my time until either we find her sister, or we go to one of those agencies and let them figure out what to do."

"I think we have reached that point. Do we even know what her sister's name is?"

Kate laughed. "You know, we never asked her." She turned to Marisol and said, "*Cómo se llama tu hermana?*"

Marisol smiled. "Graciela."

Kate smiled. "Your parents sure picked out beautiful names for their daughters. *Bonita. ¿Cuántos años tiene tu hermana?*"

"*Veintiuno.*"

"Twenty-one? She's much older."

Lawrence sighed. "This girl has been through so much. Hey, we're going away from the ocean now. Will this go straight to 101?"

"Yes. Route One veers north around here, sorta bypassing Oxnard."

They drove past miles of strawberry fields, then offices and warehouses and finally a toilet paper factory before they finally got on the 101. They were back again next to the ocean right after passing through Ventura. "Isn't La Conchita the place where they had a landslide that destroyed the town?" Lawrence asked as they drove by a funky looking beach town of sorts right on the freeway.

"Yes. I think there were two or more of them."

"When was the most recent one?"

Kate Googled. "2005 was the one that killed ten people. But it says here that it was actually the continuation of a landslide in 1995."

"Ten years later and they call it a continuation?"

"That's what it says. Not a smart place to have a home. They expect more landslides all the time. But I guess those two happened after unseasonable rainfalls."

"The town isn't even right on the beach. It faces the highway and they have to cross it to get to the beach."

"What beach?" Kate asked, watching the surf meet the rock reinforcement along the freeway. "I'll bet the houses are cheap, though, compared to the surrounding towns."

The cliffs came close to the freeway again, and then fell back to a mesa. Ahead were orchards and greenhouses interspersed with homes. "Here's Carpinteria," Lawrence announced. "Shall I get off here?"

"Get off at Casitas Pass Road and then go down Carpinteria Avenue to Linden. Left on Linden and it's just a few blocks to the city beach."

"This is such a nice town." They drove down Linden Avenue to where it dead-ended at the beach and parked.

Kate got out of the car and motioned to Marisol to get out also. Marisol opened her door and ran into the sand all the way to the water. She took off her shoes and stuck her toes in. "*¡Mira! ¡Mira!*" she shouted to Kate and Lawrence. "*¡El océano!*"

"Wow, that is one excited young lady!" Lawrence gushed.

They walked up and down the beach, sat on the sand for a bit, and let Marisol play in the shallow part of the water. "Shall we get some lunch here or drive further?" Kate asked.

"What's that cute Danish town with the windmills and stuff?" Lawrence responded.

"Solvang?"

"Yeah, Marisol might enjoy that. How far is it? Maybe we can go there for lunch."

"Let me see." Kate looked at her map app. "It looks like it's about an hour. Are you hungry or can you wait?"

"I can wait," Lawrence replied. "How about you?"

"I can too." She turned to Marisol. "*¿Tienes hambre?*"

"*Sí.*"

"*¿Puedes esperar una hora?*"

"*Sí.*"

"Except didn't you want to look at the farms here in Carpinteria?" Lawrence chimed in.

"Yeah, but I didn't do my homework yet. I figure we could go to Solvang for lunch and I can do some research while we eat. Then we can stop back in Carpinteria on the way home. We could eat dinner here."

"That's fine. I just thought since we were here . . ."

"Are you needing to get home for anything? We might not get back until after eight."

Lawrence grinned at her. "Retirement. Remember? Freedom." They got to their car and got in. Lawrence started driving back up Linden through downtown Carpinteria. "Am I going back to the 101?"

"Yes. We'll go north through Summerland, Montecito and Santa Barbara until we get on 154 to Solvang."

"Isn't Montecito where Oprah lives?"

"Among other famous rich people."

"I think there are plenty of rich people, famous or not, in all of Santa Barbara County," Lawrence added. "Where was Michael Jackson's Neverland Ranch? Was that in Montecito too?"

"I'm not sure." Kate scrolled through her phone. "Actually it's north of Los Olivos, near Solvang."

"Is it still like an amusement park, even though Michael Jackson is dead?"

"I don't think so. I think it's for sale but they're asking a lot."

The road climbed higher and higher until the ocean was just a silver sheet below. The Channel Islands peeked over a fog bank on the horizon. Cresting on San Marcos Pass, they dropped down into a golden, oak-studded valley backed by still more high mountains. They reached Solvang and found it filled with tourists. As soon as they drove into the downtown and Marisol saw the windmills she shouted, *"¡Mi hermana estuvo aquí!"*

"Does she see her sister?" Lawrence asked excitedly.

"No, I think she used past tense. Her sister *was* here."

"¡Mi tarjeta postal!"

"Postal? What's she saying?"

"Oh. I think she means postcard. One of her postcards from her sister must have been from Solvang and she recognizes it! Do you remember seeing one from here?"

Lawrence shook his head. "No. I just recall the Golden Gate Bridge, Disneyland and Monterey Aquarium."

"Oh," Kate said dejectedly.

"Maybe she lost it. I don't think Marisol would mistake this place. Maybe Graciela lives here. Or did . . ."

"Yeah, I suppose." Kate changed the subject. "Shall we make this a true Danish experience and eat lunch at the Copenhagen Sausage Garden?"

"Absolutely!" Lawrence said as he parked the car. Marisol beamed as she looked at the cute storefronts and the people dressed up in their Danish outfits. "This is like Disneyland to Marisol," he added.

Kate laughed. "But a lot cheaper."

They went inside the restaurant and sat down with their menus. "Are we going to do this right?" Lawrence asked. "Eat sausages and drink beer?"

"Might as well make it as authentic as possible. Anyway, we need to introduce Marisol to food other than tacos, pizza, and hamburgers."

"Just tell her we are ordering her hotdogs," he chuckled.

"Let's have a pretzel with our beer to start. I love those huge pretzels."

Lawrence ordered and Kate Googled cannabis in Carpinteria. "There's a place called CARP Growers. They might be knowledgeable about all the farms in the area. Maybe that would be a place to start."

"Do they have an address?"

"Yes. And a phone number. It looks like an office address on Casitas Pass Road, the exit off the freeway we were on this morning. I think it might be in that shopping center that had the supermarket."

"So do you want to call or just stop in?"

"Let's stop in first." The waiter brought their beer and pretzel and a coke for Marisol. They were hungrier than they realized and finished the pretzel quickly.

"I guess we should have ordered one for each of us," Lawrence said.

"Well we do have sausages coming also."

"But we need to save room for dinner. I have my eye on that Corktree Cellars we passed when we drove back from the beach."

"Beer for lunch and wine for dinner. Will we be able to drive home?" Kate teased.

Lawrence grinned. "I'm sure if I can't, you will."

They used the restrooms, paid the bill, walked around Solvang and were back in Carpinteria by four. "I hope someone's still in the office," Kate said as they parked in the shopping center and walked to the office of CARP Growers.

"Looks like someone is here," Lawrence said as he opened the door. "Well, the door's unlocked, anyway." They walked into the office and a man was just turning out the lights and gathering his phone and jacket.

"Are you open?" Kate asked.

"I was just leaving. Can I help you in some way?" the man said.

"I'm not sure." Kate explained the situation briefly, asking if he had any ideas on how they could find Marisol's sister, Graciela.

"Well, first off, it must be an illegal farm if she isn't documented," the man replied. "No one who's jumped through all the hoops and is paying taxes would risk hiring illegals."

"Oh," Kate murmured.

"And although I do know where some of the illegal farms are around here, I'm not comfortable telling you where they are. I'm sorry."

"I understand," Kate answered. "It was a long shot, anyway."

The man nodded. "Good luck."

They left the office and walked back to the car. Lawrence asked, "Do you want to just hang out some more at the beach or drive around looking for marijuana farms? Or go home?"

"It's kinda crazy to drive around searching for farms that no one wants to tell you about," Kate sighed. "And it's a little early for dinner, but the traffic will be horrendous if we head south now." She gazed around the parking lot, thinking this was not how she wanted what had been a very pleasant day to end. "Let's go walk on the beach. Then we can go to the Corktree and have a glass of wine and maybe an appetizer." She leaned into Lawrence. "Oh hell, let's take a long walk so we can eat a real good meal."

Lawrence looked down at Marisol who was watching them intently. "Think she won't be bored with that?"

Kate turned to Marisol. "*Playa?*"

"*Sí! Sí!*"

"Yes, I think she's up for that," Kate said, giving Lawrence a quick kiss.

23

"MAYBE WE SHOULD LOOK FOR THAT SOLVANG POSTCARD," LAWRENCE ASKED WHEN THEY GOT HOME. "Maybe there's something written on it that we somehow missed when we had Lucy read them."

"That's an idea." Kate went to Marisol's door and knocked.

"*Sí?*" Marisol replied.

Kate opened the door and went in. "*¿Puedo ver las tarjetas postales?*" Then she remembered she was trying to teach Marisol English and added, "Can I see the postcards?"

Marisol got her backpack and took out the pile of postcards and photos and handed them over. Kate looked at the postcards and found one of Solvang. She tried to read the card, but knew she would do better using her computer to translate the Spanish words. She looked at the other postcards and saw the same ones Lawrence had mentioned plus Solvang and the San Diego Zoo. Then she looked at the photos again. The family photo looked to be taken in Tijuana. It was probably about five years old because Marisol looked to be about seven and Gabriella looked to be about sixteen. Then she looked at the picture of the young women. "Lawrence!" Kate took the picture and ran out of the room. "Look!" She found him in the kitchen and shoved the photograph under his nose.

"What? Yeah, this must be Graciela and some friends. What about it?"

"Look at the sweatshirt one of them is wearing!"

His eyes widened. "SBCC. Oh! Santa Barbara City College!"

"So we were on the right track."

"Maybe," Lawrence hedged. "But she could have gotten the sweatshirt anywhere."

"Well, it's worth looking into. Maybe we can find someone at the school who recognizes the girl who's wearing it."

Lawrence laughed. "Kate, Santa Barbara City College probably has an enrollment of twenty thousand!"

Kate dropped the photo onto the counter and turned away. "I'm trying the best I can . . ."

He put his arm around her. "Okay. Okay. I know a couple of people who teach there. I'll see if they can help in some way." He looked at the photo again. "They all look Latina. Maybe the school has some records of DACA students. At least that would be a reasonable place to start."

Kate perked up a bit. "I'll ask Marisol if she knows if her sister goes to college."

"Wouldn't she have told us that?" Lawrence asked. "She doesn't seem to know much about what her sister does here."

"I'll go ask anyway." Kate left and came back a few minutes later. "You were right. She doesn't know. She did say Graciela has been in America for five years, though."

"Then she could qualify as a DACA student. But how in the world did she get enough money to pay a coyote. That's a real mystery to me."

"Well, call your friends."

Kate and Marisol were watching a Disney movie on television when Lawrence entered the living room, holding the picture of Graciela and her friends. "Would you ask Marisol if it's Graciela wearing the sweatshirt?"

Kate looked up how to say it. *"¿Es esta tu hermana?"* she asked as she pointed to the photo of the girl wearing the sweatshirt. Marisol shook her head no and pointed to one of the others. Kate looked up at Lawrence. "It doesn't mean she doesn't also go there?"

"True. Are you coming to bed soon?"

"As soon as this is over."

Lawrence waited until Kate came to bed before telling her what he had found out from his phone calls. "There is a program at SBCC for DACA students. He said he would ask them tomorrow if they have a student registered whose name is Graciela. But it won't be easy. Like the elementary school, they don't readily give out information."

"I understand why," Kate sighed, "but in this case it's so frustrating."

"Maybe this will pan out in some way for us. By the way, I have a lunch tomorrow with some of my old colleagues and it'll probably drag on for hours."

"Maybe I'll take Marisol to the beach. She loved it so much."

"Not back to Carpinteria?"

"No, I'll show her my old house in Venice and where I used to teach. And we can walk the boardwalk. She'd enjoy the circus atmosphere I'm sure."

"That'll be nice for her. What are you going to do about school?"

"I'll call Mrs. Flores in the morning and see if there are any developments. I'm not sending her back—there or any school—until they assure me she will be safe."

"Good plan. Now, how about a celebration of sorts," Lawrence said as he reached for Kate, his eyes twinkling.

"Mmm," she murmured back. "But what exactly are we celebrating?"

"Well, how about just celebrating us?"

"You're definitely worth celebrating." She kissed him and they fell into their comfortable lovemaking rhythm.

Marisol came into the kitchen the next morning, dressed and holding her backpack. "*¿Escuela hoy?*"

Kate looked up from the table where she was typing on her laptop and shook her head. "I need to call the principal first to make sure ICE agents won't come." She looked up the Spanish translation dictionary, but wasn't able to find an exact translation. "I need to *llama a la directora.*" Marisol nodded that she understood and sat down at the kitchen table. "*¿Qué quieres comer?* What do you want to eat?" Kate asked.

"*Huevos y pan tostado,*" Marisol answered.

Kate smiled, thrilled that Marisol finally felt comfortable to say what she wanted instead of just agreeing to eat whatever was put in front of her. "Eggs and toast it is."

Kate took the eggs out of the refrigerator and then hesitated and took out her phone. "*¿Quieres aprender cocinarlos?* Do you want to learn to cook them?"

"*Sé como concinarlos.*"

"I imagine you know how to cook a lot of things," Kate smiled. "Be my guest." Kate gave her the eggs and let Marisol take over the cooking and toasting the bread. Lawrence walked in and smiled at Kate when he noticed Marisol standing at the stove. "Would you like Marisol to make you some eggs?" Kate smiled back.

"I'll just have coffee. It's going to be a big lunch if I know these guys."

Kate nodded and went back to reading on her computer. Marisol didn't even have to be told where the dishes were or to clean up after herself. Her mother must have taught her well. Kate waited until nine to call Mrs. Flores at the school, knowing that the principal liked to be outside welcoming the kids when the building opened. She dialed the number and the clerk put her right through. "Oh, Kate. Hello. How are you and Marisol?"

"We're fine. I've gotten a little more information out of her. She wants to go back to school. Do you know anything yet about whether it's safe for her?"

Mrs. Flores sighed. "I did find out what happened. One of the students in her class is the son of a prominent administrator in Immigration and Customs Enforcement. Apparently the boy told his father that he had a new girl in his class who didn't speak any English. His father is apparently good friends with one of the LA School Board members and that's how he got the information and sent the agents here."

Kate was furious. "What's with the board member? Doesn't he or she know about the policy of not reporting undocumented kids?"

"Of course she knows. You never know what the real story is. My guess is that there's some political shenanigans going on."

"Probably this guy donated to her campaign and she owes him!"

"Could be something like that. But there is some good news. This particular student doesn't have the best behavior record, so perhaps we can use that to give us some leverage with his father."

Kate snorted. "Like leave Marisol alone and we won't suspend your son for his infractions?"

"I didn't say that," the principal answered and that said to Kate that she was right on target.

And she certainly understood why Mrs. Flores did not want to admit to it.

"So do you think we can send Marisol back to school?"

"I still want to talk to the district Office of General Counsel again. I'll let you know this afternoon."

"Thank you," Kate replied, still reining in her anger at the situation. She vowed to find out who that board member was and look into it, but then realized that it would not serve her or Marisol well to get involved like that. She hung up and went to find Marisol to take her to Venice Beach.

They spent the day on the boardwalk, watching the acrobats and musicians and perusing the booths of trinkets for sale. They got their feet wet in the ocean and had lunch at a pizza place. Kate took her for a long walk by the house she had lived in twenty years ago, the high school she had taught at, and then walked along the canals. It was a full day and Kate enjoyed a day not struggling with trying to translate all her thoughts and questions into Spanish. Marisol didn't need any explanations. She could just gaze at everything and take it all in.

They got home about four thirty and Kate called Mrs. Flores who hadn't called her back yet. She was concerned that the principal would be leaving for home soon and Kate wanted to know if Marisol could attend school the next day. The clerk said that Mrs. Flores was on the phone and would call her back when she was finished.

Lawrence walked in the door just as Kate's phone rang. Kate put up her finger to silence Lawrence so she could answer. "Hello?"

"Kate. It's Mrs. Flores." The principal sighed. "I don't have an answer for you, I'm afraid. I mean you could send her to school and we could take our chances, but this father wields a bit of influence, I guess."

Kate sighed back. "What do you think we should do?"

"Her teacher and I will do everything in our power to stop any agents that might turn up, but I can't guarantee something similar won't happen again. It's your decision."

"Let me talk it over with Lawrence and I'll let you know in the morning, either by phone or in person if we decide to bring her."

They hung up and Kate turned to Lawrence. "Well, here's the latest."

24

KATE AND LAWRENCE DECIDED NOT TO TAKE THE CHANCE OF SENDING MARISOL BACK TO SCHOOL. Marisol was clearly disappointed, despite knowing the danger. For the time being Kate decided to focus on Marisol's reading and English skills, the latter with some suggestion from Mrs. Flores. She sat at the kitchen table with Lawrence, sipping coffee and making notes on points she wanted to discuss with Mrs. Flores. Lawrence looked up at her from the Los Angeles Times. "Do you have those photographs and postcards or did Marisol take them back to her room?" he asked.

"I think she has them," Kate answered. "Why?"

"I want to look at them again and see if there are any more clues. We missed the sweatshirt before and we might find out more from reading the postcards now that we have a little more background information."

"Do you want me to get them or will you?"

"You are much better with the Spanish translations than I am," he answered. "Do you mind?"

"No. I need to clear my mind a little, anyway." Kate went and knocked on Marisol's door, scrolling through her phone as she did. *"¿Puedo ver las fotos y las tarjetas postales?"* she said as she opened the door.

Marisol was in bed, looking at them with tears streaking down her cheeks. "Aw, sweetie," Kate said as she climbed in next to her and put her arm around her.

"Gracias por todo," Marisol sniffled as she leaned into Kate's shoulder.

"You're welcome." They sat quietly for a minute and then Marisol handed Kate the pictures and postcards.

"¿Piensas que mi hermana está muerta también?"

Kate looked for the translation and then sighed and shook her head. "No, I don't think your sister is dead. We will find her." She looked it up and added, *"Encontraremos a Graciela."*

Kate took the items to Lawrence and they both looked at the photograph of the young women. They all looked Latina and seemed to be in their early twenties. "Hey, can you read the sign on the building they're standing on the steps in front of?" Lawrence asked as he squinted and pulled it up closer to his eyes.

"It's a nice building. Gorgeous Spanish architecture. Oh my goodness! I think it says Montecito Union School!"

"Montecito? Like where we just drove through yesterday?" Lawrence asked excitedly.

"I think so." Kate tapped on her phone. "Oh, yes, this is a huge clue!" Kate exclaimed. "I guess we have another trip up the coast coming up."

"Today?" he asked apprehensively. "Let's wait until tomorrow."

"You don't have to go. Marisol and I can go. The school is on San Ysidro Road and I remember seeing a freeway exit for San Ysidro so it should be easy to find."

"Are you sure?"

Kate kissed him. "Yes. Really. It's not a problem." She gathered the photos and postcards and went into Marisol's room. "Let's go here. *Aquí.*" She pointed to the school building in the picture. "*Es una escuela en* Montecito."

Marisol smiled. "*¿Una nueva escuela?*"

"Oh, not a new school for you to go to. *Para tu hermana.*"

Marisol looked at her quizzically. "*Ella es muy grande para esa escuela.*"

"I know she is too old to go to school. *Vámonos.* Let's just go." It was too frustrating to look things up on her phone and try to explain everything to Marisol in Spanish. Maybe if they got her a phone . . . but then Marisol would have to read well enough to use a translator app. Well, at least she could call if she got into trouble. Then Kate's mind jumped to Google Location. She could know where Marisol was at any time, even if she couldn't call. The whole long heart-wrenching search after the ICE incident wouldn't have had to happen; Kate would have known where she was. Kate rushed back to the kitchen.

"Lawrence, we need to get Marisol a phone."

"That's a good idea," he said as he poured himself another cup of coffee. "Wish we'd thought of it earlier."

"I just realized with Google Location we could know where she is anytime."

Lawrence took a sip of coffee. "Do I get put on surveillance, too?"

Kate raised an eyebrow. "No. You're a big boy. Or should I be curious?"

"Nope."

"Anyway," Kate continued, "I think I'm going to go do that and then go on to Montecito."

"Are you going to get her a prepaid phone or put it on our plan?"

"I guess just put it on our plan."

"And buy her a phone? Isn't that kind of expensive?"

Kate narrowed her eyes, trying not to say what had come to her mind, but she blurted it out anyway. "Why are you being like this?"

"Like what? I was just wondering if we find her sister and she moves in with her, are we going to continue to support her?"

"Like we can't afford to help her even if she isn't living under our roof?"

"Jeez, Kate. I just never thought it out before. Food, clothes are one thing. A contract makes one think—differently."

"Like marriage?" Kate replied, a bit coldly.

"For better or for worse," Lawrence countered. "Look, Kate, just because I happen to say something you don't like doesn't make me a nasty man. I really care about Marisol and a phone is a good idea. I trust you'll proceed with the thought that we have no idea what the future will bring."

Kate looked away and tapped her nails on the counter. "They probably have used phones."

"An excellent idea."

Kate turned back. "I don't doubt your compassion, Lawrence. Most men your age—"

"My patience is pretty thin at times. We can't pretend otherwise."

Kate nodded. "Yet you waited for me through my stint in the Peace Corps."

"Well, I felt a little more sure of the outcome."

"It's a bit more stressful now isn't it?" Kate asked softly. She approached him and gave him a little kiss. "I'm sorry."

Lawrence smiled down at her. "We'll get through it. I've got some people to call about this ICE situation with the school board."

Kate looked at him quizzically. "You mean your friends that told you about that Immigration Center for Women and Children?"

"Yeah, and some others. I just want to find out what resources are out there and what, if any, recourse we have if ICE comes after her again. I have the names of a couple of immigration lawyers to talk to."

"You know it's going to cost you if you talk to lawyers. They will bill you for a five minute phone conversation!"

"Not these."

"Why not these? Who are they?"

"Well, one is an old student of mine," Lawrence replied.

Kate looked at him skeptically and shrugged her shoulders. "Sounds like you have something over them."

Lawrence laughed. "Maybe. The other is a cousin of my first wife."

"Have you even talked to this cousin since she died?"

"Not much . . . and not recently. Probably not since Danielle was born six years ago."

"You never told them you got married again?"

"Oh, I don't know. Maybe I did. Or maybe Michael and Carla did. Why all the questions?"

"No real reason," she shrugged. "Would you let Marisol know we'll be leaving in about half an hour if she wants to shower?"

"Sure if you tell me how to say it."

"You can't look it up yourself, Mr. PhD professor?" she grinned.

"I can try, but you are better at the technology and the Spanish than I am."

Kate patted his head. "I'm sure you can do it." She winked and left.

Lawrence went to his computer and typed the words, 'You and Kate will leave soon' and wrote it down. Then he put in 'Do you want to shower first?' and wrote that translation. He tore the paper off the pad and knocked on Marisol's door. "Marisol?"

"*Sí?*"

He opened the door and read off his paper, "*Tu y Kate se irán pronto. ¿Quieres bañarte primero?*"

Marisol smiled broadly at him and said, "*Estás hablando Español.*"

Lawrence smiled back and nodded. "*Un poco.*" Apparently Marisol didn't want to shower first because she left the room to find Kate.

Kate and Marisol stopped at the Verizon store near the UCLA campus and Kate got Marisol set up with the phone that they had a special deal on. The phone was free and adding her to their plan was only about twenty dollars extra. Marisol must have had a phone in Mexico because she knew just what to do. "I'll add these to your contacts," Kate said as she put in the three numbers: hers, Lawrence's, and Juanita's. They were on the 405 in less than an hour.

The traffic started to thin out after switching to the 101 and getting past Sherman Oaks and most of the San Fernando Valley. Kate glanced over at Marisol whose eyes and fingers had not left her phone since they left the store. "*Gracias por mi teléfono,*" Marisol said into her phone. Then she turned to Kate and said, "Thank you for my phone."

Kate grinned and said, "Oh my! I didn't know there was a voice app that would translate for me. This certainly makes life easier!" She reached into her purse and took out her own phone and handed it to Marisol. "Put it on mine?"

Marisol said into her microphone, "Put it on my phone." She waited a few seconds and turned to Kate. "*Ponla en mi teléfono. Si.* Yes."

Kate settled happily into her seat and enjoyed the drive while Marisol continued playing with her phone. They got to the San Ysidro exit in Montecito about an hour later. Kate remembered that the address for the school was 385 San Ysidro Road and they got to the school in just a few minutes. She pulled into the parking lot and couldn't help but admire the beautiful grounds. It didn't surprise her, of course, that a place like Montecito would have a lovely school. The tax base was probably quite substantial and these parents would have nothing less. But she was still quite shocked at the amount of playing fields and playground equipment for one elementary school with less than four hundred students. Kate had always taught in poorer neighborhoods, both urban and a smaller town in northern California. The divide between the haves and have-nots was quite obvious.

"I'm hoping you can help us," Kate said as she approached the clerk in the school office. She took out the photograph and placed it on the counter in front of the school secretary. "This young woman is Marisol's sister and we are trying to find her. Do you happen to know her? Her name is Graciela Sandoval."

The secretary looked at the picture and shook her head. "No, I'm sorry. Does she have a child that attends our school?"

"Oh, no. It's just that the photograph was taken in front of your school so I thought that perhaps you would recognize her."

"No, but I do recognize this young lady." She pointed to one of the other young women in the picture. "I don't know her name, but I believe she's a nanny for one of our families. She has come into the office a few times."

"Oh! If we could talk to her, maybe she could help us find Graciela."

"I would have to think about what family she works for. I can ask around. Could you leave me this photograph?"

Kate looked at Marisol and realized that was out of the question. "I'll get a copy made and bring it to you. Could you direct me to a place where I could get the copy made?"

"Sure. There's a UPS store and a CVS on Coast Village Road."

"And where's that?"

The clerk looked at her a bit warily. "Oh, you're not from here?"

"No. I'm from Los Angeles."

"Well, the easiest would be to get back on the freeway going north and get off at Olive Mill, the next exit."

"Okay. Thanks." Kate took Marisol's hand as they left the building. She took out her phone and pressed her new app and said, "The lady might know one of the girls." Then she read off the phone. "*La señora podriá conocer a una de las chicas.*"

Marisol grinned and pressed her own app and said "*¿Encontraremos a mi hermana?*" The app answered, "We will find my sister?"

Kate shrugged and smiled. "I hope so. *Yo espero que sí.*"

They got the copy made and brought it back to the school secretary. She took down Kate's phone number and promised to call as soon as she had any information. Kate called Lawrence to update him. "Maybe she's a nanny too?" he asked.

"Maybe," Kate agreed. "I bet it would be a lucrative job in Montecito. It would certainly pay better than picking fruits and vegetables, but maybe not more than working on a pot farm. Do you think I should stop in at Santa Barbara City College with the picture? Maybe show it to your friend there?"

"I don't think that would be necessary. I'm waiting for his call back, as well as from the lawyers. Why not just come home and we can figure out the next step."

"I guess you're right. See you soon."

They got in the car and were back on 101 when they passed the Carpinteria exit. Marisol called out, "*¿Playa?*"

Kate looked at the time. "Sure. We can stop at the beach." They spent the rest of the afternoon

walking on the sand and wading in the water before
heading home.

25

A FEW DAYS PASSED WITH NO RETURNED PHONE CALLS FROM THE SCHOOL SECRETARY OR LAWRENCE'S LATEST CONTACTS. Marisol's predicament was almost forgotten as they went about typical family activities. After dinner Sunday, Kate and Lawrence were watching 60 Minutes and Marisol was playing games on her phone when Kate's phone rang. "It's Rachel," she said. Lawrence looked confused. "My friend we met in Anza."

"Oh. That seems like a million years ago," Lawrence said, shaking his head.

"I know," Kate sighed. She started walking into their bedroom. "Hello, Rachel."

"Hi Kate. Have you found out anything more about Marisol's situation?"

"Some," Kate sighed and then got Rachel up to date with all that had happened since they talked.

"That's a lot," Rachel responded. "You have some solid leads."

"Leads, yes. But I'm beginning to get discouraged about them going anywhere."

"Well, I might have some more for you. Not sure if it'll help, but it's another possible direction to go in."

"Great. What have you discovered?"

"I've been doing a little research and talked to some of my friends in the, um, underground network. Yolanda reminded me, also, that you should probably check the farms in Lost Hills."

"Where is Lost Hills?"

"Northwest of Bakersfield. Not far off Interstate 5."

"Why Lost Hills?" Kate asked.

"There's a huge migrant population working on all the farms there," Rachel answered.

"We tried that route, stopping in Tranquillity and Firebaugh. They don't like to talk, understandably. And we don't have any reference to Lost Hills like we did for the other towns."

"The difference might be that Lost Hills is along the underground network."

"Underground network?"

"Remember the Underground Railroad during the Civil War? It's like that for undocumented immigrants fleeing north to Canada."

"Oh, I see." Kate got pensive. "So maybe Marisol's sister was there, even if she isn't there now?"

"Well, that and just the fact that there are so many farms employing them in that area. It's one of the first places immigrants go because there is so much work."

"Any ideas on how to begin my search there?" Kate asked.

"Maybe now that Marisol is talking and you have that translation app, she might have a memory of someplace or something." Rachel took a deep breath. "But be careful."

"What do you mean?"

"It's not just the migrant workers that don't want to talk. Their bosses are not thrilled at being interrogated either. They have their own things they'd like to keep hidden."

"Thanks, Rachel. And thank Yolanda for me also."

"Sure. Keep me in the loop." They hung up.

Kate went back to the living room to tell Lawrence what Rachel had said. "It seems like another crazy wild goose chase to me," Lawrence responded warily.

"I'll start with looking up some of the farms in the Lost Hills area and see if Marisol reacts to any of the names of the farms."

"You know I'm not keen on going back to the Bakersfield area."

"I don't blame you. I can go alone. It would only be a few hours drive. I can do it easily in one day." Kate opened her laptop and looked for farm names. "Remember that scandal with the Wonderful Food Company? The ones that make Pom, the pomegranate drink that the billionaire couple made all those false health claims about?"

"It rings a bell."

"Paramount Farms is theirs and it's the largest supplier of pistachios in the world. The Wonderful Company also makes Fiji water and they're big citrus growers too. I'm going to show Marisol pictures of their products and see if something rings a bell for her." Kate put up several pictures of products from the Wonderful Company on her screen and brought her laptop over to where Marisol was sprawled on a chair. *"¿Trabaja tu hermana en Lost Hills?"*

Marisol spoke into her phone's app and then turned to Kate, "I don't know." Kate showed her the pictures of the nuts, the Fiji water and Pom drink that she had on her computer screen. *"¡Papá!"*

Kate turned to look at Lawrence and found him as shocked as she was. Marisol had never brought up her father much before this at all. "Your papa worked for this company?" She looked at the translation on her phone. *"¿Tu papá trabajaba para esta empresa?"*

"¡Sí! ¡Mi papá!" Marisol started to cry.

"¿Él murió aquí? He died in America?"

"Sí." Marisol sniffled. Kate put her arm around her and turned to Lawrence. "I wonder if he sent some things to Mexico like the nuts or drinks and that's what she recognized."

"Seems like it," he responded. "I guess this is big, then. Do you want me to go with you?"

"It's okay. I know you'd rather not."

"Well, I'm guessing we don't have to go through Bakersfield to get to Lost Hills . . ."

Kate looked at her phone. "Nope. I guess we then have a plan for tomorrow."

"It's better than sitting around here waiting for possible calls from a bunch of lawyers."

"You know, I'm going to call Juanita and see what she thinks about how to approach this."

"I think you'd be better off talking to Consuela and Javier. They are in the business."

"That's a great idea. Wait, did we get their phone number?"

"I don't think we did."

"I'll call Steve in the morning. I should be able to reach him through the Ybarra Farm number."

"Why not try tonight?" Lawrence asked. "It's still early enough. I doubt farms are on a Monday through Friday nine to five schedule."

"I'll try." Kate found a number for the farm and dialed. It went to voicemail and she left a message. "Should I try to talk some more to Marisol about her father? I don't want to upset her more."

Lawrence shrugged. "I don't know what to tell you. It would be helpful to get more information, but I'm afraid she might clam up again."

"I know. Well, maybe I could just ask her a few questions." She talked into her Google Translation app. "Do you know how he died? *¿Sabes cómo murió?*"

"*En un accidente en la granja.*"

"Did she say an accident on the farm?" Lawrence asked.

"Yep. I'm guessing she doesn't know more than that. I'll wait to ask her any more questions, I think."

"Probably best."

"I'd like to call Juanita and Lucy and get their take on all this."

"The more information the better," he replied.

Kate went back to the bedroom to make her calls and returned to the living room as 60 Minutes was ending. "Juanita knew about the network and said that Lost Hills was a good possibility. Did you know about the underground network?"

"Not really," Lawrence answered. "I mean it makes sense. They are people that house the migrants so they don't get picked up by ICE?"

"I guess it's also to help them escape to Canada."

"Is that what they want? Can't blame them, other than the cold weather."

"I guess Canada is more welcoming than we are. At least they didn't build a wall!"

Lawrence shook his head in disgust. "Let's not get into politics. Only makes us crazy."

"Kind of hard not to when ICE agents are out to ship Marisol back to Mexico." Kate could feel herself getting angry. "But you're right . . . let's keep our eyes on the prize. Focus on helping Marisol as best we can." Her phone rang. "Oh it's Lucy calling me back." She returned to the bedroom.

When she came back out to the living room, Lawrence and Marisol were sitting in front of the television watching a Spanish station and eating bowls of ice cream. "Uh oh, you caught us," Lawrence chuckled.

Kate laughed. "Are you understanding the TV show?"

"No, but apparently it's a comedy because Marisol giggles at it a lot."

"Lucy thought Lost Hills was a good idea too, but also thought we shouldn't give up on the Central Valley towns where the postcards were mailed from."

"You mean go back there again?" Lawrence asked.

"Well, we didn't go to Stevinson and didn't really talk to anyone in Firebaugh. I guess we didn't give those towns that much of a chance." Lawrence inhaled and let his breath out with an obvious touch of annoyance. "I know you just want our lives to get back to normal," Kate retorted, "but we've taken it this far . . ."

"I know, I know. I guess I'm just thinking we should all give ourselves a break and stop looking for Graciela. Let's just keep Marisol and find her a better education situation where she can learn English and not worry about ICE agents coming for her."

Kate gazed at him and then flashed a little knowing smile. "That may very well be what happens. But I think we should keep looking for

Graciela until we've exhausted every possibility we can think of. That's all."

Lawrence stood and gathered his and Marisol's empty bowls. "I guess I'll turn in. Another busy driving day tomorrow."

"So you're coming with us?"

Lawrence smiled. "Did you really think I wouldn't?"

Kate kissed him. "I wouldn't blame you if you didn't want to."

"We're a family. We stick together. You, me and Marisol." He kissed Kate and leaned down and kissed the top of Marisol's head. "*Buenas noches.*"

26

THEY WERE ON THE ROAD TO LOST HILLS BY NINE. They would have liked to have left earlier, but traveling during the morning rush wouldn't make them arrive any earlier. As they drove up Interstate 5 Kate got a call back from Steve Ybarra who was happy to give her Javier's number and Kate called him to update him on all that happened since they visited at his house. "Apparently her father worked at a big pistachio farm in Lost Hills and was killed in an accident there."

"I heard about that," Javier said. "It was a big story among the migratory workers. A guy was crushed by machinery."

"When was that?" Kate asked.

"It must have been a couple of years ago."

"Hmm. Not too long ago to offer some clues," Kate mused aloud. "Was it a man old enough to have a twenty year old daughter?"

"I think so. It wasn't a young kid or anything. I don't remember exactly, but you could probably find out when you're there."

"Do you know anyone there, by chance?" Kate asked hopefully.

"Not really. Maybe Steve does. I'll ask him. But didn't you already talk to him?"

"Just to get your number. I didn't go into details."

"Tell you what. I'm meeting with him in a little while. I'll tell him to call you."

Lawrence looked over to Kate when she closed the call. "So what did he say?"

"He remembered an accident about two years ago. A farmworker was killed by some sort of machinery."

Lawrence frowned. "What a way to go. Well, it's a good lead, anyway."

"He's going to have Steve call me. Maybe he knows someone at the farm who could help us."

"Was it that farm that makes the Fiji water and the Pom juice?"

"I assume so. I didn't ask if it was the same farm. But it doesn't really matter. It was a big thing around there, so it's likely anyone there will know the details."

"Except that anyone who actually works on that farm would likely say little if they valued their job."

"True. Still, it's no secret."

It was after eleven when they arrived in Lost Hills and Steve still hadn't called. They decided to go get a cup of coffee and hope that he would call soon. Lost Hills was not exactly teeming with hip cafes, so they settled for a Denny's. Steve called shortly after they sat down. Lawrence had also put the translation app on his phone, so he tried to have a conversation with Marisol while Kate went outside to talk to Steve. *"¿Quieres huevos?"* Lawrence asked.

Marisol said, "No thank you."

"Do you want to speak in English instead of Spanish?" he responded.

She poked at her phone and then said, "I need to learn English."

Lawrence smiled and nodded. "Yes you do."

"Steve gave me the address of a farm where he knows the owner," Kate said as she rejoined them. "He said to just go there because he would be a hard one to get a hold of by phone. He's old school and doesn't carry a cell phone."

"Is it in Lost Hills?"

"Yes." They ordered a large muffin for Marisol and coffee for themselves.

"She can sure eat a lot for being such a skinny kid," Lawrence said. "Didn't she already eat breakfast?"

"She just had cereal," Kate answered.

Back in the car, they drove through the actual ag workers' town of Lost Hills—not the travel franchise version along the Interstate—and then turned north and drove several miles through orchards of almonds and pistachios. They arrived at the farm and got out of the car. It was huge and no one was seen in the vicinity of the various sheds and offices. Hearing noises in the distance, they started walking in that direction through what seemed like an endless almond orchard. The trees had been shaken, the nuts had been picked up from the ground, and the trees looked barren and tan. They hadn't been watered in a while and the dust rose in clouds around them. Eventually they came to a plot where the trees were being bulldozed for a new planting. They could see some workers cutting the trunks and larger limbs to wholesale as firewood. Most of the tree remains were being bulldozed into huge piles that would be shredded for a biomass plant nearby.

"Well, we finally found someone," Kate puffed, slapping the dust off her jeans.

"Are you going to talk to them?" Lawrence asked. "Will they talk to you? And in Spanish or English?"

Kate chuckled. "So many possibilities! Well, let's give English a try first. Then I guess I have my trusty Google Translator App." Kate poked at her phone and then turned to Marisol. "We will ask them if they knew your father and sister. *Les preguntaremos si conocen a tu padre y a tu hermana.*"

They trudged over the broken ground and reached the workers. All eyes were on Marisol, seemingly out of deference to the adults with her, and much to Lawrence and Kate's surprise, Marisol spoke first. The workers responded in rapid Spanish that Kate couldn't translate fast enough. Marisol was nodding as they continued speaking while Kate and Lawrence looked on in shock. They had never seen Marisol behave so maturely and assertively. "They're having a real conversation," Lawrence whispered to Kate.

"Amazing. Look at our little Marisol!" she replied proudly.

"*Gracias,*" Marisol said to the workers and turned to her phone, typing feverishly. Then she turned to Kate and Lawrence. "They don't know them but heard about the accident. They said my sister left the area after that."

"So we know they were here at one time. That's helpful, I guess." Lawrence looked at Kate waiting to see if she agreed with him.

"Not if we don't know where she went afterwards," Kate answered. She spoke into her translator app. "Do they know where Graciela went?" Then she turned to Marisol and said, "*¿Saben adónde fue Graciela?*"

Marisol went back to the workers and talked for a few more minutes and then came back to where Kate and Lawrence were standing. "*Ella fue con su novio. Él preguntará a su hijo,*" she spoke into her phone.

Marisol showed Kate the translation and Kate read it aloud to Lawrence. "She went with her boyfriend. He will ask his son."

They watched as one of the men made a call and talked briefly. He then approached Kate and offered his phone. She took it, surprised that he handed it to her rather than Marisol, but spoke into it. "Hello," she said tentatively.

"My dad said you wanted to know where Graciela Sandoval went?"

Kate breathed a sigh of relief. The man's son spoke English. "Yes. Her younger sister has been looking for her since she crossed the border."

"I am friends with the guy she went with, but I don't know where she is right now. I know they went to some other farms in the valley and then wound up in Santa Ynez, over the mountain from Santa Barbara. But they broke up and that was like more than a year ago."

Kate looked over at Lawrence and winked. "Santa Ynez," she mouthed. "We were on the right track in going to Solvang." She spoke into the phone. "Do you think she's still there?"

"I really have no idea."

"Were she and her boyfriend working on a pot farm there?"

"Uh, maybe," he replied reluctantly. "I'm not sure."

Kate realized that for all he knew, she could be an ICE or a drug agent looking to break up illegal pot farms. "Thank you so much. You've been a great help. Do you think it would be helpful if I spoke to your friend, the ex-boyfriend?"

"I said they broke up. Do you keep up with your exes?"

Kate forced out a chortle. "No, of course not." She realized that he wasn't going to say anymore, but hoped something might change his mind later. "Could I give you my phone number? If you hear anything or if your friend has any more information, you or he could call me?"

"I guess."

Kate gave him her number and hung up the phone. "Thank you so much . . . *gracias*," she said to the worker. The man nodded and went back to work. She turned to Lawrence. "Well, I guess we go back to the Solvang area."

"Well, it's a lot more appealing than this," he replied, waving at the destruction all around him. They started walking, but Lawrence was the first to notice Marisol wasn't following. He turned and saw her sniffling and wiping tears off her cheeks. He turned back and squatted by her, putting his arm around her shoulder.

Kate looked over and sighed. "Oh the poor girl. It's only natural after all that effort she put forth." She came up and caressed the top of her head and eventually Marisol calmed down. They walked back to the car slowly.

"Do you want to go to Santa Ynez now? On our way home?" Lawrence asked as they drove away from the farm.

"Let me check the map and see how long it would take. Hmm, there's no real direct route from here. It's definitely not an 'on our way home' stop."

"Probably just as well. I mean, we don't know for sure that she's still there and how do we even begin to look for her? It's not like illegal pot farms are going to be obvious."

"Maybe we'll get lucky and the ex-boyfriend or his friend will call me back." She let out a big sigh. "It's so frustrating," Kate lamented. "It seems like we are just waiting for all these people to call us back."

Kate turned around to glance at Marisol in the back seat. For the first time since she'd gotten it, her eyes were not glued to her phone. She was gazing out the window. *"¿Estás bien?* Are you okay?"* Kate said to Marisol, patting her knee.

Marisol nodded and smiled, though her cheeks were wet. *"Sí.* Yes."

"Let's go home," Kate said to Lawrence. "We can go to Santa Ynez another day."

27

MARISOL WENT STRAIGHT TO HER ROOM WHEN THEY GOT HOME. Kate went out to get a pizza for dinner, hoping that would brighten Marisol's mood, and Lawrence went to the kitchen to make a salad. The whole household was pensive and apprehensive, not sure how to process what they had learned that day or how to proceed. They ate in silence, all three lost in their own thoughts. Marisol went back to her room when she had finished while Lawrence and Kate cleaned up. "I think I will call Mrs. Flores again and see if she thinks it's safe for Marisol to return to school," Kate finally said.

"That's a good idea," Lawrence replied. "She was very happy there and it will give her a chance to be with other kids."

"After today's emotional highs and lows, I think it's better to look for Graciela without her in tow." Kate's phone rang and she picked it up to see who was calling. "Oh, it's Lucy. Hey there," she said, walking into the living room.

"Hi Kate. What's the latest on Marisol?" Kate told her what they had learned that day. "I'm hoping the ex-boyfriend calls me. Actually, I wish some of these other people would call back, too."

"Well, I had another thought," Lucy said.

"What's that?" Kate asked eagerly. "Any advice is more than welcome."

"It's about that fake birth certificate. I know they can be bought online or through other channels, but I've heard that many times, they belong to family members."

"So you think maybe that Lourdes girl is related to Marisol?"

"That's what I'm thinking. It might be another avenue to try."

"How? Call the hospital in Fresno?"

"I don't know, but you could start by just Googling the names, Lourdes as well as the parents listed on it."

"It's worth a try."

"Might be a dead-end," Lucy conceded, "but it certainly wouldn't hurt."

"No it wouldn't," Kate agreed. "We've been so focused on the postcards and photos that we hadn't given the birth certificate another thought." She hung up and went to the kitchen to tell Lawrence and then went back to the living room with her laptop to Google. Not surprisingly, nothing came up, since Lourdes was young and her parents might be undocumented and therefore invisible. Kate decided to call the hospital in the morning. She wasn't sure what she would ask them since the birth certificate was twelve years old. But maybe there was a sympathetic soul working there who could do some research and sleuthing. She knocked on Marisol's door and opened the door hesitantly. "Can I come in? *¿Puedo entrar?*"

"Yes."

Kate smiled as she opened the door, happy to hear Marisol using English. She spoke into her translation app, "Can I see the birth certificate? *¿Puedo ver el certificado de nacimiento?*"

Marisol reached into her backpack and took it out. She handed it to Kate. *"¿Por qué?"*

"¿Es Lourdes tu prima? Your cousin?" Marisol shrugged. *"¿Una pariente?* A relative?" Kate went on.

"No sé," Marisol responded with another shrug.

Kate took the birth certificate and left Marisol's room. She returned to her computer and looked up the address of the hospital, trying to decipher if it might be in a Latino neighborhood, not even sure why. Was she just going to knock on doors in the neighborhood of the hospital where a girl was born twelve years ago and ask everyone who answered if they knew her? She was not exactly good at this detective stuff, even if she had read a lot of crime novels. Lawrence came into the living room from the bedroom. "I got a call back from my friend at Santa Barbara City College."

"And?" Kate asked.

"Nothing. I mean no Graciela Sandoval registered."

Kate sighed. "Oh well, it was kind of a long shot. Just because some girl she's with is wearing a sweatshirt . . ."

"I still wish you'd contact one of the agencies that work with undocumented immigrants. They may know ways to find her that we haven't thought of or don't have access to."

"Yeah, I think you're right." She smiled sheepishly. "This is getting to be way out of our league, even if we have gained some information. I think I'll go to bed and read. I need to put my mind on something else."

Kate called the school at 7:30 the next morning, hoping the school secretary would answer that early, even if the principal wasn't there yet. She was in luck. Mrs. Flores was there and assured Kate that she thought it was safe for Marisol to come. She had thought out a plan if the agents showed up. She went to tell Marisol whose grin gave Kate confidence that this was indeed the right thing to do. She found Lawrence in the kitchen making coffee. "Mrs. Flores thinks it will be fine to send Marisol."

"That's good."

"I'll bring her and then come back to make some more calls. What are your plans?"

"The gym this morning. Then I'm not sure. I hadn't made any since I didn't know how long we'd be gone."

"I need to go back to the gym too but I think I'll wait until I can be more consistent about going. I'll probably jog after I drop her off. I could at least get some aerobic activity."

Kate took Marisol to school and got back from her run about ten. She set up her laptop on the kitchen table as she felt that today was going to involve a lot of calling, researching, and emailing and wanted to make it as comfortable and organized as possible. The hospital was less than accommodating. Not only would the person she talked to not give out any information, they were short with her and it kind of pissed her off. She spent most of the morning looking up Fresno County and Fresno City rules and regulations as well as birth certificate information websites. Nothing was very helpful. She finally broke down and called some agencies, but it was hard to find any help from them on the phone. She wrote a bunch of emails to any agency she found online that might help, without giving out any names except her own. She called the Montecito school secretary back, but she was busy and couldn't talk. Her frustration was starting to get her riled up so that when Lawrence got home she was grouchy and irritable. "Any luck?" he asked as he entered the kitchen and took a bottle of water out of the fridge.

"It's worse than no information. No one seems to want to help."

"Just because it's our priority doesn't mean it's theirs."

"I know. I'm just frustrated."

"Did you eat lunch?"

"No."

"That's part of your problem, I'm sure. You probably have low blood sugar."

She smiled at him. "You're right. And actually I never ate breakfast. What time is it?"

"One."

"I'll make something. What would you like for lunch?" she asked.

"I'll have it later," he replied. "I want to shower first."

Lawrence left the kitchen while Kate made a sandwich and went into the living room to eat it. She turned on the television as a diversion and saw that the local news was on. They were covering an ICE raid at a family's home in Boyle Heights that had turned violent. The agents had chased the father/husband and shot him when he tried to escape. "Damn!" Kate exclaimed in horror. "Lawrence?" she called.

Lawrence came in with a towel around his waist. "What?"

"Look at this!" she cried.

He watched for a minute and sighed. "Don't law enforcement officers have better things to do than harass people?"

"I've got to do something to protect Marisol from this. I—I think I'll look into adopting her!"

"Whoa," Lawrence replied, hooking up his towel. "I'm guessing that's not an easy thing to do."

"Well," she frowned. "I can at least see what it entails."

Lawrence shrugged and sighed, "Whatever." He went back to the bathroom. He resigned himself to the fact that Kate was an idealist who was going to persevere until she got answers. And he loved her for that.

Kate went back to her computer and stayed on it until it was time to pick up Marisol from school. The kids were just being dismissed and Mrs. Flores was in her usual spot at the door, saying goodbye to each and every one of them. Marisol wasn't among the first group and that worried Kate a little, so she went up to the principal to ask if everything had gone well. "Oh yes, Kate. We read the riot act to the classmate who had tattled to his daddy. He won't be doing that again."

Kate laughed, remembering her own days as a teacher and how well guilt worked as a deterrent to bad behavior. Marisol came running up at that moment, full of smiles and exhilaration. "*¿Cómo estuvo la escuela hoy?* How was school today?" Kate asked her, having looked up a couple of phrases before leaving home.

"School is fun," Marisol answered, speaking slowly, but proudly. Kate gave her a hug. "Go to beach today?" Marisol continued.

Kate looked at her phone to see what time it was. "Yes we could do that," she answered and nodded as she spoke, just to be sure Marisol understood.

"To Venice?" Marisol added.

"Sure."

"Ice cream."

Kate laughed. "Oh, you want to go to Venice to get ice cream on the boardwalk?"

"Yes. *Sí.*"

They got in the car and Kate was surprised to find parking just a few blocks from the beach. "I guess two-thirty on a weekday is actually a good time to go to the beach. Not as many people." Marisol looked at her quizzically, but Kate decided there was no need to translate that, so she didn't bother.

First stop was the ice cream parlor and they ambled down the boardwalk while eating their cones. "Miss McCoy!" Kate turned around to see who in the world would be calling her by that name. A handsome Black man about thirty came over with a toddler in his arms. "It's me, Malcolm!"

"Oh my goodness!" She hugged him. "And who is this?"

"This is my daughter, Aja."

"I don't believe it! A lot has certainly happened since I saw you last." Malcolm had been her student and Kate had run into him on a few other occasions when her father, Finn, had ended up living in the senior residence where Malcolm worked.

"How long have you been home from the Peace Corps?"

"Oh, about a year. Time flies. This is Marisol, by the way."

Marisol had been cooing at Aja and extended her arms up to her. "Would you like to hold her?" Malcolm asked Marisol.

"She doesn't speak English," Kate explained, but it didn't seem to matter. Aja squirmed to get out of Malcolm's arms and into Marisol's.

"Are you in a hurry?" Malcolm asked. "We could go sit on the sand and catch up."

"Sure." Kate turned to Marisol and said as she pointed to the sand. *"Playa?"*

"Sí. Yes." Marisol put Aja down and took her hand to walk together to the beach.

The children played in the sand while Malcolm told Kate about how he and Savali adopted Aja and Kate told him all about Marisol. "So now we're trying to figure out what to do next," Kate finished, almost breathless.

"Any ideas where her sister might be?"

"We suspect a pot farm rather than general field or orchard work. She would have to be earning a lot of money to pay the coyote and I assume there is more to be made there."

"Have you considered the Emerald Triangle?" Malcolm asked.

"Yes, but none of the evidence points there. The closest connection comes from a postcard of Solvang and a group photo in front of the grammar school in Montecito. I understand there's a lot of cannabis growing north of Santa Barbara."

"Yeah, both legally and illegally. Being that she's likely illegal, so would be her employer."

"I know. And those, of course, are the hardest ones to find."

"Hmm. Maybe Dutch knows someone who grows there."

"Who's Dutch?" Kate asked.

"A pot farmer I know in Garberville." Malcolm grinned. "He's sort of a far out connection of mine."

"Far out is fine with me." Kate laughed. "Do you have his number?"

"I have his email." Malcolm scrolled through his contacts. "Is your phone number the same as it was before you went to the Peace Corps? I still have that number."

"Yep."

"Cool. I'll text you Dutch's email."

Marisol and Aja approached them and flopped on the sand next to them. "*Ella huele*," Marisol said and held her nose for emphasis.

"Ah, the universal language for baby stink," Malcolm laughed. "I need to get ready for work, anyway. Savali gets home about four and then we switch roles. I work in the evening and she watches Aja."

"That works out then."

"Yeah, but I'm not getting any documentaries made, which is what I'd rather be doing than waiting tables. But . . . all in good time. Having children puts a damper on a lot of things." Kate pondered that statement for a moment, realizing how true that would be for her and Lawrence as well if they kept Marisol.

They stood and hugged. "Thanks for Dutch's email. Let's keep in touch. I know people always say that, but maybe we can babysit sometime. I'm sure Marisol would like that."

"I'd like that, too!" Malcolm grinned.

Kate and Marisol walked back to the car and got home just as Lawrence walked in the door with groceries. "We ran into Malcolm on the boardwalk!" Kate exclaimed. "Lots to tell you but we might have a good lead. I'll tell you later. First I need to write an email."

Kate spent the rest of the evening checking her email every ten minutes, but there was no answer from Dutch by the time they went to bed. "Hey, it's harvest time, isn't it?" Lawrence speculated as he turned off the light. "He may be too busy to check emails."

"Yeah. I just hope I didn't end up in his spam file. But you know what? Marisol is happy and back in school, so another day is no big deal."

Lawrence studied the reflections in the ceiling from the streetlights outside. "I still think we need to contact an agency that deals with this."

"I did email a few this morning," Kate said proudly. "I just need to tread carefully. It's so hard to trust things on the Internet these days."

"You think ICE agents are trolling these sites?"

"Who knows what they are capable of."

Lawrence pulled Kate to him. "Things will work out."

28

THE NEXT MORNING KATE DROVE MARISOL TO SCHOOL AND THEN DECIDED TO JOIN LAWRENCE AT THE GYM. They even went out to lunch afterwards, taking a step back to when it was just the two of them. Kate tried hard to get it out of her mind and to focus on being alone with Lawrence, but she wasn't too successful. She did make a point of not checking her email on her phone, waiting until they got home to check on her computer. Dutch hadn't answered, but a couple of the immigration agencies did. Those emails didn't sound very encouraging, however.

"I'm going to pick up Marisol. Do we need anything?" Kate asked.

"Not that I know of. No word?"

"Nope." Kate gathered her phone and keys and was about to leave when her phone rang. She answered as she walked out to the car. "Hello? Yes, this is she."

"I'm calling from the Montecito Union School. I wanted to let you know that we did find a teacher who knows the young woman wearing the sweatshirt. She didn't know any of the others."

"Really?" Kate asked excitedly. "Do you have a name and contact information?"

"I'd prefer to give her yours, if that's okay."

"That's fine. But could you please tell her the situation so she understands that we are looking for Marisol's sister and she is apparently a friend of hers?"

"Yes. I will tell her. I'll get back to you as soon as I can, but it may take a while to track her down. The teacher who recognized her said she thinks she has picked up kids, but she isn't sure whose kids. She's probably a nanny for one of our families. But it could have been awhile ago and she may not be here anymore."

"Thank you. I appreciate it." Kate hung up, discouragement creeping back in. She picked up Marisol and immediately went home to get back to her computer, but still nothing from Dutch. She went into her contacts and called Malcolm, knowing he wouldn't be going to work until after four. "Malcolm? It's Kate."

"Miss McCoy?" he replied.

"C'mon Malcolm," Kate laughed. "You're an adult now. You can call me Kate."

"Okay," he chuckled. "You're right."

"I emailed Dutch but haven't heard back and wondered if you had a phone number for him."

"I don't think I do, but I'm sure Jed does."

"Jed knows him?" Kate asked.

"Oh yeah, they're good buddies. We brought Homer up there after the senior residence closed. You remember Homer? The guy with Parkinson's?"

"Yeah, I do remember Homer. Well, I will call Jed then. I have his number still, I think. Let me see." She looked at her contacts. "I have the number for the columbarium and a number for his wife, Monica."

Malcolm laughed. "He's crossed the line into the twenty-first century. He now has a cell phone. I'll share his contact info with you."

"Thanks Malcolm." She hung up and smiled, remembering how Malcolm and Jed had met on the boardwalk in Venice when they were both homeless.

She got the text from Malcolm and called Jed. "Hello this is Jed Gibbons."

"Hi Jed. It's Kate."

"Kate! How are you? Oh no . . . is it Finn? Did something —"

"Dad's fine."

"Thank goodness. How was the Peace Corps?"

"Has it been that long since we've talked? Wow. That seems so long ago. It was great, but I've been back in Los Angeles for almost a year."

"Well, what can I do for you?" Jed asked.

Kate relayed the whole story of Marisol and said, "I ran into Malcolm who told me to get in touch with Dutch in Garberville because he might know some farmers in Santa Barbara County, but he only had an email for him. He hasn't answered my email, so I wanted to call. Malcolm said you would have his phone number."

"Yeah, let me find it for you. I don't think Dutch is growing much pot anymore, but he might know some people down there." He gave Kate the phone number. "How is Finn? I haven't talked to him in a couple of months."

Kate then realized that she hadn't talked to him lately either and she hoped he was fine. He was in his eighties, after all, although healthy as a horse. "Dad is the same old curmudgeon."

Jed laughed. "Isn't that what we love about him? I need to finish locking up and get home. Love to see you if you come up this way in your search for Marisol's sister."

"You bet. And please call if you get down here too." They hung up and Kate immediately dialed the number Jed had given her for Dutch.

"Yes?" Dutch answered.

"Hello, Dutch? This is Kate. I emailed you recently. I'm a friend of Malcolm's—"

"Oh yes. Sorry I haven't gotten back to you yet. I'm not that great at keeping up with email."

"That's okay. I hope you don't mind that I called you. I got your number from Jed."

"Hey, a friend of Jed's and Malcolm's is a friend of mine. No worries. So you were asking if I knew any growers in the Santa Ynez area?" She, once again, told Marisol's story. "Yeah," Dutch replied. "That's a good possibility, especially in that county. I do know some growers there, but I'm not comfortable giving out their information. I'm sorry.

I'll email you the contact information for a legal grower in the area and maybe he could help you."

"Thanks Dutch," Kate replied, trying to hide her disappointment. "Much appreciated." She went to the kitchen and found Lawrence and Marisol cooking dinner together. "How cute is this!" she smiled.

"We're a great team," Lawrence grinned. "With her on that app, we get things done in no time." He started laughing. "Why, she's way better with that app than you are."

"Young people usually are," Kate replied good-naturedly. She then relayed her conversations with Jed and Dutch and gave Marisol an abbreviated version – just that they would be looking for her sister on some farms near Solvang, the windmill place.

After dinner, Kate went to her computer and found that Dutch had sent the contact info for the legal grower. She went to the kitchen to find Lawrence finishing the dishes. "So when are you thinking of going to these places?" Lawrence asked.

"Tomorrow."

He laughed. "So much for leaving things alone for a while."

Kate shrugged. "I have some new information so I want to get on it."

"Do you want me to go with you?"

"No, because I don't know how long I'll be and you'll probably need to pick up Marisol from school."

"True, but I'm not sure I like you going to these places alone."

"Excuse me?"

"Look," Lawrence countered. "Dutch may be a great guy, but you don't know where this contact will lead you. Some of those farms are run by Mexican cartels."

She softened. "Duly noted, but you saw some of the places I went in Africa when I was in the Peace Corps."

"I know but —"

"Please Lawrence. I've lived most of my adult life alone. I'll be fine."

He sighed. "Well, I know I'm not going to change your mind . . ."

"Correct." She smiled. "But I love you for caring."

"And I love your persistence, even if it is annoying sometimes." He kissed the top of her head and left.

She looked at the information Dutch had sent her and went on Google Maps to plan the trip. She was considering when to call this contact when her phone rang. Unknown caller. Normally, she wouldn't answer those, waiting to see if they left a voicemail. But since she was waiting for calls from people not in her contacts, she answered. "Hello?"

Five, maybe ten seconds of silence passed before a male voice said, "Is this Kate?"

She hesitated. "Yes."

"I'm Eduardo."

Kate waited for him to explain who he was, but he was silent again. "Um, okay. Do I know you?"

"I was Graciela's boyfriend a while back."

Kate leaped up and ran to find Lawrence as she talked. "Oh, thank you so much for calling me."

"I'm not sure how much I can help you, though. I haven't talked to her in a long time."

"Anything you can tell me will help. Where did you go after leaving the Lost Hills farm?" Kate glanced over at Lawrence and he nodded.

"We went to a bunch of different farms in the valley until a buddy of mine told me about a pot farm looking for trimmers so we went there."

"Was the pot farm in the Santa Ynez Valley?"

"Well, we tried a few. We traveled around the state, but yeah, we ended up there."

"When was that?" Kate asked.

"Uh, I don't know for sure . . . maybe a year ago. That's where we were when we broke up."

She motioned for Lawrence to lean down so he could listen in. "Is she still there, do you think?"

"I don't know," Eduardo replied. "That's the last I talked to her."

"Were you with her when she sent the money for her sister to come?"

"No. I didn't know she wanted her sister to come. She was saving a lot of money though."

"Had her mother died when you were together?"

"No. She was in Mexico. Graciela sent her money all the time. She died?"

"I'm afraid she was murdered."

Eduardo didn't answer right away. Finally he said quietly, "I'm sorry to hear that."

"Did your friend tell you how I found her sister, Marisol?" Kate asked.

"He told me just that it was real important for me to call you. Not really why."

"You have been extremely helpful, Eduardo. I really appreciate it."

"Okay. Well, I gotta go."

"Oh, one last thing. Do you have a phone number for Graciela?"

"I don't know if it's the same number, but I'll give you the one I had." He recited a phone number and Kate said it aloud and pointed to a paper and pencil on the table for Lawrence to write it down.

"Thanks again, Eduardo." They hung up and Kate flopped onto a chair, exhaling loudly. "Well, we have been on the right track, I guess."

"Maybe you should join the police department as a detective," Lawrence laughed.

"I'm going to tell Marisol what's going on and have her make the call to this number. Let her be the one who talks to her sister first!"

"Kate—" But she was already in the hall.

Marisol was playing with her phone when Kate burst into her room. Kate started to tell her the news and then realized that she was speaking in

English and Marisol didn't have a clue what she was saying. "*¿Qué?*" Marisol asked.

Kate started to look for her translation app, but then decided it would be easier to have Lucy tell her. After explaining what was happening, Kate gave her phone to Marisol so Lucy could speak to her. Kate watched Marisol's eyes widen and a huge grin spread across her face. She jumped up out of bed and leaned into Kate who put her arm around her and squeezed her shoulders. Then Marisol handed the phone back to Kate and looked at her expectantly. "Hi Lucy! You need to see her face! So excited and happy!"

"Well good luck! Let me know what happens."

Kate hung up and was about to dial Graciela's number when she realized the paper was still in the kitchen. She ran to get it, excitedly shouting to Lawrence what Marisol's face had looked like after Lucy told her the news. She grabbed the number off the table and added, "Do you want to be there when she calls?"

"I don't think that's—" But Kate was gone again. He hesitated and then slowly followed.

Kate dialed the number and handed her phone to Marisol whose smile was a mile wide . . . until it wasn't. She handed the phone back to Kate with a confused expression on her face. Kate put the phone to her ear and heard the telltale words, "The number you dialed has been changed, disconnected or no longer in service. If you feel you have reached this message in error, please check the number and try your call again."

Kate handed the slip of paper to Lawrence. "Could you read me the number? Maybe I dialed it wrong."

Lawrence bit his lip, took a deep breath and read out the number. Kate redialed, but this time she kept the phone, shaking her head as the same message repeated. Marisol couldn't have looked sadder. She flung herself onto her bed and sobbed into her pillow. This was the first time Kate had really seen her this heartbroken and lay down next to her, holding her close. Lawrence tiptoed out of the room.

29

LAWRENCE OFFERED TO TAKE MARISOL TO SCHOOL, SO KATE WAS ON THE ROAD THE NEXT MORNING EVEN EARLIER THAN SHE HAD PLANNED. She had hoped to miss the rush hour traffic on the 405 and the 101, but there really wasn't any rush hour anymore in Los Angeles. Every hour was rush hour. So she more or less crawled along until she was past Calabasas. Eduardo had texted her a few farms, but the addresses were vague.

She eventually arrived in Buellton, a town on the edge of the Santa Ynez Valley right off the freeway. She hoped to find someone who seemed likely to know where illegal pot farms were located. This was also wine country, but the scale of the ag industry was tiny compared to what she had encountered in the San Joaquin Valley. Even in Buellton tourism obscured the daily grind of the fieldwork and she didn't know where to begin. She decided to head east into the tourist mecca of Solvang, hoping that the anonymity of serving the throngs of visitors might make maids and servers more relaxed—or that she might connect with someone selling on the sly.

She parked and started walking around, searching for young folk who looked not only likely to know, but also willing to share information. She pretended to be interested in buying an eighth of an ounce, but didn't get very far until a couple of people suggested she look out for a certain guy and where he'd likely be. And there he was, sitting on a bench in the middle of the bustle, an oversized gold, green and red beret on his ash blonde dreadlocks. "Do you have any idea where these are?" she asked handing him the list of farms she had written down from Eduardo's text.

He looked at it. "Not really." He flashed her a crooked smile. "Did you try Google?"

"I don't think they're upfront like that."

The guy chuckled. "You're probably right."

"I'm looking for someone. Graciela. She was here with a young man, Eduardo, about a year ago."

He looked at her skeptically. "What kind of trouble are you looking for?"

Kate sighed. "None. Her little sister fell into my care. It's a long story . . ."

"I'm sure."

"Their father was killed in a machinery accident in Lost Hills and their mother was murdered in Tijuana."

"That sucks." He drew in a long breath. "Yeah, I recall a guy and a girl who fit into some of that story, sorta. That accident. Gruesome."

"You talked to her?"

"Nah. She was real quiet."

"How about the guy?" Kate asked.

"He had told me about the accident."

Kate tried to keep her excitement in check. "Which farm was this at where you knew them?"

"Well, let me see . . ." He pulled on his beard. "I've worked at a lot of places, here and there." His eyes settled on her purse. "My mind's pretty hazy, you know."

"I can imagine," Kate murmured, opening her purse and rummaging for her wallet. She took out a twenty. "Will this help you remember?" she asked.

He somehow managed to look both offended and pleased with himself. "Yeah, that helps a little. Cebada Canyon, off 46, this side of Lompoc." He squinted up at her. "Don't drive myself, so don't know the address. You're a cool, resourceful lady. You'll figure it out. Hope you find her."

"So do I," she said as she turned to leave.

"Hey," he said, flashing the folded bill between his fingers. "Thanks."

Kate nodded. "Thank you."

Kate returned to her car and sat in the driver's seat, scrolling over the map on her phone. Cebada Canyon wasn't that hard to find, but as she zoomed in she could see all sorts of lanes going off it. She quickly zoomed out so as not to feel overwhelmed at the impossibility of it all, and started back to Buellton on 246. Traffic was heavy between Solvang and Buellton, but thinned out to just a few cars as she continued westward over a patchwork of crops flanked by low hills. Signs of habitation were few and far between. She felt discouraged by this, and even a bit uneasy over the sense of isolation. Her phone warned her that Cebada Canyon was coming up, so she took her foot off the gas and rolled over onto the shoulder. She looked up the narrow, lumpy ribbon of pavement disappearing into the platinum colored hills. "Oh, what the hell," she muttered to herself. She cranked the steering wheel and drove off up the road that soon hugged hillsides as it climbed. Road cuts revealed a soft sandstone-like soil dotted with water-worn stones and shells—almost like a slice of desert if not for the dry oaks waving on the slopes, and the greasewood and oaks scattered below along the dry creek. No one else was on the road, and she focused mostly on the soft edge breaking off to her right and the eroding cliff on her left.

Kate felt unusually nervous and wondered why. She reminded herself that she was no timid driver and focused on the crest of the canyon ahead. Suddenly it was hard to steer. She turned the steering wheel one way and then another, but the car only responded vaguely, as if somehow floating. "Shit. A flat tire?" She stepped on the brake and the car came to a stop in fairly normal fashion, but the weird rolling, jarring motion continued. Ahead the cliff started slipping into the roadway like quicksand—a flotsam of rocks and vegetation riding the slide like a surfer. A dull roar like the sea or a car in motion filled the air. She stared in disbelief as the road ahead was covered in a layer of debris. She had been in many earthquakes, but never while driving and certainly never out in the middle of nowhere.

First the noise stopped . . . then the motion. Then there was dead silence, as if everything was holding its breath, interrupted occasionally by falling pebbles and stones. Kate opened the car door and stepped out—and felt the earth tremble again in an aftershock. She braced herself against the rocking car until it passed, and then looked back from where she came. A similar landslide had spilled over the road about a quarter mile back, that one perhaps worse because she could still see streams of rock and debris moving. She turned and walked up to the slide in front of her, feeling unsteady as another minor aftershock passed. This landslide was relatively minor, perhaps eighteen inches deep, but when she stepped onto it her feet sank into the loose material. She wasn't at all confident that it wouldn't either sink down or slip off the road, or even if the road was stable. Far ahead she thought she saw a crack or short ledge running along the pavement, so she decided the car was safest where it was.

She pulled out her phone, but unsurprisingly discovered there was no service, more likely due to the isolation and terrain rather than an outage. She considered walking down to 246, knowing someone would soon pass by, but that plan would take her far away from her original intention, perhaps for an extended period of time if the earthquake had caused widespread damage. She locked her car and started walking up the canyon.

After wading and stumbling through the landslide and walking along what was indeed a short ledge where the roadway had sunk down, Kate found herself at the top of the canyon. Still no phone reception, but at least here the sea breeze breathed a little life into the landscape. Occasionally she heard a meadowlark or an insect buzzing. She had forgotten her water bottle in the car and tried to keep her mind off her thirst as she trudged along. The earth continued to roll from time to time, and she worried that the first quake had merely been a foreshock to an even larger one.

She couldn't pretend anymore that she wasn't scared. There were no cars . . . no houses . . . no people. This must have been how Marisol felt when they'd found her that day. Maybe she should stay by the car. Someone might come along, but it could be days before they would look for survivors way the heck out here. She had the water bottle, but she hadn't thought to bring food. She could probably survive a couple of days without food, and she could sleep in the car, but it probably got quite cold at night. Why did she tell Lawrence not to come? He would have thought to bring food. He always planned for things so much better than she did. Wait, wasn't that camping gear still in the car from their trip with Marisol back to where they had found her? Lawrence did always think of everything.

She hurried back to the car and found the tent and sleeping bags still there. She started feeling better, smiling at her good fortune in finding such a wonderful man, but then another aftershock! The car started slipping and she decided that sleeping in the car would not be a good alternative. Perhaps actually setting up the tent somewhere would be better. But where? She was also afraid of things falling on her or her falling into the ground. Well, she had to do something. She took the tent and sleeping bag out of the car, got her bottle of water and started trudging back to the top of the canyon. Somehow she felt it was safer for her to do the falling than being in a position where things could fall on top of her. She needed to be away from trees and areas where rock avalanches might happen.

She saw an open area and decided to try to set up the tent there. She took the tent out of its bag, but when she looked for the pegs, they were not in the bag. Oh great! It had been so long since they'd camped, neither she nor Lawrence had thought about checking. Well, so much for this idea. She left the tent and bag, not wanting to lug it around, and set off with just the sleeping bag. At least she had that. She was starting to doubt her decision. Maybe she should just keep walking, if only to look for a safe place to curl up in her sleeping bag.

She walked for what seemed like hours through a couple more minor aftershocks. Finally, off in the distance, she saw a house. She dropped the sleeping bag, not wanting to hinder getting to the house as quickly as possible. The house remained small in the distance for some time, but finally she was able to discern the various crops around it: avocados on the slope above and grapes and blueberries below the house. It was quite a showplace, like Steve's in Tranquillity. At least it felt inviting, and Kate cut through the vineyard instead of walking the sweep of the driveway. She was exhausted from the combination of nervous and physical fatigue and approached the grand front door without much thought to her intrusion. Her knock was answered by the loud barking of what seemed like large dogs, and shortly thereafter the door opened to emit a joyous, frenetic furry twosome joined by a forty-something year old woman.

"Sorry to intrude," Kate smiled, wiping the hair out of her face, "but my car is stuck between slides down in the canyon."

"Oh, so it is blocked," the woman replied. "I was afraid that would happen. Nasty quake, wasn't it?" The dogs were still barking and running circles around them. "Don't mind Abbott and Costello here. Come on in."

"Do they fit their namesakes?" Kate grinned as she stepped inside.

"Absolutely. My name is Samantha, by the way," she said, holding out her hand.

"I'm Kate."

"It looks like you could use a glass of water, Kate. Or wine."

"Both!" Kate laughed. "If that was a full offer."

"Of course," Samantha laughed back. "I've already started on mine. Only two everyday wine glasses got smashed. Follow me. You can use our land line if you like, as I'm sure you discovered, cell service is at best spotty around here." She pointed to the phone on a counter in the kitchen. "You'll probably have a hard time getting through, however. Everyone is calling everyone else."

"So you guessed I'm not from around here," Kate said as she stepped over a split sack of flour on the floor.

"Well, I don't know you—although I think I'd like to. I figured if you were on your way to visit someone up here, you'd just keep walking and not come this far off the road. Here's your water to start with." Kate drank a glassful without stopping. "And the powder room is just off the entry," Samantha smiled.

"Oh, we do think alike." They laughed like old friends.

"Sit down," Samantha said as Kate returned from her visit to the powder room. "My husband is out checking irrigation lines right now, but maybe later he can take the tractor out and see about freeing up your car, if another neighbor hasn't gotten to it first." Samantha brought Kate a glass of wine.

"So what have you heard about the earthquake?" Kate asked after taking a sip.

Preliminary magnitude, 6.3. It was west of here, offshore. Not as big as the one that happened in the same area back in the 1920s, so it shouldn't be a shock to anyone, no pun intended."

"Was it felt in Los Angeles?"

"Apparently, but not enough to cause much concern, let alone damage." Samantha swirled the wine around in her glass. "Is that where you're from?"

"Yes. At least I don't have to worry about my husband, or . . ." Kate hesitated, always at a loss to describe the relationship. "Marisol."

"Your maid?"

"Oh, no!" Kate laughed. The wine was already causing her to take such an inference lightly. "I'm not in that class. Marisol is a darling Mexican girl I'm caring for at the moment. It's sort of a long story . . ."

Samantha took a sip. "Is that why you're here?"

Kate stared at her. "Well, yes. How did you guess?"

Samantha shrugged. "Just a hunch. I'm rather intuitive at times."

"I'm looking for her sister, Graciela."

"Who is working on a farm that isn't exactly on the up and up?"

"So this has happened before?" Kate asked.

"No. Well, no one has come asking around here before, anyway. It's just that of those types of farms around here, a few are managed by Mexican cartels, and that fits your scenario nicely. They exhibit a veneer of neighborliness if it's to their benefit, but don't go poking into their business. Especially if you're a stranger and a woman."

Kate fiddled with the stem of her wine glass. "Really?"

"Really. I think they'd take particular delight in a woman."

Kate felt a chill run down her spine. "But I talked to a young man who worked with her—"

"Who is a stoner. Like an illegal, easy to manipulate."

"True," Kate murmured. The wine was no longer having a positive effect. In fact, she felt a bit paranoid. "So what you're saying is that I shouldn't continue this quest?"

"Exactly."

At that moment Samantha's husband walked in. "Fixed a few pipes, but I'm not finished looking at all of them." He then noticed Kate. "Oh, hello."

"This is Kate," Samantha explained casually. "Her car is stuck down in the canyon. There have been some minor slides and her car is between them. Maybe you could take your tractor and clear a path for her."

"I could do that." He stuck out his hand. "I'm Greg."

"Thank you so much, Greg," Kate replied, shaking his hand.

"Have you heard anything more about the earthquake?" Samantha asked her husband.

"Not really. Just that it seems to be centered west of Lompoc."

"Oh dear!" Kate exclaimed. "I forgot to call my husband."

"Go ahead and use the phone in the kitchen," Samantha said.

It took a few attempts, but Kate finally got through to Lawrence and told him what was happening. "Did you have damage in Los Angeles?"

"Not much," Lawrence replied. "Just some shaking."

"I hope I won't have any trouble getting home. I guess the fact that it was centered offshore is a good thing, but I don't know what 101 will be like. Or more specifically, getting to 101." Kate hung up and went back into the living room where Samantha was straightening out some pictures on the wall. "Did Greg leave?"

"Yeah, he'll meet us on the road," Samantha answered. "I'll drive you to your car."

They got into Samantha's SUV. "I guess you have four wheel drive?" Kate asked.

"Yeah. You need to around here."

They got to Kate's car after a somewhat harrowing drive. There were aftershocks and the road was definitely bumpy and slippery, but the four-wheel drive SUV did fine. It made Kate a bit nervous about what the ride in her small car would be like, but she wanted to get home. Samantha had instilled a little fear in her about who might be lurking around these deserted parts, and she didn't want to get stuck anywhere else. She felt very lucky that she had found that particular farm. "Thanks so much for everything," Kate said as she got out of the SUV.

"I can wait with you if you like. The tractor doesn't go very fast. It may be a little while before Greg gets here."

"I don't want to keep you. You have plenty to do at home." Kate wanted to be diplomatic, but the reality was that she wanted her to stay.

"Well, it shouldn't be too long. Nice meeting you, Kate." Samantha drove off, much to Kate's chagrin.

Kate got in her own car, feeling more secure in there if there were more aftershocks or if any shady characters showed up. She did feel the car shake a bit more, but luckily Greg drove up without anyone else appearing. "Follow me," he called out to her as he also motioned with his hand. She obeyed.

He was able to clear a path for her fairly easily and by the time they got to Route 246, the road looked fairly unobstructed. "Thank you!" she called to him as she turned left on 246 towards Buellton. He waved back and Kate was on her way.

30

IT TOOK KATE FOUR AND A HALF HOURS FOR WHAT WAS USUALLY A TWO AND A HALF HOUR DRIVE HOME. Not because the freeways had been damaged by the earthquake in any way, nor had the cities of Santa Barbara and Ventura. It was simply the fickleness of evening rush hour traffic exacerbated, perhaps, by an eventful day. She was exhausted by the time she pulled into the condo garage and found herself leaning into the elevator button. Once inside their unit, she followed the noise of two busy people in the kitchen and tossed her purse onto the table. "Well, that was fun!" she exclaimed.

Lawrence gave her a wry grin and hugged her. "I'm glad you're home."

"I'm afraid I had to ditch the camping equipment you had put in the trunk ages ago."

"Camping equipment? Huh?"

"Long story. I'll tell you later. But thanks for being you and being organized." She kissed him.

"Okay, but I don't know what you're talking about."

Kate just smiled at him and hugged Marisol. She took out her phone to the translator app because she wanted to ask Marisol if she felt the earthquake. "I have some messages. I'm going to listen to them," she said as she left the kitchen. There were two from the secretary at the school in Montecito, a couple from the agencies she had called, and one from a Fresno phone number. She assumed it was the Fresno hospital she had contacted about the birth certificate. The agencies were absolutely no help, but the school and the hospital both had some interesting news. She returned to the kitchen and sat down at the table set out with her dinner.

"So what's up?" Lawrence asked.

"Well, the Montecito school secretary said she had located the family where the girl in the picture had worked, but she doesn't work for them anymore. She did get the girl's phone number, though, and called her and left a message with my contact information. So now we wait and hope she calls me. The one other call that might be a lead was from that hospital in Fresno."

"I thought you said they were less than helpful."

"I thought so, but apparently I was wrong. The message was just to call them back, though, so I don't know if there's any new information there."

"I guess you'll have to wait until the morning."

"Probably so. Did you tell Marisol what happened to me today? And did you ask her if she felt the earthquake?"

"Well, between both of our translation apps, we were able to have somewhat of a conversation about it. She said she had to go under her desk when the earthquake hit."

"Was there much shaking down here?" Kate asked.

"Not too bad. Certainly not like the 1994 Northridge quake."

"Was Marisol scared?"

"She said she didn't know what was going on. The teacher just told them to go under their desks so she did what she was told. Afterwards the teacher explained what had happened."

Kate squeezed Marisol's hand and smiled at her. She had wanted to get out her phone to talk to her, but realized how utterly exhausted she was from her day's activities. She wanted to finish dinner and go to bed and that was exactly what she did. She got into bed and took out her Kindle to read when her phone rang. She looked at it and didn't recognize the number. She was tempted to let it go to voicemail, but then remembered that the nanny might be calling. "Hello? This is Kate."

"Um, hi," an uncertain young female voice replied. "Uh, my name is Marina. You wanted me to call you about Graciela?"

"Oh, yes. You're the nanny in Montecito?"

"I was. Yes. Um, but I don't live there anymore."

"Are you still in touch with Graciela?" Kate asked eagerly.

"Not since I moved away."

"Do you know if she is still in Montecito?"

"I don't know. She was trying to get money for her sister to come here and worked a lot."

"Was she also a nanny?"

"Yeah, but she was planning to leave right after I did. She didn't like her family. She only stayed with them as long as she did because they paid so well."

"Do you have a phone number for her?" Kate asked, hopefully.

"I tried the number I had before I called you to see if she answered, but they said it was no longer in service."

"Was it this number?" Kate read her the number she had used for Graciela earlier.

"Yeah. That's the one I had too. I'm sorry I can't help you."

Kate sighed. "Oh you've been more helpful than you realize. It's just that it's so frustrating and discouraging." Kate told Marina the whole story.

"I'm surprised Eduardo isn't still in touch with her," Marina responded. "I thought they were still friends even though they broke up."

"Apparently not. By the way, did you know what pot farm she worked at? I'd like to contact them and see if they know where she is."

"No. Just that it was near Lompoc."

"Do you still live in Montecito?"

"No. After I got my AA from Santa Barbara City College, I went home to Riverside to find a job. It's too expensive to live in Santa Barbara."

"That it is. A beautiful place, but that's why it's so expensive. Well thanks again. If you think of anything that might help us find her, please call."

"I will. Bye."

Kate hung up and sunk back into the pillows. Lawrence walked in and asked, "Who called?"

Kate related the call with Marina. "Another dead end," she said despairingly.

"Don't think of them as dead ends. Each contact you've made has brought us closer to finding her."

"Aren't you the optimist!"

"Well, it's true. Little by little, anyway. Let's go to bed and you can call the hospital in Fresno first thing tomorrow. Lawrence pulled her to him. "I'm just glad you made it back home safely."

"You know, I haven't even thought about that. It was a harrowing experience, being in the middle of nowhere during an earthquake. It could have been a much worse outcome." They made love and fell asleep in each other's arms.

Marisol was dressed and finishing her breakfast when Kate got to the kitchen. "*¿Qué hora es?*" Kate asked, surprised that she was ready for school.

"Seven-thirty," Marisol smiled, proudly.

Kate smiled back and automatically responded in English. "Ready for school?"

Marisol looked at the translation app. "We need to leave soon, yes?"

"Yes. I slept late. I'll go get dressed." Marisol looked a little puzzled when she looked at her app. Kate thought perhaps the phrase slept late might be translated strangely. "I slept too many hours." Marisol nodded and Kate left to get dressed.

Kate decided to drive Marisol instead of walking to school. She wanted to get back home quickly so she could call the hospital. She poured herself a cup of coffee and kept her eye on the clock, waiting until nine to call. Lawrence came home and joined her in the kitchen. "You were quite the sleepyhead this morning," he said as he poured his own cup.

"Where were you?"

"At the gym. I went early. Have you called yet?"

"I'm waiting until after nine." He nodded and took his coffee back to the living room to work on his computer.

Kate watched the clock and finally dialed the number at nine-fifteen, thinking if they started work at nine they would need time to get settled. She had high hopes, but was also doubtful that anything would come of this. Why would a twelve-year-old false birth certificate be valuable in finding Graciela? "Hello, Fresno Hospital, how may I direct your call?"

Oh crap! Kate had forgotten the name of the person who called. "I'm sorry. I'm returning a call about an old birth certificate and I don't remember the name of the person to speak with."

"You need to talk to the Fresno County Office of Vital Statistics to get a copy of a birth certificate."

"No. I have the birth certificate. I'm trying to track someone down and I received a call from someone who had some information for me."

"I'm sorry but I don't know who that would have been from the hospital."

Kate exhaled sharply. "Okay, thanks." She hung up and listened to the voicemail again. "Hello. My name is Bianca Moreno. My sister-in-law works at Fresno Hospital and she gave me your name. I think I can help you find Lourdes Moreno." Kate immediately pressed the call back button. She hadn't listened carefully enough to the message last night. This woman didn't work at the hospital.

"Hello?"

"Is this Bianca Moreno?" Kate asked.

"Yes it is."

"You called me yesterday about Lourdes Moreno?"

"Oh, yes. You are Kate?"

"Yes I am."

"Lourdes is my daughter."

Kate couldn't believe what she was hearing. "Really? Oh my goodness. I'm so happy to talk to you. Did your sister-in-law explain the situation to you?"

"Yes she did."

"So you know Graciela?"

"No. I don't."

Kate's face fell. All her hopes dashed. "Oh. I see."

"And my sister-in-law said the birth certificate said that my daughter is twelve. But my Lourdes is twenty-one."

"I guess it's a different Lourdes Moreno," Kate said resignedly.

"I'm sorry. I wish I could help you."

"Is your daughter there?" Kate asked as an afterthought.

"No. She lives in Santa Barbara."

Kate immediately perked up. "Oh, then maybe she does know Graciela. She used to live in Montecito. Could I have her number?"

Bianca didn't say anything for a minute. "I will give Lourdes your phone number."

"That would be fine. I'd really appreciate it." There was silence on the other end of the line, so Kate decided to keep talking. "So what did your sister-in-law think about the ten year age difference on the birth certificate?"

"I guess she thought there might be some connection because the rest of the birth certificate was correct. It had the same mother and father names and the same month and day for her birthday."

"It would be a strange coincidence," Kate replied.

"I don't know. I suppose."

Kate sensed that Bianca was not interested in talking anymore. "Please ask Lourdes to call me as soon as possible. Maybe she knows Graciela.

Marisol lost both her parents and Graciela is her only relative." Kate thought she'd throw that in for a little sympathy.

"Okay." Bianca said and then hung up. Kate went to find Lawrence to tell him what had happened.

"So what do you think is going on?" Kate asked when she had finished relating the story.

"I don't know," Lawrence responded. "It does seem too coincidental that someone with the same name, born in the same hospital, on the same day, with the same names for her mother and her father."

"And that Lourdes lives in Santa Barbara. Oh shoot. I should have asked Bianca how long she's lived there."

"Let's just hope that she calls you soon and that she knows Graciela."

"And I'm back to waiting mode."

"Well, Marisol is happy at school and with us and we're happy to have her. So if we don't find her sister—"

"She still wants her sister," Kate interrupted.

"I know. But my point is just that she is certainly better off than if we hadn't found her."

"I guess." Kate sighed. "I'm going for a walk."

"With or without company?"

"Without, my love."

He nodded and returned to his computer screen.

31

LAWRENCE WAS EATING HIS LUNCH WHEN KATE BARGED INTO THE KITCHEN. "Lawrence! Oh my God!" Kate hugged him tightly. "I just got off the phone with Lourdes! She's Graciela's friend!"

"You're kidding!" he exclaimed. "That's wonderful news! Did she give you Graciela's phone number?"

"Yes. I tried it but it went to voicemail. But at least it didn't say it was out of service. I left a message. Oh Lawrence! We found her! It's so exciting! I almost want to run over to the school to tell Marisol!"

"Wait until you pick her up."

"I know. I'm just so happy for her!"

"Have some lunch and we'll pick up Marisol together."

"Okay." Kate started to make a sandwich.

"Did Lourdes explain the whole birth certificate thing?"

"Yes. They changed the year on it. Apparently it's not a true legal birth certificate. It's one from the hospital and they are easy to alter."

"I think this calls for a celebration. Let's take Marisol out to dinner tonight."

"We need to see where Graciela is. We may have to go to her."

"Lourdes doesn't know where she is?" Lawrence asked.

"She hasn't talked to her since she left to meet Marisol. She was afraid things had not gone well and was waiting for Graciela to call her."

"Does Graciela live in Santa Barbara too?"

"I didn't ask Lourdes that. I guess I figured I'd ask Graciela all that when I talked to her."

Lawrence grew pensive. "Maybe we shouldn't say anything to Marisol yet. What if Graciela doesn't call you back? We will have gotten Marisol's hopes up, like the last time and . . ." Lawrence's voice trailed off.

Kate didn't answer right away. She finally said, "You mean she might not have the phone anymore?"

"That, or . . ." He paused. "She might be dead."

Kate exhaled loudly. "I guess you're right. We should wait until Graciela calls and then Marisol could actually talk to her."

"I think that's a better plan."

Kate took the remainder of her sandwich into the living room. Lawrence stuck his head in and asked, "Would you like me to pick her up?"

"I would, if you don't mind." Kate wanted to gather her thoughts and put a happy face on to mask the possible scenarios she hadn't considered before.

By the time Lawrence and Marisol got home, Kate was in a better mood, but she still hadn't heard from Graciela. Lawrence raised his eyebrows at her as if to ask if she'd heard anything and Kate just shook her head. "Marisol said that her friends at school are teaching her English," he said.

"Really?" Kate said and then turned to Marisol. "What English have you learned?"

"I am twelve years old. I live in Los Angeles. My favorite color is pink. My favorite foods are chocolate and pizza." She grinned proudly.

"That's wonderful sweetie!" Kate said hugging her.

"I can read English too." Marisol reached into her backpack and took out a simple book at about a first grade level. She opened it and pointed to each word as she read. Kate and Lawrence exchanged happy glances. "Will you help me?" She asked Kate when she finished the book. "I can read your books?"

"My books? Oh, you mean the ones I bought you?"

"*Si.*" Marisol put her hand over her mouth. "I mean yes."

"Sure." Marisol ran back to her bedroom to get her books. "She seems so excited to read and speak English."

"She wants to fit in," Lawrence said. "That's all any kid wants."

"That's all any adult wants too, just to belong somewhere." Just then Kate's phone rang.

She looked at it and exclaimed, "It's her! Hello?" She grinned and nodded vigorously at Lawrence. Marisol walked in the room at that moment and Kate said into the phone, "Wait, let me put Marisol on." She handed the phone to Marisol without saying a word.

Marisol took it hesitantly and said, *"¿Hola?"* Then she screamed and fell into the couch and sobbed. "Graciela!" She spoke in Spanish so quickly that Kate had no idea what was being said. But Kate waited to take the phone and get the particulars from Graciela. They talked for about ten minutes, Marisol alternating laughing and crying, all of it joyful. Finally Marisol handed the phone back to Kate and ran into Lawrence's arms and wept. Lawrence and Kate both had tears running down their cheeks as well.

"Where are you?" Kate asked.

"I'm in Calexico," Graciela answered. "That's where I was supposed to pick up Marisol. I've been here trying to find her." All of a sudden Kate heard a voice talking to Graciela. "I have to go," Graciela said. "I'm at work and my break is over now. I will call you after I get home if it's not too late."

"You're working there? And have a place to live?" Kate asked.

"I didn't want to leave. I'm just waitressing and staying at a crappy motel. It might be late when I get off, though."

"Call back anytime. It doesn't matter." Kate hung up and went to join Marisol and Lawrence in the group hug.

They did end up going out to dinner to celebrate, but first Kate called everyone who had helped her along the way to tell them the good news. She and Lawrence explained to Marisol that Graciela would call back and they would all go to Calexico. They all waited until ten for Graciela's call, but then Kate told Marisol to go to bed. She would be seeing her sister tomorrow. Marisol went reluctantly. Lawrence waited up with Kate until he finally fell asleep in the chair at eleven-thirty. Kate stayed awake, although her eyes were closing and she too finally fell asleep on the couch at midnight. She was awakened at one-thirty and noticed Lawrence had gone to bed. "Hello?' she answered the phone sleepily.

"I'm sorry it's so late," Graciela said.

"No problem." Kate sat up.

"Do you want me to call you back tomorrow? I didn't know I'd be on so late. The dishwasher didn't show up so I had to help in the kitchen."

"It's okay. I just have so many questions."

"I do too," Graciela replied.

"But we'll drive to Calexico tomorrow and we can ask and answer them all in person."

"Okay, but my shift starts at eleven."

Kate looked at the map app on her phone. "It says it takes three and a half hours from Los Angeles."

"Not during the morning rush," Graciela reminded her. "Let's meet during my break instead."

"Okay. We'll plan to be there by then. Where do you work?"

"Applebee's on Scaroni Road."

"We'll find it. See you tomorrow." Kate hung up, tiptoed into the bedroom and slipped into bed.

32

THEY WERE ON THE ROAD THE NEXT MORNING BY TEN. Marisol was so excited that she wouldn't eat her breakfast and Kate was so busy getting ready that she didn't even think about eating. Lawrence had sat at the kitchen table as if in the eye of a storm, calmly eating his bowl of oatmeal. He then packed some protein bars and bananas because he knew their excitement would wear off after a couple of hours, likely along the desolate stretch by the Salton Sea. They listened to music on the radio and didn't say much as they went through downtown Los Angeles and into Ontario, all three of them lost in their own thoughts. Kate thought of losing Marisol if she chose to live with Graciela, but she was consoled by the fact that Marisol had packed only a few things in her backpack. Obviously she had not thought about much more than a happy reunion with her sister. The endless, dingy suburbs flashed by, palm trees and Italian cypress tall against an opaque, silvery sky. At Riverside Kate's phone dinged with a text. She read it aloud. "It's from Graciela. They changed her hours on her. She doesn't start until two now and won't be on a break until six."

"Great," Lawrence groaned. "We'll be stuck in Calexico all afternoon."

"How bad can that be?" Kate asked.

"Try a hundred degrees and nothing to do."

"It's October. It won't be a hundred."

"Okay. Ninety." He gave her a sly look.

"Well, we can eat lunch while we wait and then she'll be on her break. I know. We'll have lunch at Applebee's so at least Marisol and Graciela will be able to see each other right away."

"A meal to match the town," Lawrence frowned. "Bet there's good Mexican in Calexico. But your idea is better. We can wait until Graciela can serve us and they can talk a little while she's at our table."

"Right. Now I have to figure out how to tell Marisol all this in Spanish."

"Why not give her your phone with Graciela's text on it and let her use the app on her phone to translate English to Spanish. It'll give her good practice and something to do while we're driving."

"Good idea," Kate said and handed Marisol her phone. "From Graciela," she told Marisol. Marisol looked at her quizzically. "You translate it," Kate added.

Marisol got to work with both phones and asked after several minutes, "We will see her today?"

"Yes." Kate was going to try to explain the plan she and Lawrence had made, but it was just too daunting to have to look up every word.

Marisol would figure it out when they arrived at Applebee's and she saw her sister working. Palm Springs would have been Kate's choice in somewhere to stop for lunch, but she didn't want to add more time to the trip.

"Hungry?" Lawrence asked.

"Yes. I wish we could stop in Palm Springs where there are at least good restaurants."

"Well, I brought some protein bars and bananas," Lawrence offered. "They're in that bag."

"You're a saint. I was so busy I didn't even think to bring food." She got the food out and shared it with Marisol.

"How much longer does your phone say until we get to Calexico?" Lawrence asked.

"About two hours."

"So we'll get there about two-thirty?"

"Something like that. Should we stop for a bathroom break?" Kate turned around to ask Marisol. "*¿Baño?*"

"No."

"I'm okay for now too. How about you Lawrence?"

"I can wait, but we should stop before we get to the Salton Sea. Who knows whether we'll find one after Indio."

"Let's stop there and we should probably fill up then too."

After the date palm groves south of Coachella, the drive became truly boring and everyone was getting quite antsy. A foul, fishy wind blew off the shores of the Salton Sea and they had to set the air conditioner on recirculate to keep the obnoxious odor out of the car. Finally they reached Calexico and Kate was able to direct Lawrence to Applebee's using her map app. Marisol was beside herself with excitement when they pulled up to the restaurant. She jumped out of the car and ran up to the door, but stopped to wait for Kate and Lawrence before going in. "Look how happy she is," Lawrence said as they joined her by the door. He opened it and Marisol ran in, looking frantically around for her sister.

"Three for lunch," Kate said to the hostess. "And can we please sit in Graciela's station?"

"Graciela is not here."

"Oh," Kate said, surprised. "Didn't she get here yet? I thought she started at two today."

"Um, she did but then she left."

Marisol tugged on Kate's arm. "Where is Graciela?"

Kate shrugged and turned back to the hostess. "Why did she leave? Do you know? Is she sick?"

"You'll need to talk to the manager."

"Then would you please get the manager?" Lawrence cut in. Hunger was making him irritable.

The hostess found the manager and brought him over. "What's the problem here?" he asked.

"We're looking for Graciela," Lawrence replied impatiently. "We've driven almost four hours for Marisol here to see her sister. Where is she?"

"She came to work and quit when I told her she wouldn't be able to take a break today because there would be no one to relieve her," the manager replied coldly. "So now I'm down two waitresses for the dinner hour!"

Lawrence and Kate exchanged glances and took Marisol outside. Kate immediately texted Graciela and they sat in the car waiting for an answer. Kate tried to explain to Marisol what was going on, but wasn't sure that she understood. After fifteen or twenty minutes Lawrence said, "We need to eat something."

"I'm not going back in there," Kate sniffed, nodding at Applebee's.

"Let's just find a taco stand or something while we wait for her answer. Did she tell you what motel she was staying in?"

"No." They drove around a few blocks and found a Mexican restaurant that looked promising. They sat down and ordered what they thought would be quick. Kate had put her phone down in the middle of the table and all three of them said nothing, their eyes never leaving the phone. Their food came and they ate voraciously, having eaten so little all day. But there was still no return text from Graciela. "I'm going to phone her. Maybe she didn't hear the text alert." Kate picked up the phone and dialed Graciela's number, but she didn't pick up. Kate left a voicemail, "We are in Calexico. We went to Applebee's and found out you quit. Where's your motel?"

They sat at the table long after they had finished eating. It was too hot to walk around outside, so they weren't sure what to do. Finally, Lawrence broke the silence. "Let's go back to Applebee's and see if one of her coworkers knows where she's staying."

Kate nodded reluctantly."Okay." They got up, Lawrence threw some money on the table and they got back in the car.

"What time is it now?" Lawrence asked.

"Five."

"Seems weird that she wouldn't be more on top of her messages since she knew we were coming."

Kate sighed. "I know." They arrived again at Applebee's and Kate announced, "I'm going in alone. Maybe just one of us won't raise their hackles so much."

Kate approached the hostess again who gave her an unfriendly look. "Yes?"

"I was just wondering if you knew where Graciela was staying."

"No. She didn't work here long and I didn't know her well."

"Could you ask one of the other servers if maybe they know?" Kate asked, trying to be warm and friendly.

The hostess pulled some menus for a party that just arrived. "As you can tell, we're very busy and short-staffed, thanks to your friend." The hostess turned away and motioned for the party to follow her.

Kate started after one of the servers to ask herself when Lawrence came rushing in and plucked at her blouse. He had a huge grin on his face. "Come outside now!"

Kate followed him out and saw Marisol and Graciela sprawled on a patch of grass under the Applebee's sign, their arms entwined and sobbing loudly. Kate took Lawrence's hand, wiped her own tears and silently watched the happy reunion. The sisters finally stood and Marisol ran over to Kate and hugged her. *"¡Mi hermana! ¡Mi hermana!"*

Graciela came over and also hugged Kate. "Thank you so much for taking such good care of Marisol. I thought I'd never see her again and now to see her looking so well!" She then turned to Lawrence and hugged him as well.

"So you quit your job?" Kate asked.

"Yes." Graciela hesitated. "I-I thought if you wouldn't mind, I could ride back to Los Angeles with you. I want to get out of this hellhole, now that I found Marisol."

"Sure, but don't you have a car?"

"No. I got a ride here."

"Is this where you were supposed to meet Marisol?" Lawrence asked.

"Yes," Graciela answered. "But I guess that Coyote took her to a stash house instead so he could get money out of them too."

"We can talk on the ride home," Kate said. "Shall we get your things at the motel?"

"Yes, please."

"By the way, I left you a text and voicemail. Did you get them?"

Graciela looked down and bit her lip. "I'm so sorry. My phone's a burner and I ran out of minutes. I came back here now because we had planned to meet at six."

"Glad that's explained," Lawrence smiled. "Well, do you want to stop somewhere and put more minutes on your phone?"

"Not now. Let's just get out of here, if you don't mind. I can do that in Los Angeles. I'll find a motel there and go to the—"

"You'll stay with us," Kate interrupted.

Graciela hugged Kate again and then said, choking back tears, "You are so kind." She took her sister's hand and they walked to the car.

33

THE SISTERS CONVERSED EXCITEDLY IN SPANISH THE WHOLE DRIVE HOME. Occasionally Kate understood what they were talking about, but she didn't really try to follow or appear like she was trying to. She reclined her seat slightly and watched the desert sky turn colors as the sun set, soothed by the whine of the tires and happy chatter behind her.

They did a Del Taco drive-thru in Beaumont for dinner and were home by nine-thirty. They were all exhausted and after making sure that Graciela had a decent sleeping arrangement, they all just went to bed. Kate pulled the covers up under her chin and murmured, "I can't wait to get the full story tomorrow," but Lawrence was already snoring.

They all drove Marisol to school the next morning, and everyone got out of the car like it was opening day. Graciela gave a hug and kiss to her sister before Marisol ran off to join her new friends and tell them all about her big sister. Kate and Lawrence turned back towards the car, but Graciela just stood there, watching her little sister disappear into the school. Then she hastily turned around and smiled shyly, wiping a tear from her eye. "Sorry," she said. "I wish Mamá could have seen this day."

Kate reached out her hand. "We're in no hurry."

Graciela took her hand and they started walking back to the car. "There's so much to think about now, so much to do," Graciela sighed.

"One day at a time," Lawrence smiled.

Graciela nodded. "I can't tell you how much I appreciate all this—and for having to listen to us for hours last night on the drive back, not knowing what we were saying and not asking."

"Well," Kate hedged. "May I ask you questions after we get back home and I make a fresh pot of coffee?" She winked over at Lawrence. "Lawrence will get us some good pastry over on Fairfax."

Graciela laughed. "That sounds wonderful."

Lawrence dropped them off at the condo and Kate soon had steaming, fresh cups of coffee on the kitchen table. "Unfortunately the pastry won't appear so quickly."

"That's okay," Graciela grinned as she poured some cream into her coffee. "So what do you want to know first?"

"Let's start with you. I understand you left Mexico with your father a few years ago?"

"Well, I was fifteen and it was so dangerous where we lived in Tijuana. Jobs were few and far between there for Papi. He decided he would go to America so we saved up the money to pay the coyote." She took a deep breath and gathered herself. "Then I was raped."

Kate gasped. "Oh God!"

"It was common for girls there to be raped and sold into sex rings. So we took a chance and left without paying more to the coyote for me . . . "

"The coyote let you come with your father?"

"I had to sleep with the coyote, but at least he wasn't brutal and I could clean up afterwards in a real bathroom."

Kate reached out and touched Graciela's hand clenched around her coffee cup. "What about your mother?"

"She just hoped that she was too old and Marisol was too young to be raped." Graciela wiped a tear away. "My father and I planned to send for both of them after we had worked to earn enough money."

"That was in Lost Hills?"

"Yes. We had been able to save enough for one, but not both when my father was killed."

"And then you left that farm?"

"Yes. It was not a bad place to work, but I didn't want to stay after what happened to my father. It felt weird and hard to be there."

"So you and Eduardo went to other farms around the state?"

Graciela's eyes widened. "You know about Eduardo?"

"Yes," Kate smiled. "He's one of the few things I found out about in my search for you."

"Oh." Graciela paused, gathering her thoughts. "So, yes, we went to different farms, but then we found out about the marijuana farms and you could make so much more money as trimmers. We did that and then when harvest was over, they let me stay on and learn how to make bubble ice and BHO."

"Bubble ice? BHO?"

"Bubble ice and BHO are both hash. You make them out of what we trimmed from the pot plants. It's a different way of making it. Bubble ice or bubble hash uses ice-cold water. BHO is butane hash oil. That's more dangerous 'cause you use butane."

"So that's what people are making when the news reports on explosions?"

"Yeah. It's real dangerous, but I wanted to learn how because they paid me much more to do it."

"You weren't afraid?"

"I was. But I was determined to get Marisol here as soon as possible. Eduardo didn't like me doing it and we fought about it. That's one of the reasons we broke up. After he left they were all hitting on me and I didn't like it. One of them was nice though, and he told me about his sister who was a nanny in Montecito making a good salary and she had a nice place to live. It sounded like a good deal so I decided to go there. His sister found me a job." She laughed. "The families all want nannies that speak English and I had to learn the language quickly."

"And you speak it well, " Kate added. "You sound almost like English is your first language."

Graciela laughed. "I worked at my accent. I had already learned some as a child in Mexico."

"Bianca and Lourdes said you didn't like the family you worked for, though."

Graciela shook her head and chuckled. "You are quite a detective!"

Kate shrugged. "It was mostly the postcards and photos Marisol had that offered leads."

"Yeah, the family was just so strict and overprotective of their kids. They wouldn't let them do anything and I didn't agree with their ideas on child rearing." She took another deep breath and said in a much quieter voice. "Then my mother was murdered and I knew I had to get Marisol. I couldn't go to Mexico because I wouldn't have enough to get us both back to America. I had enough money for just her so I found a coyote and made the plan to meet them in Calexico."

"Did Marisol tell you what happened with the coyote?" Kate asked.

"He took her to a stash house and she ran away from it. Then you found her." Graciela squeezed Kate's hand.

"How long had she been on the road by herself when we saw her? Did she say?"

"She wasn't sure. I think about two days. The stash house was way out in the desert and she had just gotten to that highway where she met you."

"You two are so strong. Your parents would be proud." Kate got up and motioned for

Graciela to come to her. She was reluctant at first, but then broke down in Kate's arms and sobbed.

Lawrence had been right outside the kitchen for some time. He hadn't wanted to come in, afraid to interrupt when Graciela was so forthcoming. He finally cleared his throat and came in, presenting a pink box. "Hey, pastry for lunch?" he grinned.

Graciela straightened up, wiped her eyes, and started laughing. "Maybe I can make some sandwiches to go with them. I'm pretty hungry now."

Kate started laughing, too. "That's a great idea. It'll just take the two of us a minute. Can you wait that long, Lawrence?"

"I'll try," he replied soberly, putting the box on the table. "Maybe I'll just go lie down on the couch in the meantime."

"Pffft," Kate sputtered. "You snored half the night!" Kate and Graciela jostled around the kitchen and soon had hearty sandwiches laid out on the table. Kate related all that had happened since they found Marisol as they ate. "So," Kate finally said, "I have many people to thank and I need to call them all and tell them we found you."

"I need to find a place to live and a job," Graciela added.

"Don't worry about that," Lawrence said. "You have a place to live as long as you need it."

"You people are so kind, but you've done so much. I—"

"No worries," Kate interrupted. "What do you want to do? I mean, really want to do."

Graciela considered the question carefully before answering. "I'd like to go to school and become a teacher. But I still need to make money."

"Well, let's figure out how you can accomplish that goal and then work on getting you a job that pays well enough and gives you enough time to study." Kate glanced at Lawrence who nodded and smiled. "You know, I was a teacher and so was Lawrence. His son and daughter-in-law are also teachers."

"I know. Marisol told me," Graciela smiled.

"And Marisol told me that she wants to be a teacher too," Kate said.

"Our family has a lot of respect for teachers."

Kate rose and announced, "I'm going to make my calls now." She cast a glance at Graciela. "And you need to call Lourdes."

"And Eduardo, too," Graciela replied.

Kate and Lawrence grinned at one another. "Sounds like you need more minutes on your phone, stat," Lawrence said. "Let's go get that done first."

Kate waved her hand dismissively. "Oh, just put her on our plan. Then she can have a real phone and it won't cost her any more than having a burner."

"Yes, ma'am," Lawrence saluted.

"Well, it's true!"

"I know, I know!" he laughed. Lawrence leaned toward Graciela. "Watch out. She's just recently discovered she has apron strings." Graciela giggled and he added, "Distract her as I untangle myself."

"Someday you'll be happy I found them," Kate snorted.

"Yeah, when I'm actually old and helpless." He put his arm around Graciela's shoulder. "Come along and we'll get you set up on the family plan."

Kate blew him a dramatic air kiss and pulled out her phone to start in on her calls. Lucy came first, then Rachel. Juanita would have to wait until evening, lest Kate disrupt her work and annoy her employer. A message left with Lourdes would start a chain reaction with her mother and on to the aunt that worked at the Fresno hospital. Kate was surprised that Eduardo actually answered. He seemed very interested in her finding Graciela, even asking a few questions to fill out her short narrative. "I really shouldn't say this," Kate hesitated, "but don't be surprised if she calls you herself."

"Really?"

"Shhh. I never said a thing about it."

"Okay," he chuckled. "I really appreciate your call."

"And I really appreciated your help."

"Aw, I didn't do much."

"Never mind that. I look forward to meeting you in person."

"Yeah," he replied shyly. "Bye now."

Just then Lawrence and Graciela walked in with Marisol in tow. "You look like I just caught you talking to your boyfriend," Lawrence grinned.

"Moi?" Kate mustered. "You and your fantasies . . . Did you tell Mrs. Flores the news?"

"I did!" Marisol exclaimed with a little jump. She dropped her backpack on the floor.

"Mrs. Flores came out after school and gave me a big hug," Graciela added.

"And we managed to get Graciela's old number back," Lawrence piped.

"Amazing," Kate replied. "You know, I just thought we ought to work on Mrs. Flores about getting Graciela a teacher's aide position. Once she starts classes, of course."

"Being bilingual would definitely put her in demand," Lawrence mused, "but she'd make more money waitressing."

"But that wouldn't look as impressive on a teacher's resume. Some things are worth more than good tips."

"You've been so kind to us," Graciela asserted herself, "but I can't mooch off of you. Really, I can't. I can find a tiny something . . ."

"And you will," Kate cut in. "But that takes a job reference, a first and last month and a cleaning deposit. Money will have to be saved first. And then there's Marisol's schooling. It'll be hard to find a similar situation."

Graciela turned and gave Lawrence a sweet little grimace. "See," he grinned. "I told you so. And she's right. It's not mooching when you're serious about getting ahead in life. Accept kindness and generosity graciously."

Graciela shrugged. "Thank you. I hope to prove you right."

"You will," Kate said. "In due time." She reached out and gave her a hug and then stepped back. "I'm thinking about what we should have for dinner. Can you help? Marisol has proved handy in the kitchen, but feeding a family of four is new to me."

"Sure," Graciela smiled. "Mamá taught me how to make something out of nothing, and I'm sure there's a little more than nothing in the refrigerator."

"Well, I dunno . . ." Lawrence sighed.

"If there isn't, it's your fault," Kate laughed, poking him in the side.

"I've been a bit distracted from grocery shopping." Graciela studied the contents of the fridge and with Marisol's help, put together a Mexican casserole of sorts. Kate made a slaw with a creamy salsa dressing and Lawrence set the table with a bit more formality than usual. None of it went smoothly, but there was a lot of laughter in the process. "And there's still pastry for dessert!" Lawrence announced with the presentation of the now half empty box.

Later in the evening, while Marisol watched TV and Lawrence helped Graciela research online the curriculum and financial assistance at the city college, Kate called Juanita with the news. "Oh, it's so nice to hear a happy ending these days," Juanita cried. "What does Graciela want to do next?"

"Get a job and attend college. She wants to become a teacher."

"You know we live close to City College," Juanita said eagerly. "She could—oh what do the kids say—'crash' at our place if she has an evening class or her schedule is tight."

"What a kind thought," Kate replied. "And I'm sure Marisol will give you a glowing review."

The next day was Saturday and they spent the whole day at Venice Beach. As they relaxed and had fun, Kate realized she also needed to call Malcolm and Jed to tell them that Graciela had been found, but she found that easy to put off for another day. They met Michael, Carla and Danielle at a restaurant for dinner, where they stayed late, with Danielle and Marisol giggling and chatting while Michael and Carla shared teaching experiences with Graciela. Lawrence and Kate looked on, grinning at each other every so often. He leaned down and whispered, "I guess we have quite a brood now."

"My family has certainly grown," Kate whispered back.

They were just getting ready for bed when Lawrence's phone rang. "Who would call at this hour?" He looked at his phone. "Oh, it's Michael." He gave Kate a worried look. "Hello? Is everything okay?"

"Everything's great," Michael replied. "I didn't wake you, did I?"

"No, we're just getting into bed now."

"I couldn't wait to tell you. Carla and I were talking on the way home from the restaurant. We'd like Graciela to live with us. We'd give her room and board and a small salary, but she'd be there to help with Danielle and maybe a little housework. I have a buddy who could pull some strings and get her into Cal State Northridge, and she can even walk there from our house. He works in admissions and financial aid and he knows plenty of ways to get money for DREAMers."

"Wow, hold on, and let me tell Kate."

But she had already overheard most of the idea and cut him short. "It's a wonderful idea but what about Marisol?" They both heard Michael yelling over the phone, "Dad, I'm not finished!"

Lawrence put the phone back to his ear. "What?" Lawrence asked.

"Marisol could stay here also or with you, whichever she and you prefer. We have room for both, but I know you and Kate are enjoying having Marisol there, and her school situation seems ideal for now."

"We'll talk this over and I'll get back to you."

"Okay. We really want to do this. It feels like a good fit."

"Thanks Michael. It sounds like a great idea." Lawrence hung up and turned to Kate. "He said Marisol could live there also, or we could keep her with us. What do you think?"

"It's ultimately up to Graciela and Marisol."

Lawrence nodded. "Of course. But what do you think?"

Kate looked perplexed. "I said I thought it was a great idea."

"I'm not talking about that. How do you feel about Marisol living there . . . and not with us?"

Kate was silent for a minute. "I'm not sure. But I want to leave it up to Marisol. She would probably like being with her sister and another child. You and I are kind of old to be parents instead of grandparents."

"Would you be sad if she chose not to live with us, though?"

"Probably. I've grown to love her a lot. But, as I said, it's not my call. It's a decision I would learn to accept."

Lawrence nodded and smiled. "It has been nice having a young person around. But it's not like we'd never see her. She could stay here sometimes."

"Let's go to sleep and talk to them in the morning." Kate kissed him.

The next morning at breakfast they told Graciela and Marisol about Michael's phone call. Both girls were ecstatic about moving in with Michael and Carla. So that was that. Marisol didn't even question it. She did turn to Kate at one point and lapsed into somewhat broken English, "I will see you a lot, yes?"

Kate hugged her. "Of course, all the time. And you can come stay here anytime you want." She turned to Graciela. "And you too."

Graciela shook her head in disbelief. "This is a dream come true!"

Kate took Lawrence's hand and said, "Maybe for all of us."

"But I don't really understand how that friend of Michael's can help us. I mean, how am I going to pay for college and not get deported when I register and they find out I'm not a citizen?"

"How old were you when you arrived with your father?" Lawrence asked.

"Fifteen."

"Then you're good. DACA means Deferred Action for Childhood Arrivals. It was enacted during the Obama administration to protect children who were here before their sixteenth birthday. So you qualify as a DREAMer. Michael's friend will help you navigate the system so you can apply for DACA and go to college."

"But what about Marisol?" Kate asked.

"I think she'll qualify because Graciela is her only living relative," Lawrence answered. "But we can jump over that hurdle after we get Graciela situated. Marisol can fly under the radar. Michael and Carla have many friends in their school district where Marisol will be attending school. I'm sure there won't be a problem."

Marisol looked up at Kate and asked, "I am a DREAMer too?"

Kate hugged her tightly. "Yes darling Marisol. You and Graciela are both DREAMers."